THE HACKS OF LIFE

BY PERRY BUSBY

Buzz Word Publishing, LLC

—

Fort Lauderdale

Gail —
Thank you for the
support and friendship
over the years.

[signature]
4/24/18

Buzz Word Publishing, LLC
Fort Lauderdale, FL

For more information or to book an interview or event, contact Buzz Word Publishing at 786-910-5140 or visit our website at www.buzzwordpublishing.com.

Cover design by J.L. Woodson, Woodson Creative Studio

1   3   5   7   9   10   8   6   4   2

Library of Congress Control Number: 2017916658

ISBN 978-0-9994582-0-4

ISBN 978-0-9994582-1-1 (eBook)

Special Acknowledgments...

My editor, Monique Mensah, of Make Your Mark Publishing Services. Mo', I am eternally grateful for your creative insight and direction. The next project will not take as long, I promise.

Pam Straughter, Ann Wright, and Toni Wycoff-Adams, aka My Team. Thank you for enduring my countless edits, revisions, and wild ideas. You ladies were my rock and sounding board even when the discussions weren't about plots and scenes.

Roderick "Hank" Harrington, David Mays and Brian Stevens (B-Steve), the critique and suggestions were on point.

Eva Brock, JL King, Brian W. Smith, Lissa Woodson (Naleighna Kai) for their countless hours of mentoring, advising, instructing, and counseling. You are more than colleagues and friends, you are family.

Mary Jane Ryals and the members of the Gypsy Writers Group (Agnes Fourney, Gail Fishman, Jeffrey Mandel, Mary Wilkes, and Pat Tuthill). Thanks for patiently listening to all those clumsy, overly worded drafts.

The 4th Quarter Lounge crew: Michael Trammell, Lee Kitchen, Russ Franklin, Carlos Miranda, John Reynolds, Chris Hayes, and Magnus Hines he writer's workshop. Thanks for navigating me through the early drafts.

Ron Wiginton, a great friend, brilliant writer, and the absolute best writing instructor.

Trish McEnulty, you're the greatest!

Barbara Joe Williams and the member of the Tallahassee Authors Network (TAN), and Peggy Kassees and the Tallahassee Writers Association (TWA). The knowledge gained, and friendships established has been priceless.

Dedicated to

My parents
Carrie L. Chillis & Perry Busby, Jr.

and

Parents in law & love
Diverna C. Cobb & Tillman H. Henderson, Jr.

Lee Lundquist, thanks for making an out of the way trip to San Antonio, turn out so special.

Felicia S.W. Thomas, thanks for coming through in the clutch.

Barry Burrell, Lawrence & Patricia Byrd, Will Fleming, Ronald & Dorothy Gipson, Wanda Graves, Robin & Roderick Haynes, Tonya C. Jordan, Ena Love, Christopher "C-Moe" Moses, Larry Owens, Toby Sanders, Mark Silverman, Lloyd Sprott, Vewiser Taylor, Stephen Thibodeaux, Carolyn Wallace, and Melvin White, thanks for your support and belief in this project.

Kara Rice at Kara Rice Gallery for bringing artistic vision to this project.

J.L. Woodson at Woodson Creative Studios. Great work, bro! This is one book that I hope gets judged by its cover.

Thalia Clay-Simien, I told you I wouldn't forget.

My joys and original fans: Chelsea, Michael, Brandi, Princess, and Aubrey.

My wife, friend, and partner for life, Nancy. I may be the writer, but you are the best storyteller. Thanks for putting up with my craziness and adding your own to mix. I couldn't have done this without you.

To my alma mater, Prairie View A&M University, and all HBCU campuses. For generations, these institutions have continuously and consistently proven that an education from an HBCU is highly prized.

PROLOGUE
DURHAM, NC
DECEMBER 1954

"SIXTY ... EIGHTY ... and one mo' twenty makes three." Wes kissed the seal on the front of the crisp bill.

Neatly arranged stacks of twenty-dollar bills lined the top of his grandfather's old desk. The desk had been in the upstairs storage room at his father's law office for more than a decade. He had hauled it downstairs, applied a fresh coat of wax, and then crammed it into the tiny room that was secretly serving as his office. The desk was so big, he had to cram it against the wall opposite the door in order to make it fit inside the small room. There was just enough space left over to put a chair on either side of the desk.

"Three grand for my first case. That oughta be enough to keep Mama and J.D. quiet after I tell them I dropped out of law school last semester." Wes looked down at his newly acquired treasure and let out a deflated sigh. "Who am I fooling? All the money in the world won't stop them from hollering."

He took a metal lockbox the size of a lunch kit from the middle drawer and placed it on top of the desk.

Wes opened the lockbox with deliberate caution and gazed at the diamond ring sparkling at the bottom. A bonus payment for a job well done. Ellen Carrington, his client, had insisted on it, even though the three thousand dollars was more than their negotiated price.

"Take it; I insist," Ellen had urged after sliding the ring off her finger. "When you find your special love, give it to her."

Wes held the ring up and marveled at the stone's brilliance. The oval-shaped rock looked to be two carats, at least.

The front door closed with a thud. Not a door-slamming kind of thud, more like a forceful shut to announce one's presence.

Wes stiffened and listened intently for his mystery guest's every move. The visitor was a woman; the methodic click-clack of a narrow shoe heel against the wooden floor planks was undeniable. By approximating the distance in her stride, he concluded she was also a woman of above average height.

Wes stuffed the ring into his pants pocket.

"Marjorie, is that you?" he called out.

Marjorie, decked out in a black pencil skirt that hugged her hips in all the right places, strolled into the office, straight to the side of the desk, blocking his only avenue to the door.

A black patent-leather purse swung wildly from her wrist as she launched the first in a series of blistering salvos. "What's this I hear about you dropping out of law school? I guess I wasn't important enough for you to tell."

"Marjorie, baby, I swear I was going to tell you. In fact, I was going to tell you tonight." A tiny smile crept from under Wes's solemn expression as he plead his case.

"I can't believe you have the unmitigated gall to look me in the eye, all innocent-like, and lie with a straight face," she fumed. "Don't think for a minute I don't see that lil' ol' sneaky grin you're trying to hide."

Marjorie was a whirlwind of fire, with eyes and passion to match. The more she ranted and raved, the harder it was for Wes to conceal his delight. According to his mother, she had the physique, temperament, and spirit of a woman with Guinea roots.

"I'm smiling because I'm happy. And I'm happy because I can tell you the truth now. Finally." He held his palms out and smiled sheepishly.

"You've been lying for six straight months, and you expect me to believe your fucking conscience is bothering you now?" she shot back, unable to hide her contempt.

"I know you find my having a conscience hard to believe, but I have one. Trust me, I do." Wes looked up at the ceiling and mumbled, "Sometimes I wish I didn't, but I do."

Marjorie rolled her eyes and scoffed.

"Honest, baby, I was going to tell you everything." Wes raised his right hand revealing the Boy Scout three-finger honor salute.

"Does 'everything' include explaining why you've been sneaking around to see some white woman in Chapel Hill?" Marjorie cocked her head slightly to the right and raised her eyebrows. "Well, does it?" Her voice began to quiver.

Gripped with shock from hearing her latest revelation, Wes started stammering. "Who … who … told you that? I'll bet it was Vic. Did he tell you?"

"Never mind where I heard it or who told me. Is it true?" Tears began to drop from her high, angular cheeks.

Wes reached for her by the arm to bring her closer. Marjorie yanked loose and folded her arms.

"Don't touch me. Just answer the question. Is it true?" Tears the size of Tic-Tac mints flowed down her brown cheeks.

[iii]

Wes stepped closer and enveloped her in his arms.

"Yes, I've been seeing a woman in Chapel Hill."

Marjorie shoved hard against his chest, breaking free from his grasp. "How could you? Vic was right about you. I should've listened to him."

"Vic? I knew his two-timing ass had something to do with this." Wes laughed with contempt.

"Leave Vic out of this," she objected. "He's done nothing wrong, other than be a good friend."

"Snitching on your friend to his girl is not my idea of a good friend. Vic can kiss my ass, but I'm sure he'd much rather kiss yours."

Marjorie did a hard eye roll. "Don't try to change the conversation. How long have you been sneaking around to see Miss Prissy Ass in Chapel Hill?"

"Listen, I don't know what all Vic told you, but it's not what you think. The white lady I was seeing, Miss Prissy Ass in Chapel Hill …" He made a pair of air quotes with his hands. "Her name is Ellen Carrington. As in Carrington Tobacco Company, the company she inherited."

"You mean the lady whose husband was just arrested for secretly trying to blackmail her? You're the anonymous source the cops have been praising for helping them solve the case?"

Wes nodded. "She was my client. That's what I wanted to tell you. I dropped out of law school to start my own detective agency. I didn't want to tell you until I completed my first case. I was going to tell you tonight. I promise."

He dug into his pocket for the ring and then dropped down on one knee. "I was going to tell you … and then ask you to marry me."

A starburst of metallic white light radiated from the stone as it sat atop a polished platinum band.

"What do you say, Marjorie? Will you marry me?"

Marjorie's eyes grew as big as headlights. Her mouth flew open, but nothing came out. Suddenly, an ear-piercing shriek filled the small office. Tears of pain quickly turned to sobs of joy. An embarrassing grin stretched across her smooth, golden brown face.

"Oh, Wes, it's beautiful!" She slid the ring on and waved her hand like one of those hand models on a commercial. "But there's no way we can afford this, because—"

Wes stood up and held her close. Wiping the last few drops of tears from her cheeks, he looked her squarely in the eye. "Marjorie, don't worry. We can afford it. It's already bought and paid for."

Marjorie held her hand out, admiring the ring. Suddenly her approving smile went limp. A small furrow crept across her forehead. "Wes, is this ring hot?"

"No." Wes snickered. "I'll have you know I bought that with hard work, sweat, and tears."

Marjorie flung her arms around his neck and planted a juicy lip-sucking kiss that covered his lips with smeared red lipstick.

"I'm the happiest woman alive. I've got a beautiful ring and a generous man, who I know will be the world's best husband and father."

Captivated by the warmth of Marjorie's embrace and the intoxicating scent of her perfume, Wes rocked and hummed while she talked on and on. Then he stopped as her words began to soak in.

He leaned back and gave her a curious stare. "Did I hear you right? Did you just say 'father'?"

The glowing bashful smile on Marjorie's face said it all. "Yes," she gushed.

Marjorie wrapped him in a bear hug squeeze. "If it's a boy, I want him to be just like you."

"And, if it's a girl?" Wes asked between small kisses on her neck.

"I want her to be just like you. I want all of our children to be just like you."

Looking up at the ceiling, Wes contemplated Marjorie's wishful thought and replied, "Humph! Lord, help us."

CHAPTER 1

CHARLOTTE, NC
MONDAY, JANUARY 18, 1993

"PHIL, I DON'T understand a damn thing you just said. But it doesn't take a rocket scientist to know it ain't good," Wes said in a hushed, gruff tone as he leaned over the table. "Tell it to me again … this time, in English."

Phil dropped his head in frustration. *Just forget I said anything.* Giving voice to those words was tempting. It also meant he would be giving life to a lie. If the information he'd just learned was true, father or not, Wes Jacobson was just the detective to put on the case. He took a deep breath, raised his head, and tried once more.

"Last night, I was in the Underground." Phil paused when he saw the blank expression splashed across Wes's face. "Sorry 'bout that." He exhaled slowly before continuing. "I was on a bulletin board called The Rabbit Hole. It's a board where hackers compete to see who can pull off the best hack or prank on a company's computer system."

"What's the point in all this hacking? You say you're competing. What do you win?"

"You don't win anything. Well, maybe bragging rights. It's just a couple of guys fooling around. The object of the game is to see who can hack into the most impenetrable computer network or a highly prized target like a bank or branch of government. The bigger the target, the more points you get."

[1]

Wes, still not able to make heads or tails of what he'd just heard, shook his head in resignation. "How many points you get for being a damn fool?"

Phil ignored the question and continued. "Anyway, a couple of hours ago, I came across this t-file ... Excuse me; I came across a document that explained how this hacker named NoMoBoesky compromised ITI's network and uncovered something really suspicious while tracking their financial records. Based on the information I read, NoMoBoesky pranked ITI into thinking they were in trouble with the Feds over some bogus EEOC violation. He didn't want to cause a major panic, just a minor disturbance so he could track where they moved money during a crisis. He hacked into ITI and got access to their network transmission logs. From there, he found the computer and the file where they listed all their off-the-book wire transfers. ITI was still using an old network security patch, so it was just like they'd left the back door open. He found the accounts along with the passwords, and the rest is history. It wasn't quite as easy as what I'm telling you, but isn't that some crazy shit?"

"You wanna know what kinda shit it sounds like to me? The kind you don't need to poke your nose into. Shit stinks, son. You don't have to smell it to know that." Wes looked at his son and shook his head. "And why are you smiling and looking all starry-eyed when you talk about it? You look like a teenage girl after her first kiss."

"I'm not smiling," Phil objected. An embarrassed grin spread across his face.

"Explain what you just said a lil' better. I'm still not quite understanding what you're getting at."

"In NoMoBoesky's t-file, he has proof—" Phil stopped mid-sentence when he recognized his father's coded signal: a napkin-covered index finger pressed against his lips, followed by a single cough.

A group of customers walked by.

"Continue," Wes instructed after they were out of earshot.

Phil closed his eyes and took a deep breath. "This guy, NoMoBoesky, says he has proof that Intellect Technology Incorporation, also known as ITI, or to be more specific, the place where I work, was given money to cover up a problem and then cooked their books to hide it."

Wes surveyed the diner, keeping a mental inventory of the additional faces since his last surveillance check. It was a practice he performed more out of habit than necessity. Every detective developed an uncontrollable tic over the years; this was his. Any other day, he would've had a complete scan committed to memory in a matter of seconds. Today, it took a full minute. Considering the magnitude of what he'd just been told, he was glad he could remember anything at all.

"How well do you know this guy? I keep telling you, you better learn to pick your company carefully."

Phil knew the Underground was filled with rumors and outlandish people, but it was slowly becoming a source for answers. Information ruled in the Underground and Phil had benefitted from it on more than one occasion.

"I am careful, Daddy. But do you understand what I'm saying? I believe something is going on at ITI, and I believe it involves me."

The cling-clank of silverware tossed against plates filled the air as Wes digested his son's last statement. Thirty-five years of experience told him that Phil was on to something.

"You're starting to sound ridiculous now."

Wes knew his son's penchant for taking ill-advised risks better than anyone. This was Phil's first opportunity to work for a company of ITI's prestige since graduating from college. Under no circumstance was he going to give him the green light to dive into ITI's cesspool of problems.

"If you think that sounds ridiculous, then tell me if this isn't just as ridiculous: ITI called me out of the blue to interview for a job. How they got my phone number is still a mystery. Then they offered me a job in a department that I don't think existed when I interviewed. In fact, none of the people I interviewed with that day work in my department. Now, there's this guy saying that ITI hired African Americans for meaningless positions to cover up their bogus minority employment numbers. I've been at ITI for six months, which is within the timeframe NoMoBoesky says they ran the cover-up. Does that sound so ridiculous now?"

"Here." Wes picked up a menu and handed it to Phil as he beckoned for the waitress. "Phil, I'm not saying this NoMo, whatever the hell you say his name is, is making all of this up, but the whole thing sounds farfetched to me."

Phil never looked up when the waitress arrived. He was still trying to decide whether to order a bagel or a waffle with all the fixings.

"Let me see now, Wes, darling; I know you want a bagel, pumpernickel, lightly toasted, plain cream cheese on one side, honey-walnut on the other, and a small OJ." The waitress jotted on her pad as she rattled off the order.

Phil continued to mull over the menu. He had a habit of eating a lot when he was nervous. His mind said bagel, but his stomach screamed for the Bagels Galore Delight, a morning feast consisting of a waffle, two scrambled eggs, hash browns, and bacon.

"Phil, honey, I believe a Bagels Galore Delight would do you good this morning. Don't you agree?" the waitress asked rhetorically.

"I believe you're right," Phil conceded. He looked up for the first time as he handed the waitress the menu, and nearly jumped from his seat. "Whoa, Grace?"

CHAPTER 2

GRACE LANCASTER, by all accounts, was a warm-hearted southern girl from Sumter, South Carolina, with good intentions and an irresistible charm. She was forty-five, had flawless maple brown skin and a shapely physique that made younger women jealous and older women cautious. Phil assumed that was one of the reasons why his mother didn't like her, that and the fact that three years ago, his father had opened an office in Charlotte, hired Grace as his receptionist-slash-office manager, and then kept both a secret for nearly a year.

Phil watched Grace's voluptuous hips and butt sway in a syncopated rhythm as she walked away. She had a way of mesmerizing a man without being deliberate. The left corner of his mouth turned upward in an unconscious, suggestive smile.

"What are you smiling at?" Wes directed his query more toward the lustful grin he knew all too well than to Phil specifically.

"Huh?" Phil replied, shaking himself free from his hypnotic trance. "I wasn't smiling. I mean I didn't know I was smiling."

"Well, you were. And if you know what's best for you, you'd better not let your mama see her lil' man smiling like that."

As far as Phil could remember, his mother had never been rude to Grace whenever they were in each other's company, but their public displays of kindness were strained at best. Phil also noticed that his father acted peculiar and managed to stay busy in an uneasy kind of way during those moments.

"By the way, I sure hope you didn't mention any of this to your mama. You know you can't hold water when it comes to her."

"I just found out a few hours ago. You're the only person I've told. Besides, when would I have had the chance to say anything to Mama?"

Wes laughed mockingly. "Phil, we both know there is no way in hell you showed up on time to breakfast this morning unless your mama called and reminded you. Hell, you probably forgot I was even coming to town."

In addition to the main office in Durham, Wes had offices in Charlotte, Richmond, Virginia, and the District of Columbia. Work had brought him to Charlotte, and a phone call to Phil two days prior had led to their current early-morning confab.

"I haven't talked to Mama, I swear." Phil stuffed a generous portion of syrup-soaked pancakes into his mouth.

"Humph!"

They ate in silence, each waiting for the other to continue the conversation. Phil wanted to talk about ITI, but the door to that discussion was closed. He decided on his next topic of interest. He leaned over the table and whispered, "Daddy, what's going on with you and Grace?"

The question caught Wes by surprise. With the subtleness of a drill sergeant, he sidestepped his inquisitive son's hot seat question and mounted an offense of his own. "What did you just ask me? I know goddamn well you didn't just say what I thought you said. Just because those folk across the street gave you a job, doesn't mean we're peers. It sure as hell don't give you the right to pry into my business. That's for damn sure! And why the hell are you whispering?"

Phil leaned back and raised his arms—palms out—in surrender. "I just wanted to know what kind of case you were working. It must be important if you're using Grace on cover. C'mon, you're using *Grace* on cases now? Really?"

Wes brushed the question off with a wave of his hand. "Nothing but a Jack on the loose." That was the code for a cheating male spouse—a female spouse was a tumbling Jill. "Besides, Grace used to be a really good waitress at one time, so she was excited to do it. She's provided some good intel so far."

"Is it someone at ITI?"

"No. And I didn't ask you to breakfast just to talk shop. You've got your own career ahead of you now. There's no need to concern yourself with the business. If I'm not mistaken, I was handling things before I let you tag along. I'm sure I will be able to make it without you. Trust me."

A chilled silence blanketed the table, like the quiet of a city the morning after a blizzard. Grace refilled their coffee cups. "Like father, like son." She shook her head and left them to their muted discourse.

"Phil, the last thing I want you to concern yourself with is Wes Jacobson & Associates. That is my responsibility, mine alone. I expect you to show those people across the street how good you are and quit making a big deal out of nothing. I'm sure there's a good explanation to all of this."

"I'm not making a big deal out of nothing. Most of the black people I've met have been there less than a year, like me, just as NoMoBoesky described."

Wes sat up straight and gripped the table on each side. He spoke with resolute calmness. "There are people in this country who aren't ready for all the changes that are happening around us, son. They are too wrapped up in their biases and bigotry. They will take well-intended events, like the one at ITI, and turn it into something evil or wrong. You're a whiz when it comes to those computers. That makes you a valuable asset. I don't care what credible information anyone claims to have; you were hired because they recognized your talent. So, let me be crystal clear. Don't—I repeat—Don't do anything to mess up this great opportunity. Do you understand me?"

Phil sighed. "I hear you."

"I mean it, Phil. Sometimes, things aren't what they appear to be when we look at them with our natural eyes. I keep telling you, you have to look at things with your third eye. Your inner eye. It's the eye that allows you to comprehend justice, love, and redemption. I suggest you pay closer attention to where you go digging for information. Too many people fought so young black men like you could have access to positions like the one you have. Your presence at that company is a sign of the *justice* your grandfather and others fought for. It was *love* for your generation that enabled them to persevere through those bitter times. Their hardships paved the way for privileges your generation takes for granted. Furthermore, the fact that you are working on those sophisticated computers is the *redemption* for all the black men who were told they didn't have the capacity to come up with brilliant ideas."

Phil didn't bother to object. He recognized the familiar glare in his father's eyes, the one that said this topic was closed to any and all further discussion. "Yes, sir."

Phil stared at the half-eaten waffle he no longer craved. He wasn't sure what to think of his father. There was a time when his dad looked for every chance to be his hero. Now, it seemed as if he didn't have time to be anything, let alone a hero.

He pushed his chair away from the table. "I guess I better get to work."

They said their goodbyes and agreed to talk later.

Wes watched in awe as Phil strode out of the diner. Their resemblance was uncanny; his son had grown into a 6'1" replica of him. *I hope like hell my looks are the only thing he gets from me.*

An all too familiar dull pain poked him under his rib. Like clockwork, he pulled a pack of Rolaids from his pocket, popped two chalky tablets into his mouth, followed by a big gulp of water to wash down the residue. *Shiiid, who am I fooling? I see the signs plain as day.*

From the first moment he held Phil, Wes knew his youngest son was the one destined to follow in his path. For years, he'd welcomed the idea and even dreamt about the day he'd hand the keys to the business over so Phil could carry on the legacy. Then the doctor found a tumor on his stomach, and the idea no longer looked enticing. He rubbed the tender spot on the side of his stomach. The tumor was benign, but the idea of Phil following in his footsteps was a cancerous idea he was determined to nip in the bud.

God, I'm not telling You how to run Your business. In fact, we both know I am in no position to offer You any advice. However, if You're willing to extend a favor to a wretched soul, who has always tried to do Your will, can You please drive any idea this boy has about following in my shoes far away?

CHAPTER 3

T HE SUN POKED above the roof of the ITI Center and bounced off the ITI sign at just the precise angle to blind unexpected motorists. Phil exited the diner and shielded his eyes from the glare. Traffic filled the intersection as a stream of bumper-to-bumper drivers waited to enter the company garage.

Phil was halfway across the street when he remembered his attaché case was back at the diner. Although he resented the idea of facing Wes again, he was eager to set in motion a plan he had devised, one that would ensure his father read NoMoBoesky's t-file. Phil knew that if he surreptitiously placed a copy on the table, Wes would be reading it by the time he crossed the street.

He couldn't see Wes from the door, so he stood on his tiptoes and leaned to his left to get a better look. His father was still seated at the table, drinking a cup of coffee and reading the newspaper.

Phil hadn't noticed the subtle positioning of the table earlier. It was expertly located behind a white brick support column and a four-foot dividing wall with a planter on top. Although he didn't have conclusive evidence, Phil was convinced his father was behind the table's quasi-private placement.

He and his father had the same smooth pecan brown skin, except Wes's appeared more polished and radiant. Phil stared at his hands. They were ashy and looked like a chocolate bloom-covered Hershey's bar. He had been in a hurry to get to work and forgotten to lotion—again.

[11]

His father's manly, yet delicate, handsomeness was rather appealing, especially his salt-and-pepper beard. It was slightly heavier than a five o'clock shadow, but not so thick that he looked ominous to the casual passerby.

Phil heard a familiar voice behind him. It was coming from outside, near the diner's front door.

He turned just in time to see his co-worker Marvin Thompson reach for the door.

Getting cornered into one of Marvin's long-winded, meaningless conversations would extinguish any hope of his plan succeeding. Phil ran past the cashier counter like a thoroughbred on the home stretch. Out of nowhere, the crisp pages of Wes's newspaper fanned out like a peacock's tail, and let out a loud *Crrackkk!*

Phil's foot slammed against the floor, sending him headlong into the paper.

Wes jerked the paper aside. "Boy, what the hell is wrong with you? You damn near got shot!"

Phil had never known his father to carry a gun, but he knew if Wes said he could have shot him, debating whether he had a gun was irrelevant.

"I forgot this." Phil held up the briefcase.

"Uh huh," Wes grunted then buried his head back behind a section of the *Washington Post*.

Phil pushed the case's release button. The clasp remained locked. He checked the combination; the last dial was off by one digit. Phil heard Marvin and sensed him getting closer. He tried to turn the dial, but the sweat on his thumb made it difficult to grip the brass, and it slipped off. Phil grabbed the case, held it against his chest, and slowly turned to his left as Marvin and his two cohorts walked by and sat at a table in the opposite corner.

"Phil, what in the hell are you doing?" Wes peered over the top of the paper.

Phil tried the latch again. The clasp didn't budge. He glanced over his shoulder. Marvin's head was hidden behind a menu. "Huh? Umm … I was just about to leave."

"Boy, I swear you can really act strange sometimes." Wes shook his head and continued reading the paper. "Acting just like them crazy ass Mitchells," he mumbled to himself, referring to Marjorie's family.

• • • •

The elevator door was closing when Phil approached. He slid his attaché case into the small opening between the doors, and they retracted. He stepped inside and claimed a position against the left wall. Buttons 3, 10, and 18 were highlighted. He pressed 18 again.

Two white women, who looked to be in their early thirties, stood on the opposite side, chatting in a hushed tone. Based on their wardrobe and spritzed hairdos, Phil knew they weren't programmers. Female programmers were just as rare as black programmers, and the female programmers he knew didn't dress quite so stylishly. He concluded they were in the clerical pool.

A pudgy man in a too-tight blue three-piece suit—the standard issue uniform for all mid-level and executive managers—occupied the expanse of the elevator. The morning edition of the

Wall Street Journal shielded him from the non-manager types surrounding him.

The elevator climbed at a deliberate pace then stopped at the third floor. The portly sycophant walked off, continuing to read his paper, never acknowledging the existence of the others.

Phil sensed movement in his periphery and shifted his view. The brunette woman was whispering to her friend and pointing in his direction.

He adjusted his stance to get a better view.

The woman with auburn hair stood stiff as a board, the expression on her face was filled with shock and embarrassment.

The look on her face had everything to do with him. That, Phil knew for sure. By the way her friend was darting her eyes in his direction as she whispered, he was convinced her expression had everything to do with what was being whispered into her ear.

The door opened on the tenth floor. A blur of moussed brown hair rushed past Phil.

He looked on with amusement as the first lady made a hasty exit. He turned his attention to her auburn-haired friend, who was now looking like a frightened department store mannequin on the opposite side of the elevator.

Everyone stood frozen in time for a few awkward seconds until the elevator doors began to close. Phil blocked the door with his briefcase.

Such encounters weren't the norm at ITI, but they did occur often enough that he and the other black ITI male employees had created a weekly happy hour game called Dark Shadows, where they went around the table describing their latest, covertly racist encounter with a white co-worker.

Phil smirked and shook his head; he couldn't wait to tell the guys about this. He craned his neck to look her in the eye. "I think she's waiting on you."

She glanced at Phil sheepishly then looked at her friend.

The bossy brunette turned around and flipped a loose strand behind her ear. She beckoned her friend like a third base coach, waving his runner home. "Holly! Come on, Holly!"

Holly attempted to move her feet, but they felt like they were welded to the floor.

When she raised her head, Phil recognized her. She was the administrative assistant for one of the managers on his floor.

"Holly, will you *pleeeaaase* get outta there before ..." The brunette glared at Phil, seemingly convinced he intended to harm her friend. "Just come on," she demanded as she marched back to the elevator, grabbed Holly by the elbow, and escorted her out.

Overcome with embarrassment, Holly trudged off the elevator like a helpless child. She looked over her shoulder as the elevator doors were closing and managed a slight smile and a subtle wave.

"Before what?" he asked aloud after the elevator door closed. "Before I turn into an uncivilized nigger?" He thumped his chest, imitating the savages he had seen in those old Tarzan movies.

He stopped suddenly when he remembered there might be surveillance cameras watching and listening.

I better chill. The last thing I need is to get fired. I'll never hear the end of it, especially from Daddy, he reminded himself.

[15]

When he exited, a smile stretched across his face.

On second thought, getting fired might not be such a bad idea after all. If they fire me, maybe they'll tell me why they hired me in the first place.

CHAPTER 4

G RACE RETURNED to collect the dishes. Wes placed his hand over his coffee cup when she reached for it. "I haven't finished."

"Wes, you know you're not going to drink that. You always claim you taste the coffee grounds, remember?" She pulled a clean cup from her apron pouch and filled it. "Now, go on and read the sports section. I'll get your orange juice so you can eat the other half of that bagel."

Wes laughed and took a sip of the freshly brewed coffee. "So, you're a detective now?"

"No. Just a damn good waitress."

"Oh! I see." Wes leaned back in his seat, intrigued by her response. "Tell me, how does one determine *what* makes a damn good waitress? Or better yet, *who* is a damn good waitress?"

"Darling, that's a question you should ask yourself, seeing as I'm the only waitress in here that you want serving you." She started to leave then stopped and turned around. "Oh, and let's not forget who set me up with a job in this marvelous place. I recall someone begging me to come work here. What was his name? It's right on the tip of my tongue."

He polished off the side of the bagel that was covered with cream cheese then brushed the crumbs from his vest. "My orange juice, please. And remember—"

"I know, I know! No pulp in your juice."

Grace turned on her heels and headed for the drink counter, her smile teemed with confidence; she had finally scored one on him.

She adored Wes, but more than anything, she wanted him to recognize her skills as a detective's assistant … and anything else he desired.

Wes raised the cup of coffee and saluted her bodacious backside. "Grace, my dear, you are the absolute best."

Wes knew Grace wanted more. More attention. More time. More of everything he had to offer. Unfortunately, the more that she desired was going to be difficult to give or receive, especially since their relationship was built on mutual infatuation and unrestrained lust.

Having Grace around had been a blessing and a curse. She was the only one he could trust and look to for help with his current case. She was also the latest reason why things were bumpy between him and Marjorie. It was an inconvenience that came with his line of work.

Grace returned with his juice. Not waiting for, or expecting, an invitation from Wes, she grabbed a notepad from her apron pouch and sat down.

Wes's head was buried deep inside the latest edition of the *Washington Post*. He lobbed his first question over the paper wall. "Well?"

Grace rolled her eyes and exhaled with a long sigh. It annoyed her when he talked from behind his newspaper. It meant he was hiding something. "Robert came in for lunch yesterday. He had two other men with him. They—"

"The same two guys from the day before?" Wes interrupted.

"No. They—"

"Were they ITI guys? Did you see their badges? See their names?" Wes rattled off.

Grace shut her notepad and slammed it on the table. "Maybe if you put that damn paper down and quit interrupting me, I can tell you what you want to know. I know you think I'm just a waitress, but in my line of work, observing people is critical. Not only am I good at it, I'm one of the best. If you want to be a customer right now, I'll get up and leave you to your paper. But if you want me to give you a report, I suggest you put that damn paper down so I can do that."

Wes closed the paper and placed it on the table to the side. "I'm sorry. Please continue."

Upset and stone-faced, Grace remained motionless, as if she hadn't heard a word he said.

"Today, Grace," Wes huffed. After nearly a minute of silence, he could no longer contain his impatience. "You see? This is exactly what I was talking about when you asked me why I don't like working cases with women."

Grace's reticent demeanor was apparent when she continued. Halfway through the report, she realized he was no longer interrupting her, so she spoke with more candor and assurance. When she finished, she flipped the notepad shut and waited.

The chatter of nearby diners and the cling-clang of the busboy clearing plates from a table could not penetrate the invisible bubble created by Wes's silence. She looked up at the wall clock above his left shoulder. The red second hand devoured seconds with each tick. It was her turn to wait.

"What about Robert? Did he appear to be nervous or act like he was hiding something?" Wes wasn't sure if Grace could sense his despair. He hoped not.

She'd noticed. After five months of keeping tabs on Robert Berry, it was the first time in a long while that Wes had expressed an urgency and dependency for her. She knew it had more to do with the information she had, but it felt good just the same. "He didn't look nervous, and he definitely didn't look like he was hiding anything. Or should I say, he wasn't hiding any more than the rest of us." She locked eyes with him.

Ten months ago, their target, Robert Berry, had called on Wes for help with an issue. Technically, the case was closed, and Robert was no longer a client. Years of sorting through people's messes had taught Wes one lesson for sure: You never close a case until you can close the file for good. Closed cases, with more questions than answers, tended to pop up out of nowhere, with unexpected flare. Robert worked at ITI and patronized Bagels Galore on a daily basis. Wes wasn't completely sure, but he doubted if Robert was a Jack on the loose. The guy was dating a local celebrity. He'd discovered that tidbit of info soon after he took Robert on as a client. He checked out all his clients. Experience had also taught him that keeping a watchful eye on some clients wasn't just prudent; it was vital.

"Well, let's hope he stays that way, but I seriously doubt that he will."

"Why do you say that?"

Wes stuffed the last of the bagel into his mouth. He held up his finger as if to say "Give me a minute" then wiped his mouth. "Because Phil knows what's going on at ITI. I tried to throw him off the trail, but I doubt it. I know my son. He's not going to quit until he gets to the bottom of this. When that day comes, I just want to be sure he doesn't find my ass in the middle of it."

CHAPTER 5

T HE PHONE RANG as the office door flew open with a bang against the doorstop and then slammed shut. Phil tossed his case on the desk and grabbed the phone before the call rolled over to his voice mailbox.

"Good morning. ITI. Phil Jacobson speaking." He held the phone inches away from his ear while he leaned back against his desk and gasped for air.

"Good morning, Philander." The voice was serene, but the attention it commanded was absolute.

"Hi, Mama."

Marjorie Jacobson sat in front of her vanity mirror, while Joan Lunden and Spencer Christian bantered in the background on *Good Morning America*. Her robe was tied loosely around her amply proportioned mahogany frame, revealing her black bra and matching satin slip. "They must keep you really busy over there. It's been a week since I last heard from you."

Phil looked up at the ceiling in exasperation. "Mama, I was going to call you today. I promise."

"Philander, don't start your lying this early in the morning. I've known you nine months longer than anybody on this earth; so, you know I know you."

"Mama, I was going to call. In fact, I was going to call right after I got your message this morning, but I didn't have time because I had to go meet Daddy." He had retrieved his mother's message minutes before his meeting with his father. He remembered the skeptical look on his dad's face when he denied having talked to his mother. Although he told the truth, Phil suspected his father knew he wasn't being totally honest.

"Philander, I swear I don't know what I'm going to do with you and your absentminded ways."

His name was Philander Wesley Jacobson Jr., to be more precise. He abhorred the name. It was old and funny sounding. It seemed to be an unjust price to pay for the honor of being named after his father. He often wondered why his parents chose to pass the name on to him since his father seemed to dislike the name just as much as he did. Phil was the youngest of his parents' four children. How his two older brothers escaped such a tortuous existence was a mystery that had long been unsolved as far as Phil was concerned. He concluded that his parents had grown tired of the creative naming process by the time he'd come along, so they stamped his father's name across his forehead without debate or afterthought.

With the exception of his mother and MiMi, his grandmother, no one called him Philander. Most people assumed Phil was short for Phillip. He never bothered to correct them. It wasn't as if he were trying to hide anything, not deliberately. Phil didn't see the need in volunteering personal information unless it was vitally necessary, which wasn't often.

"So, what does your daddy have you up to now? It's not going to take up too much of your time, is it? What about your job? Is it going to interfere with your job?"

Marjorie was the commercial loan manager for the Raleigh-Durham region of NationsBank. Her meticulous approach to processing loan information resulted in her asking several questions at once in an attempt to hurry the process along, while also asking targeted questions to assess the borrower's strengths and vulnerabilities. If they tripped over a question, it meant they were hiding something. More than one stumble, and they could kiss their loan goodbye.

"He doesn't have me doing anything. Daddy told me he doesn't need my help anymore." The resonance of his father's decision punched Phil squarely in the gut, and his voice trailed off. Wes had given him the pardon he had always wanted, except it didn't feel as satisfying as he had imagined.

"Mmm hmm." Marjorie's voice echoed from the half-empty cup of tea she was sipping.

Phil reclined in his chair and waited for the next series of spitfire questions that was sure to come. He knew his mother was in the middle of her usual morning routine of talking on the phone, drinking tea, eating a slice of rye toast with marmalade, and applying the finishing touches of her makeup.

"I guess it's a good thing he doesn't need your help. Your hands are pretty full already. How is Ann? Is she excited about the wedding? What was the reason for the big rush again?"

Phil sat up, his face filled with shock. With all the excitement over NoMoBoesky's document, he hadn't thought about Ann and how she would be impacted. He and Ann Marie Donovan were getting married in two weeks. They had known each other for only six months, but they both believed they were ready to declare, publicly, the committed and passionate love they expressed privately. It had been a week since they made the announcement. The suddenness of time left many of his friends and family surprised, his mother especially. Marjorie greeted the news with delight, but Phil knew there was a torrent of questions lurking beneath her captivating smile, waiting to be lobbed his way. Floundering for answers, Phil resorted to a tactic he had seen his father use in similar situations.

"Fine. Yes. No big rush."

Marjorie chortled. "You are truly your daddy's child."

Phil laughed nervously. He had grown accustomed to his mother using every opportunity to draw comparisons between him and his father but never had he heard her do it with such clarity and profound awareness. By the time they said goodbye, his mother's revelation had placed him face to face with the one decision he had been avoiding.

CHAPTER 6

"*DON'T DO ANYTHING to mess up this great opportunity.*" Wes's baritone voice reverberated between Phil's ears. He understood his father's concern, but if NoMoBoesky was correct, then Jack Sherman, who was a highly respected CEO, and the company he headed were up to something unethical and illegal, not to mention Phil was being used to help conceal their fraud. If he exposed the corruption, there was a good chance he would get fired before Jack Sherman ever got indicted. He knew his parents would think he had lost his mind for sure. He stared at a silver-plated framed photograph on his desk. It was a photo of him and Ann. She was standing behind him, smiling brightly, with her arms wrapped around his neck. He was confident Ann would continue to love and stand by him if he lost his job, but he wasn't sure if she would understand the reason. He wasn't sure if he even understood.

Maybe I am being paranoid. There's only one way to know for sure. He locked his office door and retrieved his attaché from underneath the desk.

Phil could still smell the richness of the case's soft, top grain leather as he opened it. The black Winn International attaché was a gift from his mother. She'd purchased it immediately after he told her he had been hired. He brought it to work daily out of some obligation to her, he supposed. Until earlier that morning, the only worthwhile things he carried in the case were a notebook, some employee information sheets, a computer magazine, and an occasional lunch. Attaché cases weren't a required utensil for a programmer. However, it was an ideal accessory for an investigator.

He wasn't a private investigator, but he believed he knew enough about the trade to know that if you sensed something in your gut, you should instinctively follow it and find out why. At least that's what Wes always told him.

He retrieved the disk he copied from his case. He pulled out another disk. BOOT DISK was written across the front with a black marker. After he inserted both disks into the computer's disk drives, he unscrewed the network cable from the computer so no one could trace his activity.

He powered on the computer and typed a series of commands that made the green lights on both disk drives flicker. White letters scrolled up the black screen.

The doorknob rattled. Phil whirled around and stared at the door. The doorknob jiggled again, followed by repeated knuckle taps.

He typed quickly to erase the information from the monitor; then he ejected both diskettes and shoved them into his pants pocket.

Oh, damn! They're about to fire my ass!

He looked around the office and then spread a stack of paper across his desk to give the appearance that he was busy at work.

Maybe that crazy-ass white lady in the elevator convinced her friend to report me.

The door bumped against its frame as the knob twisted with more force.

I wonder if they saw me on the elevator.

[27]

The knuckle taps turned to dull thuds.

Phil wiped his balmy hands against his pants. Then he took a deep breath and opened the door.

CHAPTER 7

"**W**HAT YOU DOING in here, rookie?" Marvin barged into the office and shut the door behind him. Phil had known him since their college days at North Carolina A&T. Back then, Phil found his alpha male personality humorously obnoxious. Nothing had changed.

He was wiry and about as short as Carlton on *The Fresh Prince of Bel-Air*. He also had an unusual style when it came to fashion. His current ensemble included a pair of paisley suspenders and an oversized belt that was buckled on the last hole and looped halfway around his waist. Phil wanted to ask why he wore a belt *and* suspenders, but Marvin had a reputation for blowing things out of proportion, so he didn't bother.

"I'm working. What else would I be doing?"

Phil turned around and faced the monitor. He wasn't sure if he looked as agitated as he felt. He liked Marvin, even though he was annoying most of the time.

"Jacking off ain't working. Well, it might be for you. You probably have a hard time finding your dick and holding onto it." He erupted into that silly laugh of his that seemed to come more from his nasal passage than anywhere else.

No matter how obnoxious Marvin sounded when he laughed, Phil could not help but to laugh himself. He turned to face Marvin and held his arms up in surrender. "You've busted me." Phil got up and opened the door. "I guess you can leave now so I can get back to finding my dick."

"I'm leaving. I just came by to tell you that they're opening doors around here for your boy."

"What do you mean?"

"I waited for you in the lobby this morning, but I didn't see you. You were probably dragging in late like all these other niggas around here, running on colored people's time."

Phil remained silent.

Marvin started explaining how his manager had stopped by his office the previous day and asked to meet with him the following morning. He made sure not to omit any detail. "I stayed up all night preparing notes," he said with cocksure bravado.

Marvin had graduated two years before Phil. He never missed an opportunity to remind Phil that he had more corporate experience. He salivated over the idea of getting a manager's promotion and was determined to make it into the managerial ranks, no matter the cost.

"So, what happened?"

"I didn't know what the meeting was going to be about, but I walked into Steve's office this morning, ready for anything. As soon as I sat down, he told me I was being promoted to team leader for the next release of Red Sun. I'm in charge of reviewing the technical specification documents. What you got to say about that?"

"Man, that sounds like your kinda shit! How many people on the team?"

"Two," Marvin boasted.

"Let me get this straight; you're saying you have two people reporting to you? Or are you saying that you are one of the two people?"

"Yeah, it's two people: Janet and me! But her ass is reporting to me."

Phil could sense that Marvin was becoming defensive. They slapped hands and bump-hugged.

"Look, man, I'm happy for you, and I know you're going to bust your ass to make sure that shit is tight."

"PJ, you know I'm going all the way nuclear on this shit! They're not going to know what hit 'em!" He stood in his Eddie Murphy *Raw* pose. "Oh yeah, and your boy finally closed on that crib in Silver Meadow Lakes over the weekend. That's where most of the ITI managers live, you know."

Phil leaned back against his desk and crossed his arms. "No shit? I've seen those houses; they're more like mansions."

"Yeah, and you know the ladies love a man who has his own castle. Keep hanging with me, junior; you'll learn everything you need to know to make it in this world." Marvin broadened his stance as much as his diminutive frame would allow as he reveled in his accomplishment.

Phil shook his head and laughed. "I guess I have a lot to learn."

Marvin headed for the door, but Phil blocked his path. "Before you go, tell me one thing. If you didn't know why Steve wanted to meet with you, what kind of notes were you preparing? And why were you up all night making notes for a meeting that you knew nothing about?"

"You think you're so smart, PJ. I guarantee you, you will be reporting to me one day."

"See, now, that's your problem. You don't recognize talent. Because if you did, you would know that I'm too talented to work on a two-man team that requires no talent."

"Kiss my ass, rookie!"

Phil laughed as he opened the door. "You won't be a manager for long if they hear you talking like that."

"Later for you, Mr. Smart Ass." Marvin jabbed Phil on the arm before walking out.

Phil locked the door, then hurried back to his desk and re-inserted the diskettes. A few keystrokes later, the document was back on the screen.

He analyzed each sentence and processed each paragraph, looking for something, anything. He knew Marvin's previous position hadn't required much skill. It consisted of running batch jobs on the mainframe computers and then hand delivering the printouts to the designated department. Marvin could never explain what information was in the reports or how the reports were being used.

Now, out of nowhere, they're asking Marvin to be a team lead? That doesn't seem right.

He leaned closer to the screen, hoping to find an answer, a clue.

He didn't want to hurt Marvin's feelings, but the promotion made no sense. Several months prior, someone in the Underground had intercepted a message sent to ITI's board of directors and posted it on several BBS boards. The letter stated that due to low sales, Red Sun was being phased out. Phil sat back and looked at the screen.

Whatever I do, Daddy's not going to like it anyway. I'm gonna need some help, though.

The vibration from the pager buzzing on his hip shook Phil from his thoughts. He nudged the pager from its holder. It was his sister, Roxy.

The second unconscious smile of the day crept across his face. He kissed the pager. "That was quick!"

CHAPTER 8

AFTER WORK, Phil stopped by the community center where Ann Marie worked to tell her he needed to change their plans for the evening. He wasn't prepared to tell her about ITI, so he told her he would be busy on a work-related project. The guilt he felt for telling the lie was forgotten the moment he and Ann shared a hot, steamy kiss. A kiss that soon led to Phil's pants gathered in a heap around his ankles and Ann's panties balled up in a chair while the two embraced in a heated, heart-thumping quickie on her desk.

• • • •

Phil threw his car keys on the kitchen counter and headed straight for his computer with a large pizza and a twelve pack of Michelob in tow.

He stored the beer in a small refrigerator next to his desk and then settled in for another long night. First, he uploaded a program file to MystikalGremlinz, the SysOp for a bulletin board known as Game Asylum.

Phil didn't think he was being watched but decided it would be better to safeguard his calls just the same. Instead of dialing Game Asylum's access number, he ran a program that connected his modem to the local telephone company's Central Office. Once he made entry into the CO, he removed his name and number from his caller profile; then he proceeded to reroute his call through a maze of relays, switches, and exchanges. If someone were tracing his calls, the circuitous routes would be too time-consuming to untangle.

The Game Asylum's login screen appeared. Phil typed his username and password with one hand while he chomped down on a slice of thin crust supreme. He entered the main room then navigated to the chatroom area. A list of room numbers filled the computer screen. Phil typed "64" even though it wasn't on the list. He entered the private room where MystikalGremlinz met with his closest friends.

```
MystikalGremlinz:>  Hi  PhantomPhixer.  You're
                    early.
PhantomPhixer:>     Tried to get here sooner.
```

In the virtual world of Bulletin Board Systems, or the Underground, as Phil and his friends called it, no one had a name. You were known by your handle. Phil was PhantomPhixer.

When Phil was sixteen, Wes secured him a spot in a highly competitive summer computer program at Duke University. It would serve as the first of many occasions where he was the only African American in the group. The experience was uncomfortable until he befriended Matty and Gordo, two other misfits attending the prestigious program.

Matty and Gordo began calling Phil "Phixer" after he fixed a hard-to-find coding problem with a game they were attempting to hack. Phil decided on PhantomPhixer as a moniker; it sounded cool and mysterious.

```
MystikalGremlinz:>  How's life in the
                    sweatshop?
PhantomPhixer:>     Don't ask.
MystikalGremlinz:>  That good, huh?
PhantomPhixer:>     Tell you after I upload
                    this new patch.
MystikalGremlinz:>  You fixed it already?
PhantomPhixer:>     What's my name?
MystikalGremlinz:>  Dude, I swear you will be
                    the first person I bring
                    aboard when I sell this.
```

In the Underground, one's reputation could rise and fall quicker than the lifespan of a mosquito. Many egos were known to have been decimated, but PhantomPhixer had established a glowing and well-respected reputation for his ability to debug and enhance code.

MystikalGremlinz was regarded as one of the pioneers of the BBS software that almost all bulletin boards used. He had requested PhantomPhixer's assistance on the latest software he was developing.

As the file uploaded, Phil recounted MystikalGremlinz's excitement when he first sought PhantomPhixer's assistance with the project. "It's going to be a revolutionary departure from this raggedy platform we've been using," MystikalGremlinz had marveled in the message.

```
MystikalGremlinz:>  Thanks PhantomPhixer. So
                    what's up?
PhantomPhixer:>     Did you see NoMoBoesky's
                    latest hack?
```

```
MystikalGremlinz:> Been too busy. What about
                  it?
```

Phil's fingers skipped over the keyboard with speed and precision. He stopped occasionally to take a swig of beer as he filled him in. Phil chose his words carefully. He didn't want MystikalGremlinz to think he had turned into some paranoid freak. He held his breath as he typed his next message.

```
PhantomPhixer:>    I believe I am one of
                   those people ITI hired.
MystikalGremlinz:> Bummer! By the way, you
                   never told me you were
                   African American.
```

The thought never occurred to Phil since it went without saying in every other facet of his life. Phil realized there was a lot he and MystikalGremlinz didn't know about each other, even though they had been best virtual friends for ten years.

```
PhantomPhixer:>    Is that a problem?
MystikalGremlinz:> No. Just saying you never
                   told me. For what it's
                   worth, I also didn't know
                   you worked for ITI.
PhantomPhixer:>    So that's a problem?
MystikalGremlinz:> No. None of it matters to
                   me. Just saying I didn't
                   know any of that.
PhantomPhixer:>    What they're doing really
                   pisses me off.
MystikalGremlinz:> Don't worry about a
                   thing. I'm not supposed
                   to say anything, but ITI
                   is about to purchase our
```

software. When they do, I
will make sure nothing
happens to you.

Phil knocked the bottle of beer off his desk when he read the comment. A gooey mixture of cheese, sausage, and pepperoni stretched from his half-open mouth to the slice he held in his hand.

PhantomPhixer:>   ITI is purchasing your
                        project?

MystikalGremlinz:>   Yes. And the company.
                        Looks like we'll be able
                        to work together sooner
                        than I thought.

Phil shouted and pumped his fists. He couldn't believe how quickly things had turned in his favor. "Now, I can relax! No more worrying about ITI or lying to Ann. And, the best part, I didn't need Daddy after all. I did it on my own."

He paused. He couldn't think of anything he had accomplished. He still didn't know why ITI was secretly hiring minorities. He had no idea why they were putting Marvin in charge of a product they were going to discontinue. He surely hadn't found out how he had gotten hired.

PhantomPhixer:>   Thanks. But I've got to
                        find out what they're up
                        to. Something's not
                        right.

MystikalGremlinz:>   You're the PhantomPhixer
                        and you're great at
                        fixing bugs. What are you
                        going to do?

The blinking cursor reflected off of his eyeglasses and twinkled in the monitor as it awaited his response. Phil had never prepped a case. Roxy was much better. She saw the big picture, while he specialized in combing through the details. He'd called her after she had paged him, but she didn't answer. The cursor seemed to grow bigger and brighter as the seconds ticked away. His fingers hovered above the keyboard for half a minute; then he pecked the keys.

```
PhantomPhixer:>     I don't know.
MystikalGremlinz:>  OK. What can I do to
                    help?
PhantomPhixer:>     I don't know. I need some
                    time to sort things out.
MystikalGremlinz:>  No problem. You get busy
                    with your plan. I will
                    think of something to buy
                    you some time.
PhantomPhixer:>     Thanks MG. We'll talk
                    tomorrow.
```

Where do I start? What am I looking for? The litany of questions bombarded Phil as soon he turned off the computer. He grabbed another slice of pizza and then placed it back in the box after taking a bite. Each unknown poked and prodded Phil as he lay in bed until fatigue clouded his thoughts, and he finally succumbed.

CHAPTER 9

"WHAT'S THE STATUS on WorldNet?" Jack Sherman inquired as he stuffed down a forkful of eggs benedict. The venerable sixty-five-year-old CEO of ITI was in the middle of his daily scheduled breakfast and briefing with his two prized protégées: Stanley Bricker, his chief operating officer, and Vincent Martello, his chief financial officer.

The three were gathered around the enormous mahogany executive table at the east end of the penthouse boardroom. From the sodalite blue marble floor, with the etched-in company logo at the entrance, to the tiered crystal grand chandelier, and cherry wood paneled soundproof walls, the boardroom was the embodiment of hard work, American capitalism, and corporate power.

Vincent wriggled in his leather high-back chair. The thirty-five-year-old CFO sat dutifully on Jack's left, just as he had for the last five years. He took a deep breath and cleared his throat. "I got a call from Malcolm Graves early this morning. He wants to delay the purchase for a few weeks. A month at the most."

Jack dropped his silver fork on the Waterford crystal plate. "That little punk wants to do what?"

Vincent glanced across the table at Stanley, who stared back, his mouth partially open as if he wanted to say something. Stanley's thin, pinkish lips turned paler with each passing second. He looked as if he had stared into the eyes of Medusa.

Vincent turned to Jack, who had managed to talk himself into a conniption.

"Don't work yourself up, Jack. We don't want you having a heart attack before you retire." Vincent leaned back in his chair. "Trust me; this is not a big deal."

"Sounds like he's making a push to hike up the price, if you ask me," Stanley chimed in.

Vincent glared at his colleague and main nemesis. "I don't recall anyone asking you, now that you mention it."

A confidential memo announcing Jack's retirement had been leaked months ago. It was a well-known fact that Jack would be appointing one of them as his successor, but the choice would not be easy. Stanley and Vincent were both vying for more influence, and neither was willing to concede an inch to the other.

"Stanley's got a point," Jack acknowledged. "How do we know this kid hasn't gotten greedy all of a sudden?"

"Malcolm's not that kind of guy. Besides, he and I discussed the purchase price several times. He considers it to be rather generous. For what it's worth, he also wanted me to reassure you that there are no other potential buyers."

Vincent stood up and headed for the beverage tray in the front corner of the room.

"Then why is he asking us to delay it?" Stanley raised an eyebrow in anticipation of Vincent's response.

"He wants to make sure the latest software enhancements have been fully tested and ready when we go live. You realize this deal means nothing if the software doesn't work, don't you?" Vincent stood at the minibar, scooping ice from a sterling silver ice bucket. "Shouldn't you be concerned about our ability to bring this to market and stay ahead of the competition? I know I am."

"We're staffed and ready on my end. It's all systems go whenever you get this so-called masterpiece of an acquisition put to bed."

Jack listened as the two went back and forth. He had never married and didn't have any illegitimate children, as far as he knew. In a sense, he had adopted Stanley and Vincent as his sons. They were as different as moonshine and water, but Jack looked past the obvious and stared into the possibility. His handpicked heirs had the potential to be the most revered partners Corporate America had ever seen. However, getting both of them to buy into that belief had proven to be more difficult than anticipated.

Vincent poured a glass of Bloody Mary. He added a stalk of celery then held the glass out toward Jack. "Are you ready for your morning pick me up?"

Jack looked at his watch. "Right on time! Of course, any time is the right time for a heart-warming, tasty Bloody Mary."

"How about you, Stanley?" Vincent shook the glass and smiled. He knew Stanley didn't drink anything stronger than beer.

"No, thank you." Stanley lifted his hand from the table then pointed his middle finger skyward.

"Jack, I know you want this acquisition signed and sealed by the end of the month, but a couple of weeks won't change a thing," Vincent advised. "This month or next month; it doesn't matter because no one is paying attention to WorldNet Labs. If we hadn't leaked that teaser to the media last week, Malcolm Graves and his nerdy group of college dropout friends would still be unknown. By the time the competition figures out what we're up to, this acquisition will be a done deal."

Vincent knew Jack's storied legacy and how he had grown ITI from a small electronic parts supply company that he inherited from his father into one of the nation's leading software firms. Vincent also knew that if he wanted to pull this off, he would have to coax the old man through it. ITI was losing its competitive edge. Many of their longtime customers were moving from mainframes to the more economical personal computers. The industry had changed and so had the antiquated mechanisms for doing business. He was confident that Jack would see it his way in the end, but an extra nudge here and there for good measure always helped.

He placed Jack's drink on the monogrammed coaster in front of him and then took his seat. "Well, what do you want me to tell our soon-to-be partners?"

"In my day, once you had an agreement on the table, you followed it to the letter." Jack raised his glass and drank until it was empty. He smacked his lips. "Tell Mr. Graves he has three weeks, or this whole damn thing is off!"

CHAPTER 10
WEDNESDAY, JANUARY 20, 1993

"C'MON, PHIL. Let's go! The line at Bennigan's will be backed up if we're not there by eleven forty-five," Dana said as she leaned halfway through Phil's office door.

Phil had met Dana on their first day at ITI. She had been assigned to the quality control group as a test analyst. She had a petite, athletic build that was accentuated by an indulgent smile and tomboyish charm.

"Where's Karen?" Phil asked as the elevator opened.

Dana pushed him into the elevator. "She's waiting in the lobby. We've been waiting on you for ten minutes."

When they exited the elevator, Marvin spotted them immediately and began waving. "PJ! Over here."

Karen stood next to him. Her oblong, walnut-shell brown face was contorted with anger and despair. "If we walk fast, we can beat the crowd," she urged. She motioned with her head in an attempt to signal the others to hurry before Marvin invited himself along.

"I was having lunch with PJ, but I guess it'll be all right if you two fine, gorgeous ladies join us," Marvin said as he quickly got in stride with the rest of the group.

"Phil, you didn't tell us you had lunch plans," Dana quipped.

Phil looked at her with astonishment.

"We … are … leaving." Dana mouthed the words, pointed to Karen and herself, and then waved.

"No! Don't!" Phil shouted as he stepped between his two co-workers and put an arm around each of them. "Let's hurry. I'm really hungry!"

The three of them crossed the street, with Marvin tagging close behind, talking a mile a minute.

When they passed Bagels Galore, Phil glanced inside. He saw Grace and stopped. She was placing a set of salt and pepper shakers on a table where three men were seated. It all seemed normal until she tugged on her right ear. Phil knew that could mean only one thing: She had just bugged the table for close range surveillance but forgot to adjust the volume before turning on her earbud. Ear tugging was a sure sign of feedback.

Phil couldn't see two of the guys; their backs were facing the window. A man with a smooth butterscotch complexion stared at him but then looked away quickly. Phil had seen him around the office a few times.

So Daddy's target does *work at ITI.*

"You better not be trying to sneak off and leave us with Marvin's tired behind," Dana chided as she stood inches in front of him with a hand on her hip. "What are you looking at?"

"Nothing. I thought I saw someone I knew." Phil placed his arms around her shoulders and hurried off before Dana looked inside.

• • • •

They arrived at Bennigan's before the onslaught of downtown workers arrived. The buzz inside the tavern-styled restaurant was electric. It was the perfect hangout for networking during lunch and the best hot spot for meeting the opposite sex during happy hour.

"So, Phil, the big day's coming soon. Are you ready?" Karen asked after the waitress brought a round of water and got their drink orders.

Phil shrugged. "As ready as I'll ever be."

"How long have you two been dating again?"

"Six months," Phil said between sips. "I know it hasn't been a long time, but where is it written that you have to wait a year or longer? If you know what you want, and you find the person you've been looking for, the amount of time should be irrelevant."

"Well, I guess I haven't found that guy because I'm nowhere near an altar." Dana giggled.

"I'm with you on that, girl," Karen added. "To be honest, I think I'm going to expand my dating circle to include men of other races. Don't get me wrong; I have nothing against black men. I just think my interests are beyond what some brothas are willing to explore."

"And what might those interests be?" Marvin inquired.

"Things like salsa dancing, skydiving, and hiking, just to name a few. I believe that any guy who says he wants to marry me will have to be interested in those things as well because that's where he's going to get to know me best."

"Yeah, you better look elsewhere because I don't know any brotha who's into that shit," Marvin quipped. "Besides, no brotha I know is going to do all of that just to get to know you! You're smart and fine as hell, but your ass ain't *that* damn fine!"

The waitress returned for their orders before Karen could respond, but no sooner had she left, Karen tore into Marvin like a tornado sweeping through a trailer park. "Marvin, it is truly comforting to know that you and the brothas you know are not my type." She made air quotations when she said "brothas you know."

"In fact, I am relieved that you don't find any of those things interesting. Now, maybe you will leave me alone and quit trying to figure out if I will go out with you. You know what you are? You are one of those men that a woman can't be nice to because you think she wants to let you in her panties. For what, God only knows. The problem with you is you've lied to yourself and believe your own bullshit. You really believe that you have something that a real woman wants. Well, let me be clear once and for all. You will not get in my panties and you have nothing—and I repeat—nothing, absolutely nothing that I want!"

Marvin sat in silence with a stunned expression.

"Phil, get some glue. Humpty Dumpty over there just got cracked." Dana erupted into laughter, followed by Phil and Karen.

By the time lunch arrived, Marvin's bruised ego had healed, and his voracious appetite had taken over. "What are we doing for your bachelor party?" he asked before stuffing a handful of French fries into his mouth.

"I haven't made any plans so far. It really doesn't matter."

Marvin frowned and shot Phil a suspicious look. "Whatcha talkin' 'bout, Willis?"

"Marvin, I have had my share of good times; I don't need a big send-off like I'm going off to war and not coming back home.

[47]

I'm still the same Phil Jacobson. Marriage isn't going to change that."

"If marriage isn't going to change you, then you guys aren't going to be married long. Marriage shouldn't change you, but you should want to change for your marriage," Dana countered.

"That's not what I meant. I know this is what I want, and Ann Marie is who I want. We plan to make this last forever, like both of our parents have done."

Marvin grabbed Phil by the arm. "PJ, chill with the lovey-dovey stuff. No one is interested in that Harlequin Romance shit! What about the party?"

"I don't know of anything about a party. All I know is that I'm not making any plans."

"That settles it then. I'm in charge of the bachelor party. Leave everything to me."

Dana looked at Phil and shook her head in disbelief. "Lord, help you, Phil!"

CHAPTER 11

"DANA!" The voice sounded as if it had originated from the heavens. Its crisp, modulated bass tone echoed throughout the spacious ITI foyer.

"Who is that shouting my name like we're in the country?" Dana bumped against Phil as she turned to locate the voice's owner. Phil, Karen, and Marvin stood in the middle of the sparsely populated foyer and surveyed the room with her.

Phil spotted a man standing at the top of the staircase. It was the same guy he'd seen at Bagels Galore, the one whose table Grace had under surveillance. The man appeared to be in his late forties, extremely tall—6'7" at a minimum, by Phil's estimation—with an angular jaw, boasted by a broad smile.

"Dana, up here." The man raised mile-long arms and waved. "Do you have a minute?"

"Oh, that's Robert. Let me see what he wants before he starts screaming my name again."

Phil feigned interest in a corkboard full of notices next to the elevator while secretly observing the scene upstairs. Dana and the guy had just found a table in the court area.

I betcha that's the dude Daddy didn't want to talk about. He took note of the man's display of gentlemanly charm as he pulled Dana's chair back and invited her to take a seat. He also noticed the guy's debonair and wanton smile. Phil's chin dropped to his chest.

The ding of the elevator's bell interrupted his thoughts.

"Nah, that can't be it. Not him and Dana," he murmured as he entered the elevator.

"Who was that guy with Dana?" Phil asked Karen and Marvin after they exited the elevator.

Karen shrugged. "He works in human resources. I didn't know his name until a minute ago."

"His name is Robert Berry," Marvin blurted out as he blocked Phil and Karen's path. "He's a manager in HR. He's all right, I guess. I talked to him a couple of times and even told him I was looking to get into management. I asked him if he could offer a young brotha some advice about working his way up the ranks. Do you know what that jolly brown giant told me?" Marvin stood on his tiptoes and pretended to talk like Robert. "'The only thing I would advise you to do is work hard at whatever they give you.'"

Phil and Karen laughed and then walked on either side of Marvin's wispy frame.

Marvin blocked their path again. "I can't stand dudes like him. They get to management then act like they can't help another brotha get there. Just because Jack Sherman mentioned his name a few times, he thinks he's top shit among niggas around here. Well, his old giraffe-legged behind can bend all the way down and kiss my ass, because I'm on my way to management without him."

Karen giggled. "I figured you were a pervert."

"Humph! You won't ever catch me doing no freaky shit like that."

They came to a corridor, and Karen turned. "Just because I won't see you, doesn't mean you're not into it," she said in a confident tone, dripping with sarcasm.

Marvin watched with exasperation as Karen walked away. "Why are you so interested in Robert? He's no one special. He *thinks* he's more important than he really is, if you ask me. You know what I mean, PJ?" He looked over both his shoulders. "I can't believe he left me standing here, talking to myself. His black ass is going to pay for that."

CHAPTER 12
THURSDAY, JANUARY 21, 1993

WES READ the latest edition of the *Charlotte Observer* as he rocked in his wingback executive chair. The soft burgundy leather chair was one of his prized possessions. It was a reminder of the days when his father was preparing to litigate one of his many civil rights cases. J.D. Jacobson was a local legend and, until the time of his death twenty years ago, one of the best attorneys in the state. He was a fiery litigator. His courtroom showmanship was as compelling as his erudite arguments. Outside the courtroom, J.D. was unpretentious and pleasant. He shunned unnecessary formalities. Everyone, including his children and grandchildren, called him J.D. "I want people to respect me, not my position in life. Positions are temporary, but legacies are forever," he'd often said.

A small puddle of water gathered beneath a half-empty glass of Dewar's Scotch Sour. Copies of the *Gaston Gazette*, *Spartanburg Herald-Journal*, and *The Greenville News* littered his desk and one of the chairs in front of the desk. He started from the back of each newspaper section and worked his way forward, reading each article and circling the ones that caught his interest.

Grace had returned from the diner and washed the nauseating smell of food and coffee from her pores. A mixture of cocoa butter, orange blossom, and jasmine filled the air when she exited the bathroom.

Wes read a sentence for the third time, but the aromatic hints of honeysuckle, sandalwood, and black currant had awakened his senses. He tugged at the crotch of his trousers to find comfort from an uncontrollable erection. Lately, his erections were occurring at the most unlikely times and getting more difficult to maintain during times of intimacy. The battle of ego versus manhood had begun; so far, his ego was getting bruised badly. When Grace entered his office, he knew he was in for another fight he had been trying to avoid.

"Is it all right if I start with this stack?" Grace pointed to the stack of papers in the empty chair.

Wes peeped around the paper. "That's fine."

He quickly looked away, but the image of Grace in a flimsy tank top and her unrestrained honeydew-sized breasts, hanging in mid-air as she bent over, were already etched into his memory.

Grace cut and arranged articles by the newspaper sections in which they were printed: "State," "Local," "Business," "Real Estate," "Society," and "Obituary." There was even a "Recipes" section.

"I'm not sure what you see in some of these articles," she said.

"I keep telling you, the newspaper business is not about journalism; it's about the business of propaganda. They put the news that sells up front and tuck the important news in small columns on the back page."

"That doesn't make sense. Why print it if no one's going to read it?"

Wes took a deep breath and folded his paper. "Because that allows them to cover their asses when people complain and say they didn't know."

"It sounds confusing. Seems to me you would want the most important news up front." She shook her head and continued to cut and sort the articles.

"They are giving them the important news first. The only problem is the newspaper is determining what's most important. By the time people get past all the so-called big stuff, they're too frustrated and worn out to read about the important stuff that's really affecting their lives."

Wes stood up and adjusted his pants. Grace's lightly powdered breasts grabbed his attention the second he saw the imprints of her nipples as they pressed against her thin cotton tank top. "I'm going to the kitchen. You want anything?"

"Lemonade, please." Grace held up a photograph and studied it. "Who are these people?" she shouted.

"Which people?" Wes asked when he returned.

Grace was bent over his desk, looking at a photograph under a magnifying glass that was attached to the desk lamp. Her Tar Heel blue terry cloth running shorts exposed the bottom of her firm butt. Wes closed his eyes and shook his head.

"The people in this picture." She held up a black-and-white photograph of a tuxedo-dressed gentleman standing between two bleached blond socialites in strapless evening gowns and diamonds.

"I don't know. Here you go." He handed her a glass filled with ice and lemonade.

"Why are you holding onto the picture if you don't know them?"

Wes leaned over Grace to view the magnified image. The luscious scent of her oiled skin aroused him more. "Because pictures are good sources for hidden information. While the subject in the foreground tells one story, occasionally, you can see another story developing in the background."

Their lips brushed when Grace turned her head. She gave Wes a quick peck. Beads of sweat gathered on the nape of his neck from the inferno their body heat generated.

"So, what's the background story in this picture?"

With a seductive grin, Wes eyed the contour of Grace's almond brown face. "I don't know the full story, but I plan to find out real soon. All I know so far is that my instincts were right about Robert. His world is starting to crumble, and the background story in that picture tells me so."

"How?"

He increased the magnification of the photograph and pointed to a woman in the background. "Because that's Bonita De La Rosa."

"The news anchorwoman?"

"She *was* a news anchorwoman. Although I guess once a news anchor, always a news anchor. Anyway, Bonita and Robert have been an item for a little while now. They have also been living together for the past year."

"And?" Grace slurped her lemonade.

Wes moved his pointer to the right and began to make small circles.

"And this guy she's cuddling, the one with the million-dollar smile? He sure as hell ain't Robert."

[55]

CHAPTER 13

WES STOOD in the doorway of the kitchen, struggling to hide his impatience. He glanced at his watch. He had to make a few stops before his meeting with Robert, but he couldn't leave until he dealt with the current crisis. Wes knew he had said something wrong the moment he asked Grace to call Robert and schedule a meeting for dinner.

"I'll call you later to make sure Robert's confirmed for six thirty. Not sure when I'll be back. Depends on what I find. Okay?"

Grace nodded slowly. She rolled her eyes and looked away when she noticed Wes looking.

"See, this is why I don't like working assignments with women. It's this shit right here." Wes raised his arms in despair. "What's the problem now, Grace?"

Grace folded her arms, crossed her outstretched legs, and wagged her foot. "I thought you would have at least made some time tonight so we could talk about the case and other stuff. I guess I oughta know better than to make assumptions when it comes to you."

Wes searched Grace's forlorn face. She was a good-hearted woman, whom he'd felt compelled to rescue when he was working a case down in Sumter, SC. Wes admired the simplicity of her beauty and outlook on life. "What other stuff, Grace?"

Wes knew what *stuff*. In fact, he blamed himself for allowing the *stuff* to happen in the first place. He also shouldered the blame for letting the *stuff* go as far as it had.

[56]

"It's nothing. It's just me, I guess. I was just hoping we could have some time. Some time to talk like we used to when you first brought me here."

"What do you mean? I talk to you damn near every day."

"It's just that I don't get to see you as much anymore. Don't get me wrong, I still feel close to you and love working with you, but it's not like it was in the beginning. We still have wonderful sex when you visit, but I can tell even that's different."

"Come here." Wes pulled Grace closer and gave her a firm hug while he checked his watch. He stepped back, lifted her chin with his index finger, and stared deep into her eyes. "Grace, you know that I sincerely care about you. We both know that our relationship is more than we anticipated, but we can't go back and change the past. I know I can't give you everything you desire, so I promise to understand and accept your decision to walk away when the time comes. In the meantime, I'm asking as a friend that needs a favor, can you please call Robert? I don't want this ITI mess to get any uglier than it is already."

Grace broke free from his clutch.

"You don't get it, Wes. Everyone can't compartmentalize their life the way you do. Everyone can't fit people into little boxes and pull them out whenever it's convenient."

"I'm sorry, Grace. Really. I am. I promise you we will talk about it. It's just that I really need you right now. Honestly, I do."

The ice crackled and released its frozen snare on Grace's heart. She looked at Wes and smiled. His ability to show strength in the shadow of his weakness was the quality she admired most of all about him. It also made her extremely horny. She kissed him softly. "I know you do. I'll call Robert and confirm for six thirty."

[57]

"Thank you." Wes patted her on her behind. "I'll make a deal with you. No matter what I find after my meeting with Robert, I'll come straight back. In the meantime, why don't you go to the store and pick up whatever you want me to cook for dinner? We can even talk about the case … and other stuff."

"I'm on it. Thank you for putting up with me."

"For what it's worth, I think you might turn into a pretty decent investigator, with a little more help."

Wes checked his surveillance equipment and changed the batteries in his camera. He gathered the photograph and several files from his safe and stored them in his briefcase.

When Grace walked in Wes was standing at his desk, rubbing his chin and playing with the loose change in his pocket.

"Have you talked to Phil?"

"Not yet. I will. I swear, between Puddin', Mama, and you fussing over him, it's a wonder the boy can even dress himself."

Unable to ignore her penetrating stare, he finally looked up. Grace was leaning against the doorframe with her arms folded across her chest. Her mouth barely moved as she popped her chewing gum.

Wes huffed and threw his hand up. "I'll call him this evening. Damn!"

"Why don't you invite him to dinner with you and Robert?"

"Hell, no! Are you crazy?"

"Why not? What's the big deal about having dinner with Robert? You know everyone, from politicians to poll workers and corporate executives to factory workers. Why would it matter to Phil if you knew Robert?"

"It may not matter, but that's not a risk I'm willing to take. I don't want him anywhere near Robert. Robert Berry strikes me as a man who gets rattled easily. I told you nervous people talk and reveal things they shouldn't."

"But Phil can give you eyes and ears on the inside."

"Along with a goddamn heart attack. Have you forgotten Phil is already suspicious about how he got on over there?"

"Oh, yeah. I forgot."

Wes marveled at her naiveté; it was both appealing and annoying. Most times, it was just annoying, but he really needed her. He sighed loudly. "Listen, I haven't been honest with you about Robert."

"So we're not tailing him to see if he's being pressured or squeezed?"

"We are. Well, *you* are, at least."

Wes unlocked a steel wall safe and retrieved two brown expandable folders that were secured by a leather string wound around two clasps.

"Maybe this will help you understand things better. About a year ago, Robert approached me regarding a serious problem he'd uncovered. He was handed two folders and ordered to destroy their content. According to Robert, the order came from someone at the top. Just as he was about to dump the folders into an incinerator, he decided to look inside, even though he'd been given a warning to resist any ideas to do such a thing. Inside each folder were hundreds of applications and résumés from students who attend historically black colleges and universities. The applications and résumés were collected from the job fairs the company attended on HBCU campuses as part of their heralded diversity initiative. Robert didn't want to destroy the folders, but he didn't know what to do with them either, which is why he came to me. He knew the information was important, but something tells me he's about to find out how significant it really is."

"Are those the files?"

"Yes. I have them because ITI needs to believe they're destroyed and because I didn't want them in Robert's possession while I sorted out the problem. I arranged a meeting with a contact, who works as general counsel for the Equal Employment Opportunity Commission. I knew ITI had violated at least one section of the national fair employment policy, at a minimum. Since the applications came from students located in several states, I wanted to know if we needed to file the complaint with each state's agency or the federal office.

"Before my contact looked into the allegations, he warned me about ITI and their powerful connections. They do a lot of work for the federal government and many of our nation's allies. Their reach within the government is just as wide as it is deep. My contact told me that I had better be prepared for war if Robert and I came forward with these allegations.

"Two weeks later, Robert calls and says the same ITI executive that gave him the folders was now telling him to go on an African American hiring frenzy. Within six months, Robert had hired damn near two hundred African American workers. We decided against filing the claim, which made Robert happy because he was fraternizing with the big boys."

Grace thought for a few seconds, and then she said, "I don't understand why you're concerned about Robert being nervous. No one knows Robert didn't destroy those files and that you talked to the EEOC. ITI ended up hiring minority employees, which is what you and Robert wanted, right?"

Wes gathered his things. "I don't believe in problems being solved efficiently without a loose end turning up somewhere."

"From what I've seen, Robert doesn't appear to be phased in any way. What does all of that have to do with Phil?"

Wes shook his head. Grace had impeccable skills as a waitress and promising skills as an investigator, but he doubted if she would ever overcome her ability to be so naïve as not to connect the dots, even when it was obvious. "I keep telling you, Robert Berry does not strike me as a man who can keep his mouth shut if he is under pressure. If the right pressure is applied, he will say the wrong thing to someone, including my son."

"But what could he tell Phil that would be so harmful?"

"Let's start with him telling Phil that I submitted the application for him and that he made sure Phil's application was among those they hired. Do I need to go any further?"

"Wes, darling, what is wrong with a father looking out for his son?"

"There's plenty wrong with it because I put him in the middle of this hornet's nest. Besides, I know he only took this job to try and prove something to me. He believes I want him to come work with me, but I want to keep him as far away from PI work as possible. I don't want it to bring out the worst in him."

Grace hugged him. "Wes, you did a great thing. That's because you always look out for those you love. It's who you are."

"Yeah! Good ol' Wes!" he said as he walked out.

CHAPTER 14

THE MODEM'S BLINKING green lights turned dark and lifeless after Phil terminated his connection to the Game Asylum BBS. Phil was relieved that MystikalGremlinz had come through on his promise to buy them some time. Their search for NoMoBoesky had turned up nothing so far, but the good news was they had two more weeks to find him. Phil refused to think about the other news MystikalGremlinz had shared. There was no way MystikalGremlinz was going to sign those contracts without knowing the truth, not if he could help it.

Locating NoMoBoesky became the priority. His hacking exploits were legendary in the Underground, as was the mystery that surrounded his identity. In addition to mastering one's technical skills, an accomplished hacker had to be equally astute in identity concealment. NoMoBoesky was second to none in that department. Phil and MystikalGremlinz split their universe of sources. MystikalGremlinz took SysOps and hackers; Phil took the moles—guys who worked in small computer stores, where hackers sold and traded goods—and the remaining group of hackers.

Phil's pager vibrated against his hip as he pored over the list of contacts. He retrieved the pager from its holster with an adroit flip of his thumb and pressed the button to light the display.

93700411. It was Wes.

Phil tossed his pager on the kitchen counter and grabbed a beer from the fridge. He gulped down the cold brew and sorted through his cluttered thoughts. The wedding was two weeks away.

Ann hadn't made any demands of his time, but Phil expected that to change soon. He needed to get a lead on NoMoBoesky before week's end. MystikalGremlinz provided some assistance, but locating NoMoBoesky required a highly skilled sleuth. Wes wasn't interested, and Roxy, despite Phil's numerous attempts to contact her, had been her usual elusive self. Then there was that whole thing about Robert and the case Wes was working on. Something about it wasn't adding up. He was convinced that Robert was the target, but Phil wasn't so sure Dana was the woman Robert was having an affair with.

Phil dialed Wes's pager and punched in his number. *Might as well get it over with.*

Phil answered the phone with the exuberance of a child banished to detention hall. The lack of excitement on his end was a stark contrast to the revelry he heard in the background. Phil wasn't sure what to make of Wes's blithesome tone. They talked about work but steered clear of mentioning NoMoBoesky's document; although Phil could have sworn that was what Wes meant when he asked, "How is everything else going at work?" Finally, Wes suggested dinner the following night with Phil and his sister.

"Okay, but I'm not sure about Roxy. Have you talked to her?"

"I called and left her a message, but she hasn't called me back. You know how unpredictable your sister can be at times," Wes said with resignation.

"We've been playing phone tag too. She called and left a message yesterday. She was on her way to audition for a role in some big movie they're shooting in Asheville. The movie sounded kinda stupid, if you ask me. Something called *Forrest Gump*."

"I sure hope she gets it. I know it's a longshot, but I'd prefer she pursue acting fulltime rather than spend time with that shit she's doing now."

Phil laughed. He knew his father loved his sister immensely, but Roxy grooved to a beat that his father seldom understood and rarely liked. "I don't know all the details of what she does, but it doesn't sound like a bad job."

"I don't care what she says; those people ain't running nothing but a snatch-and-grab repo business. Giving the company some damn fancy name doesn't fool me."

"If it'll make you feel better, I'll talk to her and make sure she's not in over her head."

Wes chuckled. "Pssht! You're the one that's in over your head. Roxy has had your number a long time, in case you didn't know."

"Daddy, I know you're not talking. Everybody knows she's got you wrapped around her little finger."

"I wasn't calling you to talk about this. Let's go to the Orchard Grille. Bring Ann along. She's going to be my daughter-in-law soon; she might as well start enjoying some Jacobson family time."

"I'll tell her. She's on her way over. I'm cooking dinner."

"You're cooking dinner?" Wes leaned against the back of the phone booth and searched for Robert in the crowd. "You've learned more from me than I realized."

Phil looked at the phone curiously. "Since when did you teach me how to cook?"

"Did you hear me say I taught you how to cook? I was talking about … Never mind what I was talking about. You just need to know there's more of me in you than you realize."

"I got a table, Wes!" the voice bellowed above the other voices in the background.

Annoyed by Robert's sudden outburst, Wes glared and waved him away. "I've got to run. Don't forget: Orchard Grille, tomorrow at seven."

Phil looked puzzled after his father hung up. *I know I've heard that voice before.* He laid the phone on the counter. *Daddy was calling from a bar. I could tell by the noise in the background.* He replayed the statement over and over in his mind until the distinctively deep, rich sound of the voice filled the kitchen. It sounded like Robert Berry. *If Robert's not the Jack on the loose then who is he? And why is he meeting with Daddy?*

Phil locked away his thoughts when he heard the tingly chime of the doorbell. Ann was at the door.

CHAPTER 15

THE OVERFLOW OF HAPPY HOUR revelers spread past the steps of the bar, down to the lower deck area, where a smaller group congregated. Bodies bumped, and drinks spilled in the constant side-to-side shuffle to create a path to the payphone or restroom.

"Table's ready, Wes!" Robert shouted above the boisterous crowd.

Wes pressed his index finger against his lips and nodded. "I've got to run. Don't forget: the Orchard Grille at seven tomorrow." He hung up the phone and then waded through the throng of patrons, drowning their sorrows and igniting their confidence with two-for-one drink specials. He passed a group of guys engaged in a heated debate about whether the Blue Devils or Tar Heels would make it to the Final Four. He saw Robert seated at a table near the front, flipping through a menu.

Wes nursed his Dewar's Scotch Sour and listened to Robert jabber about his day as he chased a double shot of Jack Daniels with a Heineken. Wes waited until Robert drank half his Old No. 7 Sour Mash before he stopped his nonsensical chatter.

"Robert, do you remember the instructions I told you to follow until we got to the bottom of this shit?"

Robert fidgeted in his seat. "You said to remain calm and in con—Why are you shaking your head no? That is what you said, isn't it?"

"I told you not to bring attention to yourself. I specifically said, 'Keep everything around you consistent and under control.' Do you remember me saying those exact words?"

"That's what I've been doing."

"Doesn't look like it."

"Then I don't know what you're looking at. Things couldn't be better." Robert swallowed the last of his whiskey and set the glass down with a thump.

Wes folded his arms and cocked his head to the left. "Stop me when I'm wrong. Bonita's gone. She's over in Mecklenburg with her sister, the one married to the chief surgeon at Lakeside Memorial, the chief surgeon with single surgeon friends. Single, handsome, rich surgeon friends. Sounds like the perfect rebound for a woman in a relationship that's on the skids. How much further do I need to go before you stop me?"

"How did you ..." Robert shifted nervously in his seat. "All she does is scream, pout, and throw tantrums," Robert admitted. "Her day isn't complete unless she's angry with me about something. She'll be back in a few days."

"I wouldn't count on it if I were you."

"The problem is she can't get over the way WCNC fucked over her. Most people don't know it, but she's the only personality that raised their ratings in every time slot from six a.m., to noon, evening, and night. Those bastards at that TV station destroyed her confidence. They told an intelligent, articulate, and beautiful forty-year-old woman that she was too old and of no use. You don't want to begin to know what it's like living with the aftershocks of that."

"That is a tough pill to swallow. I still wouldn't count on her coming back, though."

[67]

"She did everything she could to keep that job. It's a shame the way they let her go after her last on-air report. Did I tell you that she fell off the camel the first time they tried to shoot that piece about camel racing at the International Festival?"

"Naaw!"

"Yeah!" Robert sucked on an ice cube. "She took that fall like a pro, just to show them muthafukas. She was hotter than skillet grease on Sunday after church, but she got back on that camel."

Wes looked at Robert, and they both broke out in laughter. Wes stopped. His demeanor was stern, but his eyes were filled with compassion. "She says you're drinking a lot. That you were beginning to remind her of her stepfather. He used to get drunk every weekend and terrorize the shit out of her and her siblings. She saw a therapist about it, but it still fucks with her, especially now."

"Pssht! Tell me something I don't know. Every time I raise a glass, she's nagging me." Robert shook his head and looked away. "She even accused me of using too much mouthwash. Claimed I was drinking it for the alcohol. How crazy is that? I betcha she didn't tell you that!" Robert frowned as the wheels of reasoning creaked and ground to a halt. "You talked to Bonita?"

Wes nodded. "Just before I came here."

"And she told you to tell me that she's not coming back?"

Wes continued to nod.

Robert cradled his chin with his hand. Alcohol and a broken heart made for an unpredictable mixture.

Wes watched in silence.

[68]

The drink specials were taking their toll, and the atmosphere at Bennigan's got rowdier and louder. Robert sat up straight after he finished his second drink. A fresh layer of inebriated swagger was painted across his face. "Well, good riddance to her no-camel-riding ass!" He raised the glass. "Waitress, another round!"

"Robert, remember … consistency … under … control."

"Hello, Robert. Surprised to see you here," said Linda Albright, a bubbly woman with dancing brown eyes.

Linda was dressed in thigh-hugging leather pants with a matching jacket, and she was sporting a sorority pin on her shirt. The taps on the bottom of her three-inch-heeled boots clicked against the floor when she walked.

Robert stood up halfway before flopping back onto his seat. "Hi, Linda. I'm just having a drink with a friend. Wes, meet Linda. Linda, this is Wes."

Linda had a delightful and inviting personality. Wes flirted with her to see if she might say anything that would make Robert uneasy. His fascination grew when he learned Linda's office was next to Robert's.

"We were just catching up on old times. The stories are the same, but the lies have gotten bigger," Wes said as he pulled out an empty chair. "Please, have a seat. I'm sure talking to you will be more satisfying. Besides, you're way more pleasant to look at than Robert."

Linda blushed. "Thank you, but I'm meeting my sorors. We meet every Thursday for girls' night out."

"A night with the girls over an evening with Robert and me? I don't blame you; I'd do the same."

Linda laughed and waved as she left. "Nice meeting you, Wes."

Wes looked at his watch. "I'm going to head out of here. Robert, don't do anything stupid."

"Wes, I don't know why you're so worried. I keep telling you that little problem I brought you no longer exists. Man, everyone has moved on."

"Tell that to my son." Wes paid the bill and tipped the waitress. He waited until she walked away before he continued. "By the way, does Phil know who you are?"

"Not to my knowledge. To be quite honest, I've never met your son."

Wes stood up. "Good. I need you to keep as much distance between the two of you as possible. Despite your assurances, I need to take every precaution to ensure my ass is covered."

CHAPTER 16

PHIL HADN'T SEEN Ann since their passions led them to a steamy encounter on her office desk. The past two days had been a patchwork of untruths and outright lies designed to keep her at ease. His conscious gnawed at him each time he called with an excuse for why he had to break another promise. It also didn't help that Ann had been understanding and supportive about it all. He reconciled each lie by justifying it as a necessary evil in order to accomplish a greater good. The next few weeks were going to be difficult; however, he was determined to find NoMoBoesky and put his suspicions to rest once and for all. He didn't want Ann to be the wife of a private detective. His mother was married to one. As much as Phil loved his mother, he wasn't looking to marry her, and he surely wasn't trying to be like his father.

They kissed passionately as soon as the door closed. Ann ran her hand across the back of his head, allowing the waves in his hair to tickle the palm of her hand. Phil rubbed the small of her back and then let his hands rest on her round behind. Ann's purse fell to the floor, spilling some of its contents and bringing a halt to their heated embrace. When he stepped back, Ann's eyes were glued to the erection bobbing up and down against his gym shorts. Phil cleared his throat, breaking her from her trance. When she looked up, a fiery passion Phil had never seen before filled Ann's eyes.

"I'll be right back," she said with a lustful assurance.

"I'll umm ... I'll get dinner started," Phil stammered as she headed for his bedroom.

[71]

Ann Marie worked as a counselor at the community center in the city's Enderly Park area. Phil had seen her several times when he taught the adult computer literacy class. Ann had a no-nonsense demeanor but all the children, especially the teenage girls, loved her and jockeyed for her attention. She had a confident charm that was inviting, but she was quick to let you know she wasn't for any bullshit. When she interacted with the children, he noticed how she morphed into one of those stern but loving mother figures, much like Marjorie and MiMi.

They met when two of Ann's friends, who were also students in his computer class, invited him over to their apartment one evening for a small social. Charlotte and Tina didn't attempt to hide their matchmaking intentions. Tina made sure Phil and Ann were coupled together the moment he arrived. She even threatened to put another male guest out because he was talking to Ann too much. After a night of talking, smoking weed, drinking Charlotte's killer daiquiris, and finally slow dragging to En Vogue's "Giving Him Something He Can Feel," Phil and Ann shared their first kiss on the patio. An hour later, they excused themselves. From that moment on, they'd been an inseparable duo.

The soothing smell of ground beef, garlic, and basil filtered through the apartment and mingled with George Howard's earthy soprano saxophone, playing "Baby, Come to Me."

The stress of the last few days was an afterthought the minute Phil saw Ann emerge from his bedroom wearing nothing but his bathrobe. Ann's curly black hair, still wet from the shower she had just taken, lay along the contours of her oval-shaped face. Her hazel-green eyes looked even more vibrant against her clean caramel flesh. Phil's heart raced as it pumped blood to his groin.

"Damn, baby, dinner's just been put on hold. I'm hungry for something else."

Ann giggled. "Where's the stuff for the salad? It's been a long day, and I'm hungry."

Phil moved behind Ann and wrapped his arm around to bring her closer. He kissed her neck softly. She moaned lightly and then leaned her head backward, letting it rest on his shoulder. The robe's sash came undone, exposing Ann's nakedness. Phil brushed his fingers against the crinkly hairs of her mound as he kissed the nape of her neck, making Ann groan much louder and deeper.

Phil's erection tugged against his shorts. Ann, standing naked in his kitchen, was a fantasy come true. Ann was pinned between Phil and the counter. She leaned back, and Phil circled her dark brown areolas with his tongue and then sucked one breast as he massaged the other. Phil made a trail of kisses from Ann's breast down to her navel. Phil tickled her navel with his tongue then inched his way to her neatly trimmed vulva.

"Mmm!" Ann rubbed Phil's head and pulled him deeper.

Ann's hot, sticky juices dripped down her thigh as Phil sucked her engorged clit. She closed her eyes and arched her back. Ann wanted Phil, but first, she wanted to feel his talented tongue inside of her. Ann gyrated her hips one minute and then bounced up and down on her tiptoes the next. She continued her sensual dance routine until her thighs clamped together in a vice grip around Phil's head. Her juices and the sleekness of his hard tongue as it slid against her walls brought Ann to her first climax.

They turned off the stove and headed for the bedroom, but only made it to the living room floor. They began in a slow, melodic motion that soon had their bodies hot and sweaty with the

[73]

intoxicating smell of uninhibited sex. Ann kissed Phil's chest and took him deeper. She gasped when the tip of his manhood touched the innermost parts of her womb. She squeezed Phil tightly with her legs and dug her fingernails into his shoulders and clawed her way down his back, all the way to his waist. Phil felt two layers of skin give way. He gritted his teeth as the air hit the streaks of open flesh. The sensation from the sting of blood against his raw flesh was pure pleasure.

Phil slid an arm underneath Ann and lifted her hips off the floor. She met his every thrust until their bodies came to a spine-tingling eruption. Phil knelt over Ann and looked at her with dreamy eyes and a big smile.

"Why are you looking at me like that? Can you tell already?"

"I just wanted to look at you. I can't believe in two weeks we'll be—" He looked at her with a curious frown. "Can I tell what?"

Ann smiled bashfully. "That I'm pregnant."

CHAPTER 17

THE SUN GLOWED like a prize-winning pumpkin at the county fair, dipping below the horizon against a purple backdrop. The hustle and bustle of downtown dwindled to a few casual strollers, looking for a moment of respite. No one looked up. Nobody noticed the bright lights in the corner office on the top floor.

Vincent sat at his cluttered desk, surrounded by framed parchments, touting his scholarly achievements: Columbia undergrad in economics, a Harvard Juris Doctor, and an MBA from Stanford. He flipped through receipts and punched the numbers into his calculator. The keys on the desk calculator sounded like a thunderstorm of raindrops hitting a tin roof as he tallied his latest expenditures.

Vincent knew Jack had risked a lot when he brought him on as CFO. He was thirty years old and had more potential than experience. When Jack asked him to locate a new line of business for the company, he didn't hesitate to take advantage of the opportunity. While IBM, Microsoft, and Apple were battling each other in court, he discovered WorldNet Labs. There was growing interest in a new platform called the World Wide Web, or the Internet, as some called it. Vincent knew if ITI developed an interface for the Internet before AOL, Prodigy, and the others, the reward would pay off handsomely. It was risky, but acquiring WorldNet and their Internet browser technology ensured that ITI would be a major player.

He ripped the long stream of paper from the calculator and stared at the five digits at the bottom. "Well, Vinny, you're down to your last fifteen hundred dollars!" He balled up the paper, stuck his tongue out like Michael Jordan, and attempted a shot at the wastebasket. It ricocheted off the front and rolled back toward him.

Vincent looked around the office. One day, he would be remembered as the person who closed the biggest acquisition in Corporate America. He was the one who had found WorldNet. He was the one who'd nurtured and cultivated the partnership with Malcolm Graves for eighteen months. When the company was confronted with that nasty EEOC allegation that everyone knew was true, he was the one who made it disappear. To say he was solely responsible for ITI's current enviable position was not an exaggerated truth.

His instincts told him that the Internet was a disruptive technology whose impact could surpass that of the television. Everything had gone according to plan: WorldNet had sold some of their equity to a bogus private investment group that Vincent had recommended, while he secretly came up with the $2.5 million the investment group needed for the purchase. It wasn't easy; he'd emptied his bank accounts, liquidated his assets, and sold most of his stock through a series of covert maneuvers.

"Three more weeks and this shit is history," Vincent said as he stuffed the bills and cancellation notices into his briefcase and then picked up the wad of paper from the floor and slammed it into the wastebasket.

Many industry insiders and those within ITI's executive ranks were convinced that the CEO office was Vincent's once Jack stepped down. Vincent wasn't interested in the job. The power he yielded already was unmatched and uncontested. He laughed as he thought about the VP of human resources and the stupid look on her face when Jack told her all hiring decisions would be handled through the CFO's office. She didn't like it, but self-preservation triumphed in the end. Most of his colleagues would have sacrificed everything to be in his position, but the way Vincent saw it, he deserved something more than being named CEO of a company that's trying to rebound. As far as he was concerned, Jack could hand the job over to Stanley immediately after they closed the deal. He had bigger and better plans.

Vincent checked to make sure the executive suite was empty before he took the private elevator down to the garage. He walked past the vacant parking space marked with blue stenciled lettering that read: RESERVED V. MARTELLO, CFO. He stopped at a black 1977 Pontiac Trans Am that was parked in a stall reserved for visitors. He'd purchased the car after his second year of college, but it looked as if it had just rolled off the dealer's showroom floor.

Vincent had accumulated a collection of cars, but none held the sentimental value of the Trans Am. The muscle car was one of the few that he owned outright. Vincent removed a handkerchief from his coat pocket and wiped one of the golden wings on the firebird decal. He revved the engine, and a symphony of pounding pistons and whirring belts filled the garage. As soon as the access gate lifted, Vincent sped out of the garage. The Trans Am's red taillights provided the only visible sign of its existence as the darkened thoroughfare enveloped the car's black frame.

Twenty minutes later, he pulled into Frank's Grille, a local tavern that served decent Italian food for those on a budget. The quaint-sized dive wasn't listed in the city's guide for fine dining, but the fare was delicious. The calzones and strombolis reminded

Vincent of his old Bensonhurst neighborhood. Vincent became a regular the day after he moved out of his downtown condo—he'd sold it to raise the money for the WorldNet stock—and sublet a one-bedroom townhouse near Eastland Mall.

Vincent saw an African American woman standing in front of a BMW, with the hood raised. Her smooth hazelnut skin glimmered under the restaurant sign's yellow, red, and blue neon lights. He knew many of his friends from the old neighborhood frowned on dating African American women, but he found them alluring, and the one standing in front of him was no exception; she was very desirable.

A screwdriver fell onto the sidewalk and rolled toward Vincent just as he approached.

"Here you go." He held out the screwdriver. "What's the problem?"

"Thank you. Just put it in there." She pointed to a small tool case that sat on top of the car's battery. "Nothing major. Just a loose spark plug," she said from underneath the hood.

Vincent laughed. He couldn't believe what he was seeing. The woman was dressed in a snug black turtleneck sweater, black boots, and jeans that hugged her long, firm legs. She wore a touch of makeup, just enough to accentuate her beauty without being a distraction. Her looks and attire expressed a stylish classiness that was in stark contrast to the red mechanic's towel she was holding and the grease on her knuckles. Vincent looked at her suspiciously. "What do you know about loose spark plugs and fixing a car?"

"A woman has to be prepared for anything to happen at any time." She gathered her tools, wiped her hands with the towel, and then closed the hood. "Besides, the last time I checked, the knight in shining armor department had a vacant sign hanging on the door."

"I'll let you in on a secret. I was late because I was getting my armor shined." Vincent smiled and extended his hand. "Hi, I'm Vincent."

His manicured hands were soft and comforting. The firmness of his grip exuded an air of confidence. "Hi, I'm Roxanne." She held on for several seconds before slowly removing her hand.

"Care to join me for dinner? That is unless you're planning to meet someone."

Roxanne twisted her lips and looked him up and down. "You're a real Romeo, aren't you?" She gave a faint smile and hunched her shoulders. "Sure, why not."

Vincent opened the door like a valet at a five-star hotel.

"Charming," Roxanne said flatly. "Where do you take a girl on the second date, Sizzler?"

Vincent and Roxanne sat in a booth along the back wall and shared stories over calzones and a pitcher of draft beer. They laughed and talked about everything from eating at Frank's to traveling and sports cars, Vincent's favorite topic. Both were careful not to divulge too much of their professional lives. Vincent claimed to work in finance for a company downtown. Roxanne did odd jobs while doing a little modeling here and there.

The waitress handed Vincent the bill.

Roxanne reached for the handwritten ticket. "How much do I owe you?"

"It's on me." Vincent swatted her hand playfully. "I have shining armor, remember?" He gave the waitress his credit card.

The waitress returned a few minutes later. "I'm sorry, sir, your card has been declined." She handed him the defunct platinum colored card.

Feigning shock at her revelation, Vincent took the card and looked at both sides. "That's strange; I just used it less than an hour ago." He looked inside his wallet. The Visa, MasterCard, and Discover cards were already closed, and the only cash he had was a five and three ones. Overcome with embarrassment, he patted and searched his pockets.

Sensing Vincent's current dilemma, Roxanne reached inside her purse and pulled out a twenty-dollar bill. "Don't worry about it, Romeo. I got it."

"I'll pay you back. I promise." Vincent apologized for the third time as he escorted Roxanne to her car. "If you'd like, you can follow me to my place. It's just around the corner."

"I pay for dinner; now, you invite me to your place to be dessert? That's charming. Real charming," Roxanne deadpanned.

Vincent waved his arms in defense. "No! No! That's not what I meant at all."

"Well, what did you mean?"

Vincent, his face awash with embarrassment from his Freudian slip, attempted to ease out of the unpleasant corner into which he'd backed himself. "I tell you what; why don't you meet me here tomorrow, and I'll pick up the tab. I promise."

"I can't do tomorrow."

"What about Saturday? Are you free Saturday evening? Come on, give a knight another chance to make it up to you. Please?"

Roxanne was charmed and tickled by his childlike sincerity. "It's a date, Romeo," she said before closing her car door.

CHAPTER 18
FRIDAY, JANUARY 22, 1993

THE LABYRINTHIAN CORRIDORS of ITI were empty when Phil strolled to his second meeting of the day. He didn't like meetings, especially the ones where everyone countered or confirmed each other's comments with information they'd overheard at some other meeting.

"As long as you attend my two weekly meetings, that's all that matters to me. I don't care what you do about the others," his manager had confided when Phil mentioned the growing number of meetings that dotted his calendar. Phil loathed corporate hobnobbing, so he limited his weekly attendance to Gary's two meetings, plus two roundtable discussions for programmers.

Four conference rooms with adjacent administrative areas were located on each floor. Phil did a doubletake and then a third for good measure when he saw Holly sitting across the hall from the conference room door. Phil wasn't paying attention to where he was walking and bumped, chest first, into the door. He hadn't seen Holly since their encounter on the elevator. She was on the phone, with the handset nestled between her ear and shoulder, while she jotted on a notepad. Holly's corn silk complexion turned beet red when she looked up and saw Phil staring.

"Hi," Phil mouthed the greeting and continued inside.

Holly smiled sheepishly and waved back.

An hour later, Phil exited the room. He looked for Holly, but she wasn't at her desk. Phil concluded it was probably for the better since he wasn't sure what he wanted to say. It was somewhere between, "Hi, my name is Phil. I don't bite," and "Hi, Holly, why are you afraid of black people?"

The red light was aglow on the phone when he returned to his office. He retrieved the message. It was Roxy. She would be joining them for dinner, but first, she needed to drop by his apartment. She had some juicy information about a job she was working.

"Don't get into any trouble. You're about to be married, remember?" she warned playfully before hanging up.

Phil replayed Roxy's message. A *Computer Shopper* magazine was on the desk to his left. The magazine was a favorite of hackers and enthusiasts because of its BBS directory, a comprehensive list of every major and not-so-major board in the Underground. He fanned the enormous pages with his thumb as he listened to the message again. He noticed a yellow Post-it note had been placed on one of the pages in the directory. An arrow was drawn to the telephone number above the note. Phil recognized the number; it was the number for The Rabbit Hole. A message was written in blue ink:

> Drop by this weekend. We need to talk.
> Room: 99
> PWD: tsunami

It was signed NoMoBoesky.

CHAPTER 19

THE DOORBELL RANG three times, followed by several raps on the door. "I'm coming! I'm coming!" Phil shouted as he rushed to open the door.

"Well, hurry up, then," Roxy said as she stepped inside. "It ain't like you overflowing with space in here." She removed her black leather jacket and laid it over the back of the couch before sitting down.

Roxy was thirty-one, ambitious, and talented as an actress and detective. Her worlds collided when she discovered Tamara Dobson in *Cleopatra Jones* and Teresa Graves in *Get Christie Love!* No matter how hard she tried to convince Wes that she was up to the task, he only allowed her to work in the office. When she wasn't trying to cajole her father into helping out on a case, she was busy with her acting.

Phil took two bottles from the refrigerator and held them up. "White Zinfandel or Michelob?"

"White Zin is cool." She turned to inspect the bottle. "I hope it's not that cheap, rotgut stuff."

Phil handed Roxy a glass full of the chilled blush then sat down. "So, what's up?"

"No, you go first. I'd rather save the juicy stuff for last." Roxy crossed her legs, her red ankle boot dangling in midair.

"There are a couple of things, but the most exciting is you're going to be an aunt." Phil looked on with a sheepish grin.

"I knew it!" Roxy shouted. "Y'all negroes can't fool me!"

"No, that's not it," Phil interrupted. "She just found out yesterday, and she just told me last night."

"Mmm hmm!" She took a sip of wine and nodded her approval. "I know what I know, lil' bro. You might be able to pull that off with Mama and Daddy, but not here. I notice everything. Ann walking around, acting all innocent and quiet and shit, and y'all 'round here fucking like rabbits. Have you told Mama and Daddy yet?"

"Not yet. I was thinking maybe Ann and I would drive home Sunday and tell them," said Phil.

"I just wanna be around when you tell Mr. Donovan you knocked his daughter up. Mr. Donovan doesn't look like the type of man who'd take too kindly to hearing you turned his daughter into a lil' freak. You might need some protection," Roxy chided.

Phil spit his beer out when he heard his sister's outlandish remark. "Girl, stop. It's not even like that. Besides, we're telling them tomorrow. We just want to let everyone know that we're still going to have the wedding as planned."

"I'm going to be an aunt, finally! Oh, my God, my niece is going to adore her Aunt Roxy," she said, giddy with delight. She downed the rest of her wine, then held the empty glass in her brother's direction.

Phil let out a long sigh and reached for the bottle. "And Mama's going to be a grandmother. Which means—"

"Which means no more discussions about being the only one in her circle without grandchildren." Roxy interrupted. Then she rolled her eyes and groaned. "Oh, God! I can hear her now,

[85]

'Rosalyn and Jackie go on and on about their grandchildren, and all I get to add to the conversation is a smile.'"

Phil looked on with astonishment as his sister imitated their mother to perfection. "I hope you know that was a real concern for Mama. From the looks of it, you can't blame her for worrying. Do you seriously think Greg wants children? The only children Rod wants are those forty or older. And you? … Well?"

"Well, what?" Roxy playfully nudged her brother. "I know your nerdy ass ain't trying to talk shit. Just because you finally getting some coochie on a regular basis don't make you Big Daddy."

"I never said I was Big Daddy. But now that you mentioned it, I think Natalie might've called me that a few times," Phil said with a devilish grin.

"What Natalie? My girlfriend Natalie? I know you're not talking about *that* Natalie. Please don't tell me that crazy heifer gave you some pussy."

"I'm sorry." Phil drooped his lip, attempting to look pitiful. He leaned over to give her a hug.

Roxy pushed him away. "I told you 'bout screwing my friends. I know you don't wanna believe me, but I'm telling you the truth; these heifers talk. They open their mouths just as quick as their legs."

"Well, I know you're not in that crowd. You haven't kept a dude around long enough." Phil burst out in laughter.

"Ha! Ha! Ha!" Roxy mimicked before hitting her brother in the chest with a lightning quick left jab.

"Girl, stop!" Phil curled into a fetal position. "I need to tell you about this other issue. It's serious. Let me show you something." Phil went to his computer room and returned with his briefcase. He pulled out a manila folder and handed it to Roxy. "This is why I've been calling. I'm going to need your help with this."

Roxy flipped through the stapled pages. "What's this?"

"A document I came across. It's from this place I hang out at on my computer. It's from this guy who's pulled off some amazingly brilliant hacks. Those pages you're holding tell how ITI covered up their discriminatory hiring practices to avoid a federal investigation. They also tell how ITI, despite being in a financial decline for the past three years, appropriated funds from an unknown source to hide the financial impact of the cover-up."

"No shit?" Roxy's eyes twinkled.

"It gets better." Phil told Roxy about the unsolicited call from ITI and his subsequent interviews. Then he revealed the item that puzzled him the most. "Roxy, I swear, I never applied for a job with them."

"Let me get this straight; you're telling me that you got a job that you never applied for or even knew existed?" Roxy shook her head disbelievingly. "Stuff like that never happens to me."

"That's not all." Phil detailed the events of the past few days, while Roxy sat wild-eyed and giddy on the edge of the couch, listening intently. "We've got two more weeks to find out what they're up to, or MystikalGremlinz will be forced to sign the contract, selling his company to ITI."

"Shut up! I think you need to talk to Daddy about this." Roxy went to the kitchen and opened the refrigerator; then she looked in Phil's pantry. "You have anything to snack on around here? I think better when I have something to chew on."

"I've already talked to him, and the way he responded, I wish I hadn't." Phil opened his briefcase and threw her a Slim Jim.

Roxy looked at the long, skinny package then laid it down. "Thanks, but no thanks. What's up with Daddy? What did you do to piss him off?"

Phil leaned against a counter and watched Roxy continue her scavenger hunt through the kitchen. "I didn't do anything. I had breakfast with him a couple of days ago and told him everything I just told you, minus the few late developments. He told me to leave it alone and don't create any problems."

"What?" Roxy found a box of cookies and shook it. Crumbs rustled against the brown wax paper inside the box. She looked at Phil with indignation before tossing the box in the garbage can.

"That's what I said. That wasn't the only thing. Guess who Daddy has working detail ... Grace! Can you believe he's got Grace doing surveillance?" Phil shook his head in disgust.

Roxy searched the kitchen cabinets and found a small pack of saltine crackers. "Don't feel sorry for her. She's just trying to work her way into Philandering Phil's heart," she said as she tore open the packet and bit into a square wafer.

"What are you talking about?"

"Don't tell me you didn't know Daddy and Grace were fooling around? Boy, Grace is in love with your daddy. The only problem is she doesn't know he ain't in love with her. She's just one of the souvenirs he's accumulated while working cases."

"What's with this Philandering Phil?"

She shrugged. "That's something I heard Mama call him once when they were arguing a long time ago. You better be careful; you might turn out just like him. You're named after him, so you must be just like him."

"I'm nothing like that!" Phil shook his head defiantly.

Roxy pressed her index finger against his chest. "Yes, you are; you just don't know it. They didn't name you Philander Wesley Jacobson for nothing."

"Well, if you really want to know, I think you act more like Daddy than any of his sons. So what does that say about you?"

Roxy got her wine glass from the counter. "All it says is that some guy is going to get his heart broken if he's waiting for me to fall head over heels in love." She returned to the couch with her crackers and wine.

"Whatever. And for the record, this conversation never happened; so, don't mention a word of this tonight. Not the baby, not ITI, not Daddy and Grace—nothing."

"Boy, I'm not saying a word. If anything, I'm going over to ITI next week and see if they want to mysteriously hire some more people. I still can't believe you got a job you never applied for. I swear, shit like that never happens to me!"

Phil clasped his hands behind his head and fell back against the sofa's cushion. "Please don't remind me." He turned toward Roxy. "So, what's your big news?"

Roxy turned to face Phil. "I know you know who Vincent Martello is, right?"

"Yeah, he's the CFO at ITI. What about him?"

[89]

"I got a new case this week. A client of mine is missing a few items from their financial portfolio. It seems that Mr. Martello was in possession of those items when they disappeared."

"What kind of items?"

"A 1959 Ferrari 250 GT California Spyder, worth $750,000, and a 1978 Lamborghini Countach LP400S, worth $250,000. Mr. Martello is a bona fide car enthusiast, who has an expensive taste for exotic cars."

"Who is this client and what is it, exactly, you and your partners do for your clients? Daddy's bent out of shape about it, saying you're in the repo business. I told him I would talk to you and make sure everything is on the up and up."

Roxy laughed. "I know he thought that was funny."

Phil nodded. "You know he did."

"Our clients maintain financial portfolios in excess of fifty million dollars. My partners and I recover assets that have mysteriously disappeared from those portfolios. Since I do this on the side, I only deal with assets that are valued between a hundred thousand and a million dollars; they're much easier to locate."

"How do you go about recovering these assets?"

"It takes good detective work and, occasionally, some great acting. You would be surprised by the length at which rich people will go to hide their valuables. Daddy keeps calling it repo work, but it's not. This is not like those people who hide their cars at their cousins' or grandmothers' houses. I'm talking about people who are willing to pay pirates to stage an ambush and sail their yacht to the Canary Islands just so they can get the money from an insurance claim. There have been occasions where Gulfstream IVs have fallen off the radar in midflight. I tell you, rich people act worse than poor people when it comes to letting go of their possessions."

"Are you sure it's safe?"

"It's a piece of cake. By the time they realize what I'm there for, I've already located and gotten what I came for."

"Let me get this straight. Vincent Martello is hiding some cars because he's behind on his payments, and you're going to find out where he's hiding them so you can recover your client's assets?"

Roxy gave a dismissive shrug. "Yeah."

"Sounds like you're trying to repo his car." Phil laughed.

"You're missing the whole damn point. Not only is he hiding his cars, but he sold his condo, and his bank account looks worse than mine, and mine is ugly. He's broke, I'm telling you. Doesn't that sound strange for a chief financial officer?"

Phil took the manila folder from the coffee table, put it back into the briefcase, and closed it. "Yeah, I guess you're right. You think it has anything to do with what I just told you?"

"I'm not sure." Roxy smiled when she thought about her first encounter with Vincent. "He doesn't strike me as the devious type."

"How can he not be devious? He's hiding two damn cars, Roxy."

"I'm saying he doesn't appear to be the type that would do something like the stuff you're talking about. This guy is truly broke. He's struggling. He couldn't afford a ten-dollar meal." Roxy shook her head. "I'm telling you something doesn't make sense."

The doorbell rang. It was Ann.

"Not a word of this around Ann. I haven't told her about any of this," Phil said before he got up from the couch.

"Don't you think you should?"

"I'll tell her later."

"You're sounding like Daddy now." Roxy gave Phil a look that had "I told you so" written all over it.

They piled into Roxy's BMW and headed for the restaurant. As they were riding, Ann complimented Roxy on her boots.

"Oh, I just got these today. Daddy bought them for me."

"You didn't tell me you saw Daddy today," Phil interjected

"I didn't," Roxy said.

"Then how did he buy those boots?"

"He's going to pay for them in a few minutes. Right after I tell him I'm a little short and need some help with my bills."

Phil looked at Roxy in the rearview mirror. "If we have a daughter, I swear I'm never going to leave her alone with you."

CHAPTER 20

THE MUFFLED CHATTER inside the Orchard Grille was occasionally interrupted by exuberant laughter and singing as waiters and patrons celebrated a loved one's birthday. The intoxicating aroma of charbroiled steaks, grilled salmon, and glazed apples with cinnamon and hints of nutmeg made even the finickiest of eaters salivate.

Wes basked in the joy that every father feels when he gets to spend some time with his children, and it's not crisis related. He stirred the last of his Dewar's Scotch Sour in a lazy motion. Roxy and Ann sat on either side, and Phil sat across the table. Time, like a current raging unpredictably along the ocean's floor, had carried the children swiftly beyond his protective grasps. For a brief moment, he traveled back to when the kids huddled around to hear about his detective adventures. The stories were made up and woven together by a trove of half-truths, exaggerated tales, and outright lies, but he enjoyed them just as much as the kids.

Ann looked radiant in the room's soft, ambient light. The reflection of the table's candlelit centerpiece caused her eyes to twinkle as she sat, captivated by Wes's stories. She laughed and rubbed her belly with care as Wes and Roxy recounted old stories, despite Phil's many objections.

Phil was apprehensive about the evening the second Ann rang the doorbell, but his fears quelled as the night progressed. Wes was happier and more relaxed than he had been earlier in the week, and Roxy was being Roxy. She charmed and entertained everyone, from the waiter to the toddler sitting at the next table. His stomach quivered when she made a quip about hoping to one day become an aunt.

The waiter brought their desserts. Phil had just eaten his first spoonful of bananas Foster when Roxy lobbed her first salvo.

"Daddy, Phil tells me that you're working a case involving some guy at ITI." She closed her eyes and moaned as she chewed a warm, gooey fudge brownie and vanilla bean ice cream. "Ann, grab a spoon and try some of this. It's delicious."

Phil sat motionlessly. He looked across the table and swallowed hard when he saw Wes's clinched jaws and steely gaze. "I … I said you were working a Jack case and I thought it was someone at ITI. That's all I said."

"Mmm hmm," Wes said as he took a sip of coffee.

"Yeah, that's all he said." Roxie took a few more bites from her brownie and looked at Wes quizzically. "What I can't figure out is if this Robert Berry person is the Jack on the loose, why was he meeting with you last night?"

The question caught Wes off guard. He looked at Phil and Roxy and snickered. "I see the both of you still like playing detective. If you must know, I'm investigating a couple of bogus worker's comp cases for an insurance company. They believe the claimants in these cases are being aided by someone on the inside. Mr. Berry thinks I am an adjuster, looking for a little business on the side. He hasn't bitten, but I believe he will. I didn't want Phil to get excited and start snooping around because I don't know how twisted this mess is on the inside. He brought me some wild, off-the-wall scheme he'd found with his computer, and I told him to leave it alone because I don't want him fucking up my case or his career. Are both of you satisfied now?"

Phil could hardly bring himself to look at Wes. He nodded. "Yes, sir." He did not attempt to hide his indignation when he looked to his left and glared at his sister.

Roxy met his outrage with calmness, a broad smile, and a wink. "Yes, Daddy. That explains everything. Phil, I told you. You were worried for nothing."

CHAPTER 21

JACK SHERMAN hunkered down in his reading room just as he had done every Friday night for the past two years. He settled in his Broyhill recliner and read the new *Fodor's Travel* that had just arrived. The past twenty-five years as CEO had been rewarding, but it also came with an enormous price tag attached, at least by his standards.

He'd taken over the company after his father died. When the announcement was made at the funeral, Jack was surprised, more than anyone. His father had prepared a list of actions for the board of directors to carry out upon his demise. Naming Jack as the new CEO was first on the list.

The whole thing came as a shock, considering the effort his father had gone through to keep Jack and his mother far from his growing business. His parents were loving to each other and him; although, there were times when things didn't make sense, like the secret about his mother they'd tried to keep from him.

When Jack took over the company, he worked hard to prove to his dad, who he assumed was watching, that he could do the job. He grew the business by competing with IBM, HP, and DEC on lucrative government contracts.

ITI didn't build hardware; they specialized in writing software for mainframe computers. Times were changing, and their clients were transitioning to personal computers. The company was down to its last four contracts. If things didn't turn around soon, those contracts would be their last. The time was right for him to step down, and he was more than ready to leave.

Jack had already sketched out his travel itinerary. He would begin in Fortaleza, Ceará, Brazil. From there, it was on to Shark Bay in Western Australia, and finally on to Phuket Island in Thailand. It was pronounced "poo-kayt," but he preferred "fuck it." It sounded more apropos. He stared admiringly at an advertisement for Fiji vacation packages. Fiji had to be on the list. He turned the floor globe next to his chair, looking for the Lesser Antilles.

The door opened behind him as he looked through his magnifying glass.

"I'll be up for another hour or so, Henry. Pour me another bourbon. The Pappy Van Winkle's Reserve will do," Jack instructed his trusted personal valet.

"I'll pour myself one too, while I'm at it."

Jack's head shot up. William Beauregard Sherman was the younger of Jack's Uncle Harrison's two sons. To the public, he was known as Senator Bill Sherman, those within the Family called him Beau. He was a three-term senator, who had won his first term on the name recognition of his father, the governor of Kentucky. Beau was sixty and spoiled rotten. When he ran afoul of the law with his last drug case, the Family awarded him the Senate seat as a way of helping him mature.

The Family was officially known as the Confederate Loyalists Association of the New South or CLANS. The covert group's origin dated back to 1865, in the town of Pulaski, Tennessee, when a group of northern and southern aristocrats and Confederate Army veterans came together to overthrow America's Union-led government. To pull off their clandestine mission, the

CLANS used two activist groups: the Confederate Chamber of Commerce, to enterprise and institutionalize their nationalist agenda, and the Klu Klux Klan, to propagandize and recruit. The bond between the groups was more than shared philosophy; it was kinsmanship.

"Wadda' ya want, Beau?" Jack deadpanned.

"Now, how's that to act when you see your favorite kinfolk." Beau guffawed. "Okay, enough with the hillbilly hayseed lingo. We've stirred the hornet's nest on this affirmative action crap, and now it's time for you to lead the charge and pull the rug from under their asses."

The Family was committed to white supremacy, albeit from different but supportive avenues. The KKK secured the supremacy of whites within each state, while the CCC made sure the economic system of America benefited white's supremely. A month after the three organizations sealed their covenant, they realized they needed relatives to enforce the laws that would protect the white race, so the Secret Order of Law Enforcement was established and became a part of the Family. The founding members of each group took a blood oath to appoint a family member who would uphold the Family's mission. When Jack's father died, he learned about his family's role in the secret organization: his great-great-grandfather was an original member. He also discovered that when his father left him the business, it also included an appointment to chair the CCC and a lifetime membership to the Family.

"And how am I supposed to do that?"

Beau pulled out a small desk chair and straddled it. "By paying off the debt we loaned you to cover your EEOC problem."

Jack began to roll the globe slowly. "You never said that was a loan. You said the Family was pitching in because of my strong stand against affirmative action."

"Well, the game's changed, and we're going to beat these niggers in a new way. We're going to let them have some of those affirmative action positions they're screaming for, and when they get them, we'll make 'em really pay. When those niggers start believing they're living like good white folk, we'll have them, hook, line, and sinker. Now that affirmative action has given them better jobs, they're spending and buying up all sorts of stuff, claiming it's their piece of the American pie. They want to do like the song on that show. You know the one, 'Well, we moving on up ...'" Beau finished off his bourbon. "Listen up; the Family is going to need you to start laying a bunch of these niggers off. Keep a few; they'll remain grateful and work harder."

Jack knew Beau wasn't very smart. He had bullied his way into a position of power in the Family, so Jack had to follow orders. "Won't it look strange if I just fire the blacks? The last thing I need is some nosy journalist, poking his nose where it doesn't belong and exposing some document with proof of discrimination. I am not a racist!"

"You're not just going to lay off the niggers; you're going to lay off some good, honest, America-loving white people too. That's the beauty of the plan. When they get upset, we'll just say it was because of affirmative action. When we get through telling them they lost their jobs to the niggers and every other non-white group, they'll want to repeal every law that looks like it's discriminating against whites."

"But people will lose their homes. I just helped build a new community. Many of my employees, both black and white, live

[99]

over there." Despair gripped Jack. The plan was beginning to make sense. "So, you're going to make me fire them so the banks can levy their homes and write off the debt. That'll bankrupt the system."

"No, it won't. Our boys in Congress, on both sides of the aisle, will make sure of that. By the time we get through, we'll have them niggers and their liberal-loving white friends working harder and longer." Beau slapped his knee and laughed.

"When do I have to begin these firings? I have a major deal on the table that I'm trying to close, and I don't need this interference. Let's not forget that my father and I have contributed greatly to the Family. I'm due some damn respect when it comes to my family's business." Jack slid his fingers against the globe, and it began to spin slowly.

"You can begin right after your keynote address to the Chamber members at the State of the Confederacy Conference on February ninth."

"Consider it done." Jack stood and straightened his maroon silk smoking jacket. He walked to the door and opened it. "Good night, Beau. And when you report back, please tell the Family this concludes my family's contribution to their cause."

CHAPTER 22

SATURDAY, JANUARY 23, 1993

PHIL WATCHED the cursor on the screen blink on, then off, then on and off. He had just gained access to The Rabbit Hole. He stared closer at the cursor. It began as a dot but grew as big as a Chiclet and blinked on-off ... on-off ... on-off. It morphed into a gigantic bulbous white light, like the ones on the front of a locomotive. The light seemed to be headed straight for him; it wasn't blinking anymore. Phil closed his eyes and breathed slowly, allowing his frustration to subside.

Their dinner with Wes had been a disaster. Roxy had reneged on her promise and, even worse, she had done it in front of Ann. To make matters worse, Wes knew Phil had ignored his directive. Phil felt humiliated. He had no reason to doubt his father; Wes's interest in Robert Berry sounded legit. But Roxy was unmoved by her father's explanation. She claimed Wes was lying his ass off. Phil was angry with his sister and didn't want to see anything from her point of view.

He typed the password: TSUNAMI

Room 99 was a private chat room, so Phil wasn't surprised when he saw one other person in the room.

NoMoBoesky:>	Holy shit, you're PhantomPhixer?
PhantomPhixer:>	In the flesh. Well, not exactly.
NoMoBoesky:>	I am totally bugging out. I had no idea I was working so

close to the PhantomPhixer. Love your work, by the way.

PhantomPhixer:> So you work in my department?

NoMoBoesky:> Dude, do you think I'm going to give up my identity that easily? Companies have put out rewards for my identity for the shit I've done.

PhantomPhixer:> I've heard. I love your work too, by the way. So why did you want to meet me?

NoMoBoesky:> I saw the *Computer Shopper* on your desk. Plus, you are different from the other people at the office.

PhantomPhixer:> When you say 'other people' would you be referring to African Americans?

NoMoBoesky:> I guess I didn't say that correctly.

PhantomPhixer:> I think I know what you mean. Can you tell me more about the ITI hack and what you found out?

NoMoBoesky:> So you know about that?

PhantomPhixer:> Yeah. Have you figured who's bankrolling them?

NoMoBoesky:> No.

PhantomPhixer:> I believe I can help. I have information that might interest you.

NoMoBoesky:> What kind of information?

PhantomPhixer:> Let's just say ITI is on the verge of making a power move to get back on top. I can only share what I know if we meet face-2-face.

NoMoBoesky:> I can't risk it.

PhantomPhixer:> We're both risking a lot. If we can't trust each other, they win.

NoMoBoesky:> I'm not sure.

PhantomPhixer:> You know who I am but I don't know you. Seems like I've already risked a lot.

NoMoBoesky:> All right. You say when but I get to choose the place.

PhantomPhixer:> Tonight @ 9:00. Where?

NoMoBoesky:> Black Dog Tavern in University City.

CHAPTER 23

THE DOOR LATCH clicked, locking Phil inside the pitch-black abyss of Robert's office. He wiped sweat beads from his forehead with his shirt sleeve and breathed a sigh of relief. His previous attempts at unlocking doors with a lock pick had been disastrous, to say the least, but he amazed himself with the quickness and ease in which he pushed the lock's pins and rotated the tumbler. He retrieved a pen-sized flashlight from his coat pocket. The miniature light penetrated the darkness as Phil canvassed the office. The light bounced against a brown metal file cabinet in the corner to his left. He searched the topmost drawer. Phil found a folder labeled EEOC in a hanging file folder at the back. Inside the folder were applications. Copies of the photograph from their employee badges were clipped to the front. Phil riffled through the stack to find his application.

There was a knock at the door.

Phil dropped the folder and papers scattered across the floor. He knelt down and gathered them hurriedly. There was another knock at the door; this time it was louder.

"Phil, are you in there?" the voice cried out.

Phil's eyes flew wide open. He looked around his apartment, bewildered by his surroundings and glad he was no longer in Robert's office. Phil heard another knock and recognized Ann's voice. He was still dazed and groggy when he opened the door. "Good morning, baby! I'm sorry I didn't hear you. I fell asleep on the couch."

• • • •

Shirley Donovan beamed with joy when she heard that she was going to be a grandmother. Like her daughter, Shirley had dazzling hazel eyes and was full of charisma; yet everything about her screamed teacher. A seasoned elementary school teacher, over the years Shirley had employed many methods—surrogate mother, grandmother, aunt, counselor and, when necessary, a caring, mean teacher—to get the most out of her students, especially those who were prone to be wayward, lazy, or diffident. Shirley had a way of teaching you something when you least expected it, like the time she told Phil the story about her papa. He was the best plumber in the county, regardless of race. Her papa boasted about his skills until the day he discovered he was being paid less than all the other plumbers. He completed work faster than the others, so customers assumed the work he did wasn't as difficult. She said the experience taught her papa a valuable lesson, which he shared with her: "A wise man sees his knowledge as wealth and uses it to his benefit, while the fool shows everyone how smart he is and ends up penniless."

Ann's father, Charles (everyone called him Charlie), smiled but said very little. He invited Phil to join him at the table for a game of dominoes while Ann and Shirley prepared lunch. Charlie was a former college football player and an avid golfer. He stood 6'5" and looked intimidating to any unsuspecting observer, but he was a kid at heart and enjoyed friendly competition.

When Charlie found out Phil played dominoes, their relationship blossomed. Despite their growing bond, Phil was still a little uncomfortable about breaking the news of Ann's pregnancy. The way he saw it, telling another man you've been having sex with his daughter didn't make for an easy conversation.

Charlie interrupted the quietness. He spoke with a long drawl as if he was in deep thought. "So, you think you uhhh … ready for uhhh … all of this, huh?" He talked that way whenever he played dominoes.

Phil was speechless, unsure if Charlie was asking a question. It sounded more like a statement or even a taunt. Phil cleared the dry air bubble that was lodged in his throat then offered a weak, "Yes, sir."

Charlie laid his domino on the table with a loud thump. "Gimme those three sisters. You know their name, Ella … Bella … and Stella!" That was domino slang for fifteen points. Charlie chuckled. "Plenty men have said the same thing. If there is one thing I can tell you, it's this: I've been married for thirty-five years, and I'm still not ready for some things. You know what I mean?" Charlie raised an eyebrow then gave Phil an assuring nod.

"Follow that taxi!" Phil slapped the table with his domino. "Yes, sir! I'm going to be ready as best I can."

"That's about all any man can do, son. Tennis shoes and domino!" he said as he tossed his last domino on the table.

Charlie hadn't called him son before. Phil grinned and shuffled the dominoes for the next round.

CHAPTER 24

ROXY SAW Vincent's black Trans Am in the parking lot and made a U-turn at the next intersection. *Either he really likes the food here, or it's the only place he can afford,* she surmised as she walked into Frank's Grille. Before she had orchestrated their accidental encounter, Roxy discovered that Vincent ate dinner at the small pub every evening.

"There you are," Vincent beamed and pulled out the barstool next to him.

It was six o'clock, and every TV in the bar was tuned into the basketball game. The Tar Heels were in another tough battle. The frenetic crowd raised the decibel level with each trip up and down the court. Vincent leaned closer so Roxy could hear. "Let's get out of here. I have a quieter place in mind," he said.

Roxy felt his lips brush against her earlobe as he spoke. The tiny hairs on her tragus fluttered in the warmth of his words. Roxy closed her eyes, her body tingling from the sensual sensation. "Really? Where?"

"Bernardin's. I'll need to change into something more appropriate, and I'm sure you will want to do the same, even though you look remarkable already. I'll meet you there. Is eight o'clock okay?"

Roxy leaned back and smiled, exposing the dimple in her right cheek. "It's a date, Romeo. And just so you know, Sizzler isn't all that bad."

CHAPTER 25

VINCENT STOOD OUTSIDE Bernardin's, looking like one of the Times Square billboard models for Calvin Klein. His attire, a black single-breasted suit, and white cotton shirt, with the top button undone, was iconic and chic.

His suave composure contradicted the euphoria he felt when Roxy's red BMW M3 pulled up to the valet. He was considered one of Charlotte's most influential and sought-after bachelors. Dating had been put on hold once he started courting Malcolm and WorldNet; it was a luxury he could not afford. All of that changed when he met Roxanne. He knew there was something different about her the second they'd met. He was tired of the coked-up socialites, workaholic b-school grads, and the fragile beauty queens who needed constant reassuring. He liked everything about her. She was drop dead gorgeous and easy to talk to, but what he loved most was her mysterious and edgy charm.

His coal black eyes lit up when Roxanne stepped from behind the car, wearing an elegant red cocktail dress that hung off her shoulders. "Wow, you look stunning!"

"You're rather dashing yourself, Romeo," Roxanne teased.

After the embarrassing moment with the defunct credit card, Vincent desperately wanted to redeem himself, and Bernardin's was just the place. He called the owner, who was a good friend, and got a table at the last minute. The bill wouldn't be a problem; ITI had a standing account. The best part, dinner after seven on a Saturday lessened the likelihood of running into someone who would blow his cover; although, the customers at Bernardin's were much too polite to engage in idle chit chat over dinner.

Vincent opened the door. He noticed Robert standing to his left, at the coat check counter. "Robert Berry! My brother from another mother. What a surprise seeing you here." Vincent patted his friend on the back.

Roxy stopped mid-stride when she heard Vincent call Robert's name. *Phil said he was tall, but I had no idea he meant this damn tall,* she thought as she marveled at the towering man looking over Vincent's shoulder, right at her. Her heart raced even though she knew she had nothing to fear.

"Robert, I'd like to introduce you to my friend." Vincent extended a hand toward Roxy. "This is Miss—"

"Roxanne," Roxy interrupted. It was better to keep the introduction on a first name only basis. The last thing she wanted was for Robert to make her family connection.

A puzzled look registered across Robert's face when their eyes met. "You look awfully familiar. Have we met before?"

"Robert, are you trying to move in on my date with that old pick-up line?" Vincent held his solemn expression for a few seconds then let go with a broad smile and laughter.

Robert, flushed with embarrassment, could only muster a light-hearted grin.

"I'm not sure," Roxy stammered. Her heart raced. She knew her eyes, the one glaring physical trait she'd inherited from her father, was on the verge of breaching her anonymity. "People are always telling me I look like someone they know. Maybe it's because they've seen me on TV. I've been on a few commercials."

"Maybe that's it," Robert agreed. The skepticism in his voice betrayed the certainty of his words.

Vincent continued to make small talk while Robert kept a watchful eye on Roxy. She could see the wheels in his head wobbling on their axles as he struggled to connect the dots. Unwilling to assist him in his search for clarity, Roxy feigned interest in a set of portraits hanging on the wall behind the hostess station to their right. She dropped her shoulders and exhaled when the maître d' announced their table was available. Roxy turned to Robert and extended her hand. "It's been a pleasure meeting you, Mr. Berry. Hopefully, our meeting today will leave a more lasting impression," she said with a sly smile before walking away.

• • • •

Vincent and Roxy dined at a table in front of the fireplace. The cozy setting provided the perfect ambience for them to carefully peel away the layers of their concocted personas. Roxy steered the conversation to cars and the big auto show in Detroit. Vincent resisted the urge to tell Roxy about the two exotic sports cars that he owned. It didn't make sense to bring it up since she couldn't see them. He thought about calling Uncle Tony and asking him to open the garage, but he didn't feel like hearing him bust his balls. It was better not to say anything.

"Enough talk about cars. I want to know something about you." Vincent smiled coyly.

Roxanne shrugged. "I'll tell you anything you want to know."

Vincent thought for a few seconds. "Okay, how would you prefer a man to sweep you off your feet?"

Roxy laughed. The question sounded lame, but it was thoughtful. "You know, I can honestly say I've never had a man ask me that. Let me see …" She placed her finger on her lips and looked up. "Forget about the roses. They're nice, but guys do a terrible job with the presentation. They just hold them out and say, 'Here.'" She looked at Vincent. "Please don't do that."

Vincent laughed. "Don't worry; I won't."

"If a man wants to sweep me off my feet, instead of showing up at my door with flowers, he should show up with tickets for the next flight out to some private island. And instead of saying, 'Here,' he'll say, 'Come fly away with me.'"

• • • •

As they waited for the valet to bring their cars, Vincent turned to face Roxanne. "I know it wasn't Sizzler, but I hope you enjoyed our second date." He held her arms and kissed her softly. They remained silent until their cars arrived. "Can I see you again tomorrow?" he asked as he held the car door open.

"What's wrong with tonight? The night's still young." She winked and closed the door.

Minutes later, Vincent pulled up beside her and rolled the car window down. "Follow me."

Roxy stared at the Trans Am's taillights as they sped along the highway. It was time to turn up the heat. Any clues to the whereabouts of the Lamborghini and Porsche had to be somewhere in Vincent's apartment. She would have gone inside while he was at work, but a Brink's Security sticker was in the window, so she went with her next plan.

Her harmless flirtation had gotten Vincent's attention for sure. Now, she was about to hit pay dirt. Roxy rubbed her bottom lip as Bobby Caldwell crooned "Heart of Mine." She couldn't stop thinking about the soft soul-tingling kiss they shared earlier.

Roxy pulled her visor down and flipped open the mirror when she parked in front of Vincent's apartment. She applied a fresh layer of moisturizer and lipstick then rubbed her lips together. She stared at her reflection. *Whatever you're feeling, get over it and get in there and find those cars.*

CHAPTER 26

THE BLACK DOG TAVERN was a jack-of-all-trades kind of establishment, located near the university. It was housed in a renovated two-story warehouse. On the first floor was a bar and dining area. A large game room was in the back. The upstairs level consisted of a lounge area and several semi-private padded booths.

Phil looked around the room. The crowd was sparse. A group of college students occupied three tables. Mugs of beer and stacks of plates with discarded napkins littered the tables. The young ladies giggled as their testosterone-laden male counterparts competed to see who could be the most childish. Phil spotted a Pac-Man arcade game when he entered the game room and dropped a quarter into the slot.

He could hardly concentrate. Meeting NoMoBoesky was like meeting a childhood idol. The guy was a legend in the Underground. Phil shoved the joystick from left to right, but he couldn't escape the cyan colored ghost. He looked over his shoulder at the door every time it opened. When he wasn't watching the door, he was checking the time on his watch. Phil deposited another quarter, but the game ended just as quickly as the previous one. The front door hadn't opened in a while. He wondered if NoMoBoesky had changed his mind.

Time moved slower than a child waiting for Christmas Eve to end. Phil had been there twenty minutes, but it felt like an hour. He decided to look around again. A jukebox near the stairs blasted an Aerosmith song. The college students were still at the table. Their group had grown into a small crowd.

Phil went upstairs. The lounge was a huge carpeted room that was divided into two sections. The front area was furnished with loveseats, couches, and den chairs. Two floor lamps on opposite sides of the room gave the space a mellowing vibe. He saw a young couple hugging on a loveseat.

Nirvana's "Smells Like Teen Spirit" pumped through the speakers as Phil entered the second room. Six booths were arranged along the walls to his left and right. Phil walked slowly through the dimly lit room, taking quick glances as he approached each booth.

He looked in the last booth on his right.

"Can I help you?" the woman asked.

"I'm sorry. I was looking for someone I was supposed to meet here." Phil did a double take when he realized it was Holly from the elevator. She was wearing a pair of faded jeans and a Cornell sweatshirt.

"I'm sure they'll be here soon. You can wait for them here. Take a seat." Holly patted the empty cushion next to her. "I insist."

"I really can't stay long. I'm meeting a friend, and I don't want to miss him." Phil sat down.

"I won't hold you." Holly played with a bracelet while she talked. "I really want to apologize for what happened the other day. I know you think I'm an awful person but I'm not, honestly."

Phil shrugged. "It's not the first time it's happened to me. But you're the first one who has ever apologized."

"I was just mortified when Lori pulled that little stunt. She is usually a nice person, but you would not believe the things she was saying. I know I couldn't."

Phil thought about her expression on the elevator and chuckled. "I've got a pretty good idea. I could tell by the look on your face."

"You could see me?" Holly shrieked. She covered her mouth momentarily with her hands and began to blush with embarrassment.

"Don't give it a second thought."

"You know, I never thought about how tough it must be for you to work at a place like that," Holly said apologetically. "Since that day, I have felt just terrible, and I want to make it up to you."

"Your apology is enough, thank you." Phil stood up.

"So, you mean you're not interested in what I found out when I hacked into the ITI network?" Holly asked with a devilish smile.

Phil spun around. Shock registered on his face. "You're NoMoBoesky?"

"Shh!" Holly grabbed his hand. "Yes … and we've got a lot to talk about."

CHAPTER 27

"I DIDN'T GO LOOKING for this, but when I saw it, I had no other choice. Don't you agree?" Holly pleaded.

"Okay. Let's start from the beginning." Phil hoped he didn't sound too eager.

"Like I said, I only intended for this to be a prank." Holly exhaled, her shoulders slumped. "I came up with the EEOC idea only because I thought it wouldn't raise too many flags. All I needed was something to cause a spike, nothing catastrophic."

"I believe you. But ..."

"But what? I thought you just said you believed me?" Holly's worried looked turned to fear.

"I *do* believe you. It's just that I can't understand how the EEOC audit happened, when you were the one who sent ITI the initial letter, informing them that they were going to be penalized. Something's missing. You're not telling me something."

"I guess I did leave out one teeny thing." She held her thumb and index finger less than an inch apart.

"What is it? I can't help you unless you tell me." Phil moved closer. "Trust me; I do want to help you."

Holly shook her head and then rubbed her clammy hands against her jeans. "I did it. I was the one who contacted the EEOC and initiated the audit."

"What?" Phil shrieked.

"Shh!" Holly poked her head out of the booth's entrance to make sure all was clear. "I know it was a dumb thing to do. I guess I just got tired of seeing that good ol' boy network get away with whatever they want. For the record, I don't have any regrets."

"If you think you're going to hear any argument from me, you can forget about it. I'm glad you did it. What made you do it?"

Holly placed both hands, palms down, on the edge of the bench and started rocking slowly. "My dad was an engineer at the Xerox Palo Alto Research Center. His team developed the Xerox Alto. He and the other engineers at PARC fed my interests by letting me play around with the stuff they were working on. My mom went berserk; she didn't like the idea of her little girl hanging in labs, tinkering with gadgets. My dad caved in and cut off my lab privileges. Two days later, he saw how depressed I was and brought home a computer. I guess you can say I was the first Alto beta tester, even though I was only nine years old.

"I was the second female to enroll in the computer science program at Cornell. My mother objected, but Dad allowed me to enroll only if I enrolled in a secretarial program as a backup. My father warned me that finding a job in the industry would be difficult, especially without his assistance, but I was determined to do it on my own. After three years of closed doors, you're looking at the only administrative assistant with a degree in computer science."

"How'd you come up with the name NoMoBoesky?"

"It's an homage to a dear friend named Ryan. Ryan was a hacker with a love for journalism. Whenever you'd hear news of a big scandal being uncovered and the press referenced unidentified sources, nine times out of ten, they were talking about Ryan. He was the first person to uncover the Wall Street insider trading scandal. Unfortunately, his efforts to save all of us from ruin cost him his life. He never got a chance to see Ivan Boesky and the rest of his pals get convicted, so I came up with the moniker and made it a personal mission to expose guys like Boesky."

Phil looked at her with admiration. He searched for a response, but all he could say was, "Wow!"

Holly wiped a tear from the corner of her eye with the back of her hand. "He was one of the best hackers I've ever had the pleasure of knowing." She took a deep breath and let it out slowly. She stared Phil squarely in the eyes. "I really could use your help. Whatta you say? Will you help me?"

Knowing he needed help with his own undercover investigation and Holly, AKA NoMoBoesky, had given him his biggest lead so far, Phil readily agreed. "Sure! It'll be an honor to work with you."

"Oh, we're sorry!" A white couple blocked the entrance to the booth. Phil saw their surprised expressions. The man eyed Phil suspiciously then directed his attention to Holly. "Ma'am are you in danger? Is everything okay in here?"

Holly grabbed Phil's hand and cupped it firmly between both of her hands. "Yes, everything is fine. Now, if you don't mind, we'd like some privacy."

CHAPTER 28
SUNDAY, JANUARY 24, 1993

THE TWO-AND-A-HALF-HOUR drive to Durham with Ann was the comforting relief Phil needed. Between their jobs, preparing for the wedding, and his moonlighting as an investigator, the past week had given them little time to be alone. Ann radiated with the glow of an expectant mother as they talked about the wedding, her pregnancy, and raising a child. He was content with listening to her talk about cake and flower decorations, morning sickness, or anything else she desired, as long as it kept his mind off of ITI and his conversation with Holly.

He and Holly had talked until two in the morning. The Black Dog Tavern was closing, and Phil needed to unravel the twisted vines of information. What he knew so far was helpful, but it didn't shed light on how he had been hired. The audit had been initiated based on a tip from a whistleblower, who turned out to be some fictitious employee Holly had created when she submitted documents to the EEOC. The EEOC then delayed the audit the day before it was scheduled to begin. A week later, ITI started hiring minorities and women who met their quota requirements exclusively.

Phil drove up the U-shaped driveway to his parent's house and parked in front. The sandstone colored brickhouse looked different now that he and his siblings were gone. It seemed more peaceful and relaxed.

Marjorie was on the porch, watering her potted plants. "My eyes must be playing tricks on me. That can't possibly be Philander coming to visit. Ann, I must learn your secret."

• • • •

"Whew! You've got quite an appetite today, son. You must be worried about something," Wes intoned. Phil had already finished off two healthy servings at dinner and was getting ready to dive into his second hunk of Marjorie's homemade sour cream pound cake.

"Wes, leave him alone. He's just nervous about the wedding," Marjorie chimed in. "Although I must say, he's eating more like a pregnant woman than a nervous groom."

Phil stopped chewing. He looked at Ann, who met his surprised look with a shocked expression of her own.

"Ann's pregnant!" Marjorie shrieked. She placed her hands over her heart and shot Phil one of her patented "I told you so" looks.

"What? I didn't know. That's the truth," Phil attempted to persuade his mother, to no avail.

"I know one thing for certain; she's going to be a gorgeous little angel. Her mother's beautiful, and she will undoubtedly inherit the Jacobson charm," Wes beamed.

Marjorie scooped a spoonful of ice cream. "And what makes you think it's going to be a girl?"

Wes clicked the remote and changed the TV channel. "Puddin', you know doggone well I have a perfect record when it comes to predicting the sex of every baby in this family."

Marjorie looked at Ann and Phil and shook her head. "One time. He got it right one damn time."

"You need to quit lying to those children, Puddin'. You know I predicted each of these children. Your mama didn't need an ultrasound back then. Humph … They would've run my ass out of Vegas, the way I was calling it."

Phil let out a big sigh and shook his head in despair. Although he'd grown used to his parents' unpretentious and unrestrained behavior, it still embarrassed him every time they carried on like that in front of his friends.

"The child's sex is determined by the male's sperm; may I remind you. I've had three boys, and I never looked like that." Wes pointed at Phil. "That's the look I had when you had Roxy."

"And what kind of look is that? From my viewpoint, you had the same look every time." Marjorie turned toward Ann and contorted her face into a funny expression, and they both howled with laughter like teenage girls at a slumber party.

"Mama, Daddy, come on now! We're not trying to hear that!"

"Well, I, for one, hope your daddy is right," Marjorie admitted. "The last thing this family needs is to start its next generation with another Jacobson male. Please do not wish that upon Ann."

"Oh, I won't mind if it's a boy," Ann gushed and rubbed her belly.

Marjorie leaned over. "You're about to marry a Jacobson man, and if that bundle of joy you're carrying is a boy, you're going to need all the preparation you can get. You want a girl, trust me."

"Don't believe that, Ann. The Jacobson women are more than a notion," Wes opined from his chair in the den. "Lord knows I love 'em all to death but ..." He let out a whistle that lasted for several seconds.

Marjorie got up from the table and returned a few minutes later with her purse. She grabbed Ann by the arm and announced they were going shopping. Marjorie didn't need a reason to go shopping, but knowing that her first grandchild was on the way gave the outing a sense of purpose. "Sunday afternoons are the best time to shop. That's when the stores stock the shelves with their best merchandise for the well-to-do customers who come in on Monday mornings," Marjorie explained as they walked out the house.

Phil hadn't spoken to Wes since Roxy had embarrassed him at dinner. When he walked into the den, Wes was looking through the newspaper. Discarded and unread sections were sprawled on either side of the recliner.

"Ann's a beautiful girl," Wes said from behind the newspaper. "I think the two of you make a very nice young couple. Reminds me of your mama and me." He put the paper down and looked at Phil. "About the other night ..."

"Daddy, Roxy made it sound like more than it was," Phil interjected.

"How do you know what it sounded like to me?"

"Daddy, I told her what I told you. That's it. I wasn't doing anything more. You let Roxy run those games on you every time."

"First, you tell me what I'm hearing; now, you want to tell me it's all Roxy's fault." He looked at Phil and shook his head.

The conversation was reminiscent of the one Wes had with J.D. thirty-eight years ago. Back then, he was the one who was excited and didn't want to listen to his father's warnings because he thought J.D. didn't understand. Now that he was on the other side, Wes prayed Phil wouldn't do the same. "Son, there are two things I have learned in life. The first is when you look for answers to problems that don't exist, you can best believe you're going to end up with a shitload of problems that you can't solve. Do you understand what I'm saying?"

"I understand."

"I don't think you do. You better think long and hard about what you decide to chase after. Some things aren't worth catching. I've seen many a people get consumed with chasing after things they thought they needed, only to discover they had chased themselves away from the people and things that mattered most."

Phil knew Wes was trying to protect him like always, but he didn't need protection; he needed to be released. He needed to be set free from the frustration and doubt he felt each time a co-worker regarded his capabilities as being merely skin deep. Before he could prove those people wrong, Phil was convinced he needed to clear the air of his own foggy layer of doubt. "Okay, Daddy. I get it. What's the second thing you've learned?"

Wes went back to his paper. "You can't give a person anything they're determined to buy for themselves."

CHAPTER 29

MONDAY, JANUARY 25, 1993

"FASTER THAN greased lightning, the little sonofabitch flipped me right on my backside," Stanley said proudly. The three executives were seated at their customary locations around the table.

Vincent wasn't interested in Stanley's homespun tales. However, the thought of Stanley getting flipped on his butt was pretty funny, so he joined in on the laughter. He loathed when their conversations turned to wrestling. It was Stanley's way of excluding him from the discussion.

Vincent eased back in his chair and propped his chin on top of his fist like The Thinker. Watching Stanley kiss up to Jack, along with listening to his lame stories, had become passé. He only needed to hold on for one more week. After that, he didn't care how many wrestling stories Stanley told. Besides, the story he was most interested in had just gotten better.

Vincent displayed a goofy smile. His mind was a million miles away, on his own weekend sparring session. It was the most passionate, soul releasing sex he had ever experienced. Their sweaty, hickey-ridden bodies remained entwined until six that morning, when they both got dressed for work.

"That's great! I'm sure he's going to follow in his dad's footsteps." Jack leaned over and patted Stanley on the shoulder.

"Jack, I'm sure the kid's aiming for higher than second place," said Vincent.

"And this from a guy who doesn't know the difference between a half-nelson and a double-leg takedown. But if you have a minute, I'll be happy to show you how it's done." Stanley smiled like the Joker.

"Okay, that's enough. What's the status on WorldNet?" Jack ordered.

"We're good to go. Malcolm assured me they'll be ready for next week." Vincent knew Malcolm's exact words were, "We hope to have all issues resolved in time for next week," but he knew his interpretation sounded better.

"That's not good enough." Jack slammed his fist against the table. Vincent and Stanley stared in amazement.

"Jack, what do you mean it's not good enough? You said you wanted to get this done by next week, and we're on schedule to do just that. I assure you the WorldNet acquisition is as good as closed. I don't know how to make it any better than that."

"We need to lock this down *this* week. Call Mr. Graves and tell him if he wants to do business, I want a signed contract this week," Jack demanded.

"What about the bug fixes?"

"He can continue to work on the bug fixes, and we'll make the announcement the following Friday as scheduled."

"I will get right on it. And, for the record, I agree with you. We need to lock this down as soon as possible before we get blindsided by another unexpected crisis."

"Like what?" Stanley looked worried. "Would it have anything to do with that Robert Berry fellow you've been using to handle your grunt work?"

"You'd like that, wouldn't you? Just so you know, Robert's not a problem. And if he were, I'm more than capable of handling him."

Jack rapped the tabletop with the palm of his hand. "Let's not bicker over irrelevant matters. If Mr. Berry, or anyone else for that matter, poses a problem, I expect you to handle it."

"I will."

"Let's not forget you were the one who told us we could count on Berry," Stanley muttered.

"I was, wasn't I? I guess that's why I said I would handle it." Vincent stood from his seat. "Are you sure your kid didn't flip you on your head instead of your ass? Wait a minute; your head *is* your ass." Vincent laughed and hummed a bar of "Heart of Mine" as he exited the room.

CHAPTER 30

JACK HAD BEEN on edge since his meeting with Beau. His weekend had been a continuous cycle of nervous pacing and fretful sleep. Jack had had enough of the Family and their stupid traditions, and he was definitely fed up with supporting their archaic and arcane ideology. He was convinced that breaking his family's tradition of commitment to the Family was the right decision. His exit plan had been in motion for nearly eighteen months. The day after his keynote address at the annual conference, he would announce he was stepping down as CEO and chairman, effective immediately. He'd name his successor and then make his getaway.

Just as he had entered the homestretch and saw the checkered flag, the wheels on Jack's plan had been flattened by an unexpected pothole, the Family's latest demand. Thoughts of employee layoffs, home foreclosures, and personal bankruptcies haunted him throughout the weekend. On the way into the office, he decided he wasn't going to take part in their diabolical experiment. Jack's sullen look belied the depth of his anguish. The WorldNet purchase needed to be finalized by Friday if he had any chance of getting out of sight before the State of the Confederacy Conference.

Stanley drummed his fingertips on the conference table, while Jack muttered obscenities. "Jack, relax. Vincent's an asshole, but he's done a great job in bringing WorldNet and their Internet browser application to the table, even if I do say so myself."

Jack looked around the room. "I need better assurances. I nurtured this company as if it were my child. I want to make sure all is well when I step down."

"Jack, how long have you known me?"

"Thirty years, at least. I remember when you started working in the mailroom. I guess you were about fifteen years old."

"Sixteen. You've been there for me since day one, attending my wrestling matches and helping me with my grades. Jack, if you hadn't been there for me, I never would have gotten my MBA, and I sure as hell would not have been named COO."

"I appreciate your sentiments, Stanley. I was only doing what I wanted my father to do for me when I was that age." Jack wrung his hands. "The way this deal has gone, I sure don't feel like I'm there for you and Vincent now."

"Jack, that's what I'm telling you. I want to give you the same assurances you've given me over the years. If Vincent doesn't come through by Friday, I assure you, I'll have this whole mess cleared and ready for signoff by the end of the following week. I give you my word."

CHAPTER 31

P HIL YAWNED wide like a lion anticipating feeding time, as he turned the key to unlock his office door. Sleep had become more elusive with each passing day. *Damn! A week has gone by, and I feel like I'm drowning in quicksand.*

It felt like weights were hanging from his eyelids; he could barely keep them open. His sensory receptors were so worn down that he didn't notice the interoffice envelope lying on the floor until his shoe hit it and sent it spiraling across the floor. He pushed the door behind him and rushed across the room to scoop up the brown package before the door latch clicked into place.

He ignored the list of senders' names on the front and removed the folded sheet. Holly's cryptic handwritten note was short and to the point. She had a lead but needed his help. She also wanted to know if he could come by her place after work.

"The best way to cover our tracks is not to create any," he'd told Holly when they devised their communication plan.

It was the first time their stealth messaging plan—using old, non-circulated interoffice envelopes to exchange messages—had been put into action. Although it lacked sophistication, it was the least detectable. Phil placed a checkmark in the top right corner of the page to confirm and then waited until his afternoon popcorn break with Dana and Karen to drop the envelope in Holly's inbox.

So far, their plan was working to perfection.

CHAPTER 32

"DAMN, HOLLY! What the hell are you running up here?"

Phil looked around the attic that Holly had converted into an office. A futon and coffee table, littered with magazines and old takeout containers, occupied one corner of the room. "This place looks like an NSA Special Ops command center. Well, except for the futon, coffee table, and refrigerator," he chided.

Phil counted seven workstations arranged throughout the room. Number eight was on a table with its cover and motherboard removed. Cables sprouted from the back of each computer. They ran along the baseboard like a vine to a wall-mounted shelf that housed four modems, an ISDN router, and a pair of network hubs.

Holly handed Phil a legal pad. "Pull up a chair. Excuse the mess. I'm not used to having guests up here." She grabbed a sweatshirt that was draped over the back of a chair and tossed it on the futon. "Can I offer you anything? All I have is water, Coke—the regular kind, not that diet stuff—and beer."

"A beer's cool." He rummaged through the legal pad. "Why do you need my help? From the looks of it, you've tracked every ITI transaction. This is amazing!"

She returned with a beer, a Coke, and a bag of microwave popcorn. "Popcorn's all I got. I haven't gone to the grocery store in a while. I'm sure you know why."

Holly sat down and tapped the keyboard. The monitor came to life.

Phil tried his best not to stare, but he couldn't get over Holly's stark, yet delicate after-hours transformation. The heavily spritzed hairstyle she had worn earlier was now pulled back into a ponytail. The makeup had been removed, revealing her unblemished creamy white skin and thin pink lips, and the designer label business attire had been discarded for a Howard the Duck t-shirt and a pair of faded blue jeans. She had a nerdy attractiveness that bordered on appealing.

"For the past two years, ITI stock has been in a constant nosedive. Most investors stay away from companies that can't keep up with the times. The savvy ones wait so they can pick the carcass like a vulture. The company has been taking a beating financially, which is a mild understatement. Call it a coincidence if you'd like, but a month after I initiated the EEOC audit, their fortunes made a huge turn upward. Look at this."

Holly pressed the ENTER key, and a bank registry appeared on the screen. While Phil looked at the screen, she rolled her chair to the next workstation. She repeated the sequence of steps, and another registry appeared.

"Now, take a look at this one."

She rolled to the next two PCs and repeated the steps.

Phil looked at each screen. "All of these accounts received wire transfers for the same amount, on the same day, and within seconds of each other."

"That's not all. They received it from this account." She returned to the first computer and typed. "This is a transitory account. The problem is I'm having trouble tracking where the money came from to fund this account. If we find out where the money came from, maybe we'll find out who's behind this."

Holly and Phil rolled back and forth between the computers as she guided him through the maze of transactions. He was in awe of her expert skill and analysis. In her quest to connect the digital puzzle pieces together, Holly had also unlocked several of the most highly secured banking networks.

"Women are inherently good detectives. Just ask any man who's spent any considerable time with a woman. A woman can dig up information that you thought was confidential between you, God, and a dearly departed friend," Phil remembered his father saying on many occasions.

"What are you smiling about?" Holly interrupted.

"Huh? Umm … I didn't realize I was smiling. I guess I was just admiring your work."

The base of Holly's neck turned bright red. "Thank you. That means a lot coming from the PhantomPhixer." She rolled to the next workstation and began typing feverishly.

"I don't care how good they are at getting information, the minute you bring a woman on a case, you're asking for trouble." Seeing as though his father routinely employed women to assist him on cases, Phil dismissed the advice as just another one of Wes's crazy ideas.

Holly entered a string of commands. A sea of white letters and numbers scrolled rapidly down a blue screen. "Here's the black hole … excuse me, the blue hole I've been sucked into for the last week."

Phil placed his arms on his lap and leaned closer. "What's this?"

"It's the transaction log for the transitory account deposits." She pointed to a column of numbers on the screen. "And these are the routing numbers that originated each transaction. There's only one problem: These aren't your normal ABA routing transit numbers."

Phil studied the list; the sequence of numbers seemed vaguely familiar. Holly looked on with great interest. Her faint measured breaths hovered above his shoulder. The warmth from her exhale teased the hair on his earlobe, and he quivered uncontrollably. Phil closed his eyes and cleared the dry air bubble from his throat as he struggled to regain composure.

Phil shook his head in resignation. "They look like normal routing numbers to me. What makes you so sure they aren't?"

"First of all, none of these routing numbers are listed in the ABA database," Holly began. "In fact, there aren't any routing numbers in the database with these prefixes. Secondly, if you notice, none of these transactions have an account number. It's like the transactions appeared out of thin air."

Phil snapped to attention as if Holly had recited the secret words that broke the spell he was under. He peered at the screen. "You're right!"

"I am?" Holly asked hesitantly.

"Yes! Well, you're sorta right.

"What do you mean?"

"It's like you said; these aren't normal routing numbers. They're the reserved routing numbers banks use for inter-banking transfers. The banks needed a backdoor to circumvent regulations, so they created these stealth routing numbers to make transfers right under the bank examiner's noses."

"Those sneaky bastards!" Holly rocked back and forth, a look of determination filling her countenance.

Phil finished off his beer and gathered his equipment. He turned to face Holly when they reached the front door. "I'll FTP you a list of codes for NationsBank, JP Morgan, Banc One, Wells Fargo, Wachovia, and all the other major banks when I get back to my place. Once we find out which banks sent the transfers, the only thing left to do is find out who authorized it."

Holly beamed with excitement. She draped her arms over his shoulder and kissed him gently on his lips. "You're the best!"

Phil stood motionless, unsure of what had just occurred. He searched for a response among the heap of cloudy and incoherent phrases that were running through his mind. Then he noticed how her steel blue eyes twinkled like distant stars against the hallway's ambient light. Instinctively, he wrapped an arm around her waist and drew her closer.

"You're pretty good yourself," he said in a soft, commanding tone that preceded their next kiss, a longer and more passionate kiss.

CHAPTER 33

THE COMPUTER CHIRPED a few musical notes, notifying Phil that a message had arrived.

```
MystikalGremlinz:>  I'm back. So you were
                    saying you and NoMoBoesky
                    might be on to something
                    big?
PhantomPhixer:>     We hope so.
```

Phil deliberately sidestepped any mention of Holly's name. He wanted to honor her desire to remain anonymous. At least that's what he wanted to believe was the reason for keeping his relationship with Holly a secret. *We work well together. Just the two of us. That's all there is to it.* He thought it sounded convincing.

```
MystikalGremlinz:>  I hope so, dude. Things
                    are getting weirder by
                    the day.
```

"Son, please don't tell me you expect people to believe that foolishness. You know good and damn well, it's more to it than that." Phil, startled by the clarity and closeness of his father's voice, looked around the room to make sure he was alone. Things were getting weird.

PhantomPhixer:> Tell me about it. What just happened?

MystikalGremlinz:> That was Vincent. He says we have to close on the purchase this Friday.

PhantomPhixer:> Cool.

MystikalGremlinz:> By the way, it looks like we are finally going to meet each other.

PhantomPhixer:> No shit? When?

MystikalGremlinz:> Flying in Thursday morning. Thought Vincent would go ballistic when I told him the fixes wouldn't be ready, but he was cool.

PhantomPhixer:> What did he say?

MystikalGremlinz:> He said don't worry about it. Can you believe that? He said not to worry about it because they're going to wait until next week to announce it. That gives us another week to work on the fixes.

PhantomPhixer:> Sounds like a sweet deal.

MystikalGremlinz:> That's what Vincent said. He says he's never seen a guy so nervous about becoming a multi-millionaire. I guess I should be, but Phixer, my gut tells me I need to wait on you and NoMoBoesky.

PhantomPhixer:> Why? Did Vincent say something?

```
MystikalGremlinz:> Wasn't so much what he
                   said, but how he sounded.
PhantomPhixer:>    How did he sound?
MystikalGremlinz:> Extremely stressed!
                   Vincent's worked hard on
                   this agreement. I know he
                   wants to close, but it
                   sounded like it was more
                   to it than that. You
                   think you can find what
                   you're looking for by
                   Friday?
```

Phil stared at Vincent's name. After Roxy had embarrassed him in front of his father and Ann, he tried his best to store any memory of her in the recesses of his mind. *I'm much better at this than you. You know it, and Daddy knows it, too! The only reason why he said women didn't make good detectives was so I'd quit bugging him.* It wasn't working. Roxy had mastered the art of getting under his skin, even when she wasn't there physically. He sighed and shook his head in defeat.

```
PhantomPhixer:>    I'll try. NoMoBoesky has
                   hacked into Nations,
                   Chase, and Wells Fargo.
                   It's going to take her at
                   least a week to get
                   through the transaction
                   logs for every bank on
                   that list.
MystikalGremlinz:> Her?
PhantomPhixer:>    Sorry. Typo. I meant
                   'him.'
```

Phil imagined his mother in her favorite stance, leaning against the doorframe with her arms crossed as she made one of her many father-son comparisons. *"Philander! I declare, you and your father are the only two people I know who can finagle your way out of the tightest jams known to mankind. But when it comes to figuring out how you got into the mess in the first place, neither one of you has a damn clue to save your life!"*

He rolled his chair away from the desk after exiting the Underground. As much as he hated to admit it, his mother was right—again.

CHAPTER 34

TUESDAY, JANUARY 26, 1993

A N OVERSIZED YELLOW van rumbled down the driveway to the shipping and receiving area. It had a softball-sized dent in its rear bumper that looked pretty recent. A charcoal gray Camaro with dark tinted windows followed close behind, camouflaged by the van's girth. The nose of the car was so close to the dented bumper that the two looked as if they were glued together.

Their sluggish progress was a stark contrast to the van's speedy-looking logo, with red racing letters that spelled LICKETY-SPLIT COURIERS. The decals were plastered on both sides and across the back. If not for the magnet that secured them to the van, the decals looked as if they could have easily sped past it.

Inside the Camaro, Phil hurled another expletive rich suggestion. "Muthafucka, can you please speed up?" He put his palm against the horn. *Don't do anything stupid*, he reminded himself.

He searched the perimeter of the building. The cameras mounted at the east and west corners could be seen a mile away. Those were the ones the security team wanted everyone to see. He was looking for the money camera, the one that was hidden but still in plain sight. Fifty yards from the entrance, above the opening, nestled behind the sign, he found it. The small camera was mounted with its lens pointed at the entrance at a forty-five-degree angle.

Phil reached for his blue and white Dallas Cowboys cap that he kept on the back seat and put it on. He pulled the cap down until

[139]

the bill nearly covered his eyes. Suspecting that someone might be on the other end watching, he bowed his head while the car inched through the camera's view range. He bowed so low that his chin pressed against his chest, causing him to feel a dull pain. As soon as the back tires bounced over the speed bump, he lifted his head and scanned his surroundings. He spotted an empty parking space across from the service elevator and parked. He engaged the emergency brake, flipped the cap off, and waited with the engine running.

The place was bustling with activity. A forklift operator unloaded pallets of computer equipment, while some guy holding a clipboard inspected labels and flipped through pages, checking off items. In front of him, to his left, a group of deliverymen stood around a coffeepot, shooting the breeze and chewing the fat, as his Uncle Walter would say. A service elevator was straight ahead. To its right, at the end of a narrow walkway, was a set of banged up chase doors that rocked on their hinges. Shipping and receiving stayed busy from daybreak to late afternoon. It was especially busy the hour before lunch. Some drivers were known to schedule their deliveries during that hour just to ogle at the ladies as they walked out.

Phil checked the clock on the car's dashboard: eleven thirty.

"C'mon, Holly." He trained his eyes on the elevator. The red arrow above the door pointed up. "You were supposed to be here by now. Don't tell me you backed out."

He couldn't blame her if she had backed out. The thought had crossed his mind when he'd first read her note. An envelope had been waiting for him when he arrived at his office that morning. The note was short and to the point: I think I'm on to something big. Can you get away for lunch?

There were plenty of good reasons to decline the invitation. Chief among them was the risk of being seen. The last thing he wanted was one of Ann's friends telling her they had seen him riding around town with another woman, and not just any woman, a white woman.

All hell would break loose, without a doubt. The lies he'd told about working late paled in comparison to the betrayal Ann would undoubtedly feel if she found out. He knew he'd have to tell her the truth. He also knew doing such a thing would bring their wedding plans to a screeching halt.

Then there was the previous night's encounter. It was still hard to believe that a thank you kiss on the cheek had turned into a tongue-locking, lip-sucking, breast-massaging embrace.

He wasn't sure how far they would have gone had his beeper not vibrated and shocked them back into reality. In fact, he was trying hard not to think about it, because thinking about it meant he'd have to come face to face with the fear and despair he'd felt when he saw Ann's number on the pager.

Last, but not least, he worried for their safety. Things were changing in the workplace, but Charlotte was still in North Carolina, and North Carolina was still a southern state with a troubled history. Although racial rhetoric had toned down, the animus remained the same. The windows on Holly's car weren't tinted. He noticed it when he walked her to her car at the Black Dog Tavern.

Phil was startled by a rap on the driver side window. He looked to his left. Standing next to the door, with his arm resting on the roof of the car, was a security guard. He looked around to see from what direction the guard had come, and then he saw the golf cart parked behind the car.

"Are you the new fella? You were supposed to be here hours ago," the security guard asked after Phil rolled the window down. He was a chubby guy, wearing navy blue pants that were held up below his belly by a worn out black belt that was holding on for dear life. His name was Earl, according to the blue cursive letters embroidered on his shirt. Phil wasn't sure if it was his first or last name.

"No, sir. I'm looking for a job. You know if they're hiring?" Phil took a quick glance at the elevator then returned his attention to the guard. He noticed the coffee stain and donut crumbs on the guard's shirt and laughed to himself.

"Well, this is one of those, what they call, high-tech companies. We don't have a lot of general labor jobs, but who knows, they might have a few jobs in the cafeteria. They should be able to help you inside. Go through those doors over there," the guard pointed a stubby finger at the chase doors, "and go to the human resources office. You can't miss it; it's the first set of glass doors on your left."

"Thanks." Phil rolled the window up and watched as the security guard drove off in the cart with one foot hanging on the side. He chuckled. "Earl is definitely his first name."

The double doors burst open, dispensing the first group of gorgers. The downtown lunch hour had officially kicked off.

"C'mon, Holly!"

He looked at the clock on the dashboard. The extra ten minutes he had allotted for had expired five minutes ago. His heart pumped faster.

Finally, he spotted her. She was wedged in the middle of the latest crowd that had spilled through the door. His heart began to pound against his chest. Each thud echoed in his ear.

Phil released the break, pushed down on the clutch, and shifted into gear. Holly's eyes lit up. He watched her worm through a smattering of people blocking the sidewalk. Memories from the previous night shoved their way to the front again. He'd never come close to flirting, let alone engaging in anything sexual or romantic with a white girl, and Holly was the last one he imagined. Not that there was anything wrong with her; she was attractive. He just never imagined he and Holly would have a mutual physical attraction. By fate or by circumstance, they both had discovered the depth to which their attractions were willing to go.

The idea that Holly was interested in him was nothing more than an ego teaser, at best. He was convinced that her interests centered on this case. She wanted to solve it just as badly as he did. Whenever she talked about "rooting out the culprits behind this scourge on humanity"—those were her exact words—she spoke with such certainty and sincerity that it inspired him to dig deeper for the answers he wanted.

As she opened the passenger door, his thoughts raced back to the summer of '83 and the day his brother, Roderick, picked him up from computer camp and saw him sitting at a picnic table, joking around with Mary Paulson. "I don't know what it is about these white girls that keep brothers so curious," his brother had said once they were on the freeway. "Next thing, you'll be 'round here like the rest of these other fools, pounding your chest, talking 'bout you a muthafuckin' Mandingo 'cause you living out some white girl's fantasy behind closed doors. I'll tell you like I tell these other fools: Don't forget what ol' Massa Maxwell did to Mede's Mandingo ass

[143]

at the end of the movie. As for you, you'd better be glad Mama didn't see you because she'd be on you worse than Massa Maxwell."

When they exited the garage, Phil grinned and laughed softly to himself. Deep down, he knew now, just as he did back then, that his brother was right.

CHAPTER 35

PHIL FOUND a parking spot on the back row of the parking lot between a white Ford Bronco and a blue Chevrolet Corsica. He killed the engine and shot Holly a side-eye glance. "Are you sure this is the right place?"

She pulled a sheet from the stack of papers on her lap and held it up. "I'm positive. See, the address says nineteen hundred Commonwealth Boulevard. We're on Commonwealth, and look up there." She pointed to a blue entrance canopy with numbers stitched on front. "It says nineteen hundred."

"I see that, but what confuses me is the sign up there." He pointed to the sign atop a twenty-foot-high metal signpost that read, Garrison's Steakhouse.

"Yeah, what about it?"

"What about it?" Phil began to chuckle. "Are you telling me this restaurant funneled a quarter of a billion dollars to ITI?"

Holly continued to comb through her small mountain of paper, licking the tip of her finger and flipping each page by its corner. "I never said the money came from the restaurant. I said the transfer accounts at each bank that deposited funds listed nineteen hundred Commonwealth Boulevard as their address."

Phil remained silent and stared at the quaint red brick restaurant across the street. He rolled his window down halfway. An early spring wind blew a plume of hickory wood smoke against the tip of his nose and made his belly rumble. He cleared his throat to drown his stomach's embarrassing muffled growl. After all had quieted, he asked, "Has this place always been a restaurant?"

"No, it used to be a mom-and-pop furniture store." Holly looked up. "I told you that. Don't you remember?"

Between maneuvering through lunch-hour traffic, making sure their cover was secure and sorting through the jukebox of thoughts in his head, Phil hadn't heard much of anything Holly had said on the ride over. He couldn't bring himself to tell her that he hadn't been listening, so he said, "Oh, yeah. How could I forget?"

Phil looked on. The large display windows on either side of the entrance that were once decorated with living room sets, recliners, and beds, were now fitted with mirror-tinted tempered glass. A water fountain and trimmed hedges had been added to give it a more welcoming and stately appeal.

"Come on. What are you waiting for?"

Phil shook the cobwebs loose, only to discover Holly standing outside the car. "Hey! What are you doing?"

"I'm going inside."

"Wait!" Phil unbuckled the seatbelt and climbed out. "When you asked if I could get away for lunch, I didn't know you were talking about going in there."

"What's wrong with going in and checking the place out while we have a bite to eat?"

He knew by the determined look on Holly's face that debating the issue would be a waste of time. Phil grabbed his coat from the back seat and locked the car. "I don't know why I'm letting you talk me into this."

Under the tepid midday sun, they weaved through the parking lot, trampling over their stubby shadows. Out of the corner of his eye, Phil glimpsed their reflection in a truck's side mirror. An old story MiMi had told him years ago popped into his head for the second time in the last hour.

According to MiMi, the antagonistic, yet amorous relationship between Negros and whites could be traced back to a white slave owner named Matthew Middleman. Long before Thomas Jefferson coerced his way between Sally Hemmings' thighs and found comfort, Matthew Middleman had thrust Pandora's Box wide open when he bought some slaves during a voyage through the West Indies.

A wily old merchant slaver, talking fast and emphasizing points Matthew knew nothing about, convinced the Anglo aristocrat that the slaves he was purchasing were different from all the others that were being brought out of Africa. The slaver professed that those within his keep had been brought from a village deep in Guinea, and their tribe had been birthed from Mother Earth herself. Before sailing off, the old Englishman huckster warned Matthew not to let his affections run wild. "Their aura is seductive, their physique majestic, and they have an inner strength that endures the greatest of punishment. Guard your steps at all times, for I pity the Anglo-Saxon who follows his unrepentant rapacious appetite; his lustful transgression shall be an affront to Mother Earth, his recompense a rebuke from the hand of the Almighty."

Holly nudged Phil's arm. "Hey, isn't that Senator Sherman?"

"Huh? Where?" Phil shook his head, and the story receded from his memory once again.

"Right there. Standing next to the valet station."

A broad-shouldered man stood behind a black limo. Every strand of his salon-dyed blond hair fell perfectly into place. The expensive white caps on his teeth radiated under the sunlight as he smiled and bestowed superficial pleasantries on the small group of constituents that had gathered to greet him.

Phil looked at Senator Sherman and then the renovated restaurant and cars parked out front. Despite the modern upgrades, Garrison's looked to be the least likely of places one would find a showcase of luxury cars and dignitaries.

"Who owns this place?" he asked as they walked past the senator.

"I checked Mecklenburg County records; the building is owned by the Family and Friends of Jeff Davis Foundation. I'm not sure who owns the restaurant. All I know is that it's named after a nephew of Jefferson Davis. You know how these good ol' southerners love their Confederate family heritage."

Phil stopped a few feet away from the door. "That's it! We don't need to go inside. I've got an idea."

"Are you sure?"

"As sure as I am of the fact that if I walk through that door with you, I'll end up like the white girl who goes wandering off at the beginning of every horror movie."

Holly stepped back, eyes wide as a penny jawbreaker. "You can't be serious!"

"Let's just say I'm not trying to find out. Anyway, I've got an idea. I need you to find out who's on the board of directors and executive team for each of those banks. Let's see who has a connection to ITI."

They were halfway across the parking lot when Phil heard it. "Philander! Philander!"

Time stood still as the voice and recognition of the moment became clear. A chill ran through Phil from head to toe. He stopped dead in his tracks. He tried to stand up straight, but his legs felt like flimsy rubber. He turned around slowly. His mother was standing in the middle of the valet area, holding up traffic. Her charming smile exuded a tenderness and warmth that betrayed the daggers from her subtle glare.

"Hello, Mama!" Phil smiled nervously.

"Hello, Philander," Marjorie said in that familiar tone she always used when he tried to slip into the house after curfew. She turned to Holly and nodded. "Hello. How do you do?"

Phil, sensing his mother's invisible antennae rising, jumped in with a quick reply. "Mama, this is Holly. We work together."

Marjorie raised an eyebrow. "Mmm hmm."

"It's a surprise seeing you here. I didn't know you were in town."

Marjorie smiled at Holly. "Not only does my son not call me, he has the audacity to tell me to my face that he doesn't even listen to my messages. Can you believe that?"

Holly returned the smile but said nothing.

"If you had listened to my message, Philander, you would've known that I was coming down for a business meeting and to help Shirley and Ann with some last-minute arrangements. You and Ann's wedding is next week, remember?"

"You're getting married!" Holly shrieked and cupped her hands over her mouth.

"You mean he didn't tell you?" Marjorie looked at Phil with a laser-like stare.

"It never came up!" Phil pointed out quickly.

Marjorie noticed the jugular vein pulsating on the side of Phil's neck. It was a telltale sign that he was hedging the truth or outright lying. The peculiar phenomenon was a trait that had been passed down from his father. As far as she knew, neither Wes nor Phil were cognizant of the behavior, and if left up to her, it would be a secret she took to her grave.

Phil's little lie detector had given Marjorie all the information she needed. She shifted her attention to Holly. "So, Philander tells me you two work together. Are you a programmer as well? How do you like working with him? He's not getting you into any trouble, is he?"

The barrage of questions caught Holly off guard. Phil, seeing the desperation in her eyes and sensing his mother readying for the kill, stepped between them. "Mama, please stop. You're embarrassing me." He hugged and kissed her on the cheek.

Marjorie held him tight and whispered, "I don't know what you're up to, Philander, but you can best believe I'm going to get to the bottom of it when I see you this evening."

She stepped back, her patented smile back on display. She turned to Holly. "It was a pleasure meeting you. Perhaps next time, my overprotective son will allow you to tell me what it is you really do."

CHAPTER 36

"MANY STUDIES have shown that men subconsciously marry women like their mothers," Marjorie said between sips of iced tea.

Ann Marie sat across the table, chomping away on a dinner salad, taking the whole conversation in.

"I believe, without a doubt, Philander falls into that group," Marjorie continued. "He's chosen a beautiful, loving, intelligent, strong black woman ... just like his mother."

Ann blushed. "Thank you, Mama. I'm glad you think so."

"To tell you the truth, I knew you were special before I ever laid eyes on you," Marjorie confessed once the waiter walked off with their lunch orders. "If I'm not mistaken, you're the only girl Philander has ever come right out and told us he was dating."

Marjorie buttered a slice of warm bread and bit into it. The remaining piece looped and bobbed in midair with each hand gesture as she continued talking.

"I guess Philander's had a few girlfriends; I could never tell with him. The few that I suspect were serious were nice girls. They all seemed to be a little on the needy side, though, if you ask me.

"Lord knows I prayed that last lil' girl right out the door. She was a handful. Far too controlling. Do you know the first time Phil brought her home from school for a weekend visit, that child had the audacity to go into my kitchen and cook Philander breakfast?"

"No, she didn't!"

Ann's exaggerated shock was all the motivation Marjorie needed to freely express her displeasure.

"Now, that takes some nerve! You don't step foot in another woman's kitchen. I can't believe her mama didn't teach her such common courtesies. And, on top of that, she was cooking for a man that wasn't bit mo' trying to marry her lil' unruly ass."

When lunch arrived, the conversation shifted to weddings and schedules. As eager as she was to talk about her upcoming nuptials, Ann was even more eager to discuss another topic. She made a few gentle attempts to nudge the discussion in a direction that would allow her to bring it up without seeming nosy or pushy. Nothing worked.

By the time dessert arrived, Ann still hadn't found the opening she was looking for. She was on the verge of conceding defeat when she scooped up a spoonful of bread pudding that brought her discouraged palate back to life. The bitter taste of defeat gave way to a pleasure that could only come from mixing rum cooked bananas, butter, and brown sugar with ice cream. The rum set her throat ablaze as it slid down, but it was just the jolt her courage needed. She started to say something, but a flutter in her womb caught her by surprise and made her gasp. Fearing it was her last chance, Ann exhaled, rubbed her stomach, and dove headfirst into the topic she had been dying to discuss.

"Mama, the other day you said you were going to tell me something about the Jacobson men. What did you want to tell me?"

"That's a conversation we should save for another time," Marjorie demurred.

"In a few days, I'll be marrying a Jacobson." Ann caressed the top of her slightly protruding belly. "There's also a good chance this baby will be a Jacobson male. I believe this is the perfect time."

Marjorie shook her head and giggled. "Oh, my dear, you remind me so much of myself when I was your age. Philander doesn't have an inkling of an idea what a treat life has in store for him with a woman like you in his corner."

Ann blushed. "You think so?"

"I'm positive. That's the one good attribute of the Jacobson men: They choose exceptional women. *Really* exceptional women, if you ask me." Marjorie laughed.

"I'll remember that."

"You better! Because there will be days when exceptional is the last thing you'll feel, let alone remember. I'll tell you like MiMi told me; you're destined to be exceptional because the next generation of Jacobsons and Donovans now rest in your lap. I don't know about the Donovan side, but that Jacobson side will make damn sure it brings out the best in you. Trust me."

"It can't be that bad. I've fallen in love with every Jacobson I've met so far, Phil, Daddy, you—"

"I am *not* a Jacobson," Marjorie interrupted. "I'm a Jacobson by marriage. Although I guess that doesn't vindicate me since I willingly birthed a generation of them."

"Mama!"

Marjorie pointed a heaping spoonful of glazed apples and ice cream at Ann and said, "If your mama can't tell the truth about you, no one else sure as hell will."

After a pregnant pause, Marjorie continued. "Listen, I have four beautiful children, whom I love unconditionally and without restraint. I've been the best mother I could and tried to instill in all of them the best that I had to offer. What did I get in return for my efforts? Three boys who are just like their father, in one way or another."

"That's not true. I see a lot of you in Phil."

"They're not entirely like their father. They have adopted certain qualities of mine. In fact, most of their better qualities are mine," Marjorie said with a sly grin.

"Gregory wants to be just like his father. Like his father and the Jacobson men before him, he is a born entrepreneur. And, like all the Jacobson men, including my husband, he has a tendency to put work before family.

"I feel sorry for Lori, though. She wants a family. He, on the other hand, is chasing an elusive mistress called success. Now, Gregory won't have sex without a condom because he doesn't believe she's taking her birth control pills, and she's frustrated as hell."

"That's too bad." Ann dabbed a tear from her eye. Her emotions had been a mushy mess heap of late. It didn't take much to bring her to tears.

"It's partly Lori's fault. You know what they say; if you want to know about a man, ask his mother. She's the woman who knows him best and has, more than likely, corrupted him the most." Marjorie gave an assuring nod then snickered. "I tried not to meddle, but I did attempt to offer her some helpful advice. You know I just hate to see a young woman lose what she loves because of her own foolishness. She told me she had it under control, so I left it alone.

"Then there's Roderick. He acquired the Jacobson work ethic and love of jurisprudence. Like all the Jacobsons, he's a charmer and romantic. If you let MiMi tell it, the family descended from a tribe in Guinea that was known to possess special powers of charm and seduction."

"That doesn't sound like such a bad thing."

"It is if the man's idea of romance is pleasing his Johnson and safeguarding his heart. I've lost count of the number of women Roderick has pointed toward the altar before mysteriously disappearing behind his work."

"The right one will come along."

Marjorie poured cream into her coffee and stirred. "I won't hold my breath. From the look of things, he and Roxy are in a tight race to see who gets married last."

"I wouldn't be so sure about that. I talked to Roxy last night. She didn't say anything specifically, but I get the feeling she's seeing someone, and it might be serious."

"It's going to take a special man to live with Roxy. She resembles me on the outside but, at her core, she is just like her daddy and the rest of the Jacobsons. Out of all the children, she is the one who desires to follow in his professional footsteps."

Ann placed both elbows on the table and then propped her chin on top of her clasped hands. "And Phil?"

"Philander's the quintessence of his father, even though he has no desire to follow in his footsteps. They're both deceptively charming and brilliant. Like Wes, he leads with his heart rather than his head. He's going to certainly need a woman like you to keep him grounded."

"I'll do my best. I don't know if I can compete against ITI, though. They're loading him down with so much work that we rarely even talk. We used to see each other every day, but I rarely get a chance to see him anymore." The anguish Ann tried desperately to conceal bubbled over the edge. Her bottom lip trembled as tears rolled down her hazelnut cheeks, creating a puddle of salty tears.

Marjorie held Ann's hand and squeezed gently. "Come now, baby! Pull yourself together and tell me what's wrong."

Ann wiped her eyes and sniffed. "I just don't think it's right for them to ask him to work such late hours. We rarely talk anymore, and when we do, he's either working at the office or at home. Phil says things will get back to normal before the wedding, but I'm not so sure!" Another shoulder shaking wave of tears began to flow.

"Hmm ..." Marjorie mused in a tone that sounded more curious than compassionate. "If you don't mind me asking, how long has this been going on?"

Ann wiped her face. Tiny pieces of tear-soaked tissue stuck to her cheeks. "It started last week. Do you think he's having second thoughts?"

Marjorie remembered Phil's bulging jugular vein and erratic behavior. She gathered her purse and stood up. "By the time I get through with him, he'll be lucky if he's able to think at all."

CHAPTER 37

PHIL SCROLLED DOWN and up each page of the bulletin board directory with his index finger. When he got to the end, he flipped back to the beginning and repeated the process.

After narrowly escaping his mother's parking lot interrogation, he'd dropped Holly off at the office and made it back to his apartment as fast as he could. He'd been poring through the directory, looking for Civil War or southern confederacy themed boards. Holly's comment about southerners loving their heritage had given him a hunch. Five hours had gone by, and he still hadn't found anything of use, though.

He checked his watch. Dinner at Ann's would begin in ninety minutes. As much as he was looking forward to spending time with Ann and eating some of Shirley's delicious cooking, he wasn't looking forward to the conversation with his mother. She'd already called twice and left messages, reminding him not to be late.

Although she didn't come right out and accuse him of anything, he could tell by the tone of her voice that his mother suspected he was up to no good. Telling her the truth was out of the question. She would raise a fit that would last for hours. Then she'd call his father, and all hell would break loose after she found a way to blame him as well.

"Might as well get this over with," he grunted and stood up.

Phil looked down at the oversized magazine. He was halfway through the P's. He sat back down. "Ten more minutes."

In the Underground, a person could find just about anything if they searched hard enough. There were bulletin boards dedicated to everything, from programming to model car racing, to astrology, and pornography. Boards with special interests often identified the topic in their name. Others used more obscure names with coded words. The Underground had always been a reliable source in the past. Phil hoped this time wouldn't be the exception.

He turned the page, slid his finger down and up the first page, and then down the next page.

He stopped when he saw Rowdy's Raging Rebel BBS at his finger's tip. The name sounded interesting. He checked his watch. Five minutes had already gone by. He tapped the keyboard, and the monitor lit up.

"Just one quick look."

Rowdy's Raging Rebel BBS main screen appeared on the monitor. The counter in the lower left corner of the screen displayed eighty-eight users logged in. Everyone was in a private chat room. He pressed the F key on the keyboard and entered the FILES section. Two files were listed, CLANS Bylaws and Monthly Newsletter.

The bylaws were for an organization called the Confederate Loyalists Association of the New South, or CLANS. It began:

"BECAUSE...

We love the South and are pleased to be called Southerners.

> We are satisfied with our culture, grace,
> and the elegance that bears witness of
> our forefathers.
> We are honored by our heritage of courage,
> chivalry, patriotism, and of duty to God
> and country.
> We love the Confederate flag and "Dixie"
> as inspiring symbols of that heritage.
> We take pride in the leading role the Old
> South played in the Revolutionary War,
> the drafting of the Constitution, and
> the founding of these sovereign and
> united states."

The language was familiar; it was similar to much of the Confederate doctrine Klu Klux Klan leaders had espoused for years. He'd learned a lot about the KKK from his grandmother. MiMi had a million and one stories about the Klan. Phil swore he'd heard them all.

Next, he opened the newsletter. An article announcing the organization's annual conference highlighted the top of the page. It was being held on the ninth of February, the day Jefferson Davis was elected president of the Confederate States of America.

Phil was reading through the article when he saw a name he recognized.

> Why are loyal brothers of the Family,
> like Jack Sherman, being forced to hire
> these uncivilized niggers dressed in suits
> and dresses?
> Jack Sherman has been a loyal member of
> this Family. His esteemed legacy goes back
> to Pulaski. Furthermore, he has faithfully
> supported our causes over the years.

Many Family members are questioning his
loyalty to our cause, while others
question his motive for hiring 300
niggers, spics, chinks, and boat rats from
Vietnam in the past nine months. These
concerns are not perceived as
inconsequential in that these occurred
after his stalwart proclamation to support
the abolishment of this dreadful
affirmative action law.

I, for one, am confident that Mr.
Sherman will clarify the hypocrisy that is
so evident in his recent actions when he
addresses this body at our State of the
Confederacy Conference on February 9.
Humbly submitted in the valiant and
courageous name of our leader, President
Jefferson Davis, the greatest president
our nation has ever produced. LONG LIVE
THE CONFEDERACY!

Phil downloaded the first file. He prayed the SYSOP wasn't
monitoring the board's activity. As the second file downloaded, his
thoughts went back to MiMi's old story. He couldn't remember
how it ended at first, but it was beginning to come clear:

Matthew Middlemen found the voluptuously shaped
mahogany women too desirable to resist. Lust filled his mind and
loins. The old English slave trader's instructions were stricken from
his conscious as he secretly indulged in his illicit pleasures. Fearing
the loss of chattel and his uncontrollable promiscuity, Matthew
stood with fellow slave owners in publicly advancing the idea that
slavery was actually a cost that wealthy gentlemen, such as himself,
were willing to endure for the sake of advancing their young
settlement.

Matthew enjoyed himself so much with his black maidens that he introduced close friends and business associates to his newfound pleasures. As he prospered and acquired more slaves, his desire for his wife and attention to his family declined.

By the time Matthew's death was approaching, he had become an old tormented man, whose mind, heart and soul was filled with rage.

Rage entered his mind when he learned his younger sister had been planning to buy her black lover's freedom so they could sneak away to New York. In his anger, he killed his sister's lover and sent her away penniless. Rage overflowed in his heart the day he caught his wife in bed, red-faced, sweaty, and shouting lust-filled obscenities as she rode Hiram, one of his biggest bucks. He never spoke to his wife again after he laid Hiram's blood-drenched clothes in her lap. His soul filled with a fiery rage the day he discovered his daughter was the mother of the new nigger baby the nursemaid was nursing.

The old English slave trader returned in a vision as Matthew lay on his deathbed. Matthew told him what had happened and how the Almighty had tortured him. The trader laughed and explained that he had only experienced the beginning of the Almighty's rebuke. Because Matthew's transgressions had been so profound and personal, the Almighty's hand would be against him for generations; his eternal torment, to witness the chaos of his actions deep within the bowels of Mother Earth.

Phil's face lit up. After all these years, the story was finally making sense. "That's it! MiMi's *Secret Life* books!"

Just then, he heard the phone ring. Phil looked at his watch. Dinner was starting in five minutes.

CHAPTER 38

PHIL PULLED BESIDE his mother's car and killed the engine. The Donovans' garage door was still up, a good sign that they were still expecting company. Moisture from the cool air created a hazy yellow halo around the lampposts on either side of the garage. A row of large oak trees formed a canopy over the driveway. Ann's silver Volkswagen Jetta and her sister's Toyota Corolla were parked in front of the double-car garage. Marjorie's Cadillac Seville was parked behind Tracy's car.

His father had always said, "Every break costs something." He let out a heavy sigh. "I guess I better get in there and see how much this break costs."

It wasn't Ann or her parents he was worried about. He looked over at the flowers he'd picked up on the way. They were more than a peace offering; they were a token of his love and appreciation for the understanding and patience Ann had shown in his absence. Though he couldn't tell her, the flowers were also his way of saying he was sorry for what happened with Holly.

His mother, on the other hand, wouldn't be as easy to please. A simple "I'm sorry" would not suffice for being a half-hour late. He was sure to get more than an earful. This would definitely prove her conspiracy theory correct, the one where she claimed his life's goal was to make her look like a bad mother. Phil looked at the flowers again. He'd stopped at the grocery store around the corner and gotten them as a gift for Ann and a much-needed prop to explain his tardiness to his mother.

He held the flower vase in one hand and locked the car with the other.

"Philander Wesley Jacobson, the Second!"

Phil, visibly startled, juggled to keep hold of the vase. He finally secured it against his chest. The once neatly arranged tulips were hanging over the side. A few were nearly bent in half. "Ma ... Ma ... Mama!" he sputtered. "What are you doing out here?"

Marjorie, right hand on hip, with a scowl menacing enough to make a grizzly bear whimper and run, stood next to the car. The yellow glow of the lampposts added to the eeriness.

"What am I doing out here? The question you should be asking yourself is what in the hell are *you* doing?"

"I'm not doing anything, Mama," Phil pleaded, his tenor voice now a falsetto. "I don't know what you're talking about."

"Philander, I have no intentions of putting my feet under these people's table and breaking bread while you're off doing only God knows what behind Ann's back with Sally what's her name. I truly believe you are intent on proving to people that I am some kind of bad mother."

"Holly. Her name is Holly."

"Sally ... Polly ... Holly. It's all the same, dammit! Ann says she hardly sees or talks to you anymore. That poor girl cried her heart out at lunch because she thinks you don't want to marry her. From the looks of things, I can't say that she's wrong."

"Mama, nothing's going on between Sally—I mean Holly—and me. I promise!"

Marjorie looked at her son's neck. She couldn't see the vein clearly; it was too dark. "Humph!"

"I know I've been working crazy hours, but all of that's about to change real soon. I promise. Mama, I want nothing more than to marry Ann and raise our child. That's why I'm late. I stopped at the florist and ordered these." He held up the vase of flowers.

Marjorie smiled and then burst into laughter. "You are truly your daddy's child. They're pretty."

"Thank you."

Phil kissed his mother and let out a small sigh. He put his arm around her waist and began to escort her inside.

They had taken a few steps, when Marjorie asked, "So what are you and Holly really working on if it's not work? Where is your sister in all of this? Does this have anything to do with the case your dad is working on?"

Phil stopped.

"Before you say anything, let me remind you. I've known you nine months longer than anyone walking God's green earth. I know when you're lying." Marjorie stared straight ahead.

Phil took a deep breath and exhaled. "Mama, it's nothing. Really. I thought Daddy was working on something, but it turned out to be a worker's comp investigation. As for Roxy, I haven't heard from her, and I really don't care if I ever hear from her again. Mama, she embarrassed me in front of Ann!"

Marjorie dismissed the comment with a wave of her hand. "Get over yourself, Philander. If Roxy embarrassed you as bad as you say, then why is Ann crying her eyes out over you?"

Phil grinned sheepishly. "You're right."

Marjorie wrapped an arm around Phil's shoulders and hugged him closer. "I'm always right, and don't you forget that."

They continued walking. Phil thought about the article in the CLANS newsletter and MiMi's handed down tale. "Mama, do you remember those old books that MiMi called *The Secret Life*?"

"Sure, I do." Marjorie wrinkled her brow and looked at her son out of the corner of her eye. "What made you ask about those old things?"

"Oh, it's nothing. I was looking at some stuff on my computer, and it made me think about 'em. Do you know if they're still around?"

"I'm sure they are. They're probably in the library at your father's office. You should ask him. He's coming down Thursday; you can ask him then. You should be able to catch him at the office. If not, I'm sure Grace will know where you can find him. She seems to know a lot for someone who works in a satellite office, but that's neither here nor there, is it?"

They walked in silence the remainder of the way. Phil opened the door and stepped aside to let his mother enter. Before entering, she whispered, "Philander, don't be so naïve as to believe that I don't know you're not telling me everything. And don't think for a minute I'm buying that story about going to the florist to get those flowers. I stopped at the Harris Teeters around the corner on my way here and saw those same flowers."

CHAPTER 39
THURSDAY, JANUARY 28, 1993

THE FLUFFY, golden omelet melted in Wes's mouth. "Doug is one hell of a cook. Have you tried this?" He pointed to his plate and sliced another hunk with his fork.

Mack sipped his coffee. "No. I try not to come by here too often."

"Still fighting the good fight, huh?"

Mack chuckled. "As long as they think white and I act black, we'll continue to fight."

"I know that's right. Sure would be nice if there were a few more like Doug. You don't meet too many white men like him. He's a goddamn leprechaun, I tell you."

Mack chuckled. "He is a godsend."

Mack and Wes toasted their coffee cups. "Lord, thank you for Doug," they said in unison.

"Is there anything else I can get you, gentlemen?" Grace rolled her eyes at Wes then turned to face Mack.

Wes sighed. "What did I do now?"

"Nothing," Grace said, refusing to look his way.

"Since nothing is wrong, let me introduce you to my oldest and best friend, Bobby McIntyre. This is Mack, the guy I told you who owns this place."

"I'm glad you brought that up. You keep telling me your friend owns this place, but I keep hearing Doug runs the place. Doug says it, and everyone else says it. Not one time has anyone ever said anything about a Mack. I even looked at the mail; it had Doug's name on it too." Grace folded her arms and looked at Wes like a mother who had just cornered a lying child.

"What they're saying is true. Doug does *run* it, but Mack *owns* it." Wes pointed to Mack. "Will you please tell her?"

Bobby "Mack" McIntyre was dressed in a white Adidas jogging suit and tennis shoes. A salt-and-pepper goatee and a pair of gold wire-framed glasses outlined his dark chocolate brown face.

"Wes is full of shit most of the time, but this time he's telling you the truth. Doug has full control of the place, but I am the owner." He extended his hand. "Bobby McIntyre. Pleased to meet you."

Grace flushed with embarrassment. "Please forgive me for being so rude. Is there anything I can get for you?"

"I'm fine. Thank you."

"Grace, you have got to hear how this slick sonofabitch put one over on these prejudiced white men."

Mack looked uncomfortable. "It really wasn't a big deal."

"That's bullshit!" Wes interrupted. "Back in '78, the downtown business leaders were forcing Mack, here, to sell the place because he was blocking their expansion plans. Ol' Mack fought back as hard as he could, and just when Mister Charlie and his boys thought they had him boxed in, he out slicked their asses."

Mack cleared his throat. "I really can't take credit for the whole scheme. My father started the diner, but I didn't know anything about running it. I was fighting for sentimental reasons but ran out of options and money. I had thirty days to vacate. That's when I met Douglass Clarke."

"*That* Doug?" Grace pointed over her shoulder.

Mack nodded. "Yes. The Clarke family owns the second largest tobacco plantation in the state. Doug rejected the idea of southern aristocracy and became a peace-sign-toting, weed-smoking hippy. I guess you could say he was the black sheep of the family.

"Doug came in two days before I had to lock the doors for good. He said he needed a job because it was time for him to grow up. I told him we were being forced to close and that's when he came up with his wild plan. You should've seen the faces on them rednecks when they heard Doug bought the place for five million. Then he called their bluff when he declared to use his family's wealth and influence to fight them in court. A few phone calls later, a new downtown development plan that included the diner was drafted. When the dust settled, Doug sold the diner back to me for a dollar. By then, he and the place had become inseparable, so he stayed on and runs the place."

Grace looked around. The diner was empty now, but every table would be occupied by lunchtime. "It's really a nice place. I have enjoyed being here. You should come by more often."

"He won't," Wes scoffed. "He still doesn't trust the downtown business leaders, no matter how much they talk about diversity."

"I trust them. I trust they'll do everything they can to take this land from my black ass if they find out I own it. They don't mind me making a little money because they can always print more,

[168]

but this land we're standing on, they can't make more of it." Mack and Wes tapped their coffee cups together.

"You're right about that, my friend."

"Well, I think you should come by more often and enjoy the place. What sense does it make to fight for it and not enjoy it?" Grace wiped off the table and poured them each a fresh cup of coffee before she left.

Mack watched her set the tables for lunch. "Now, that's a nice woman. How'd she end up with your pussy-chasing ass?"

"It's not like that at all." Wes stirred his coffee. "She's a very nice woman. You should get to know her."

"Where did you meet her?"

"Over in Sumter. I was down there working a case. The usual shit: Woman wants a divorce but wants to know all her husband's dirt before she files. Come to find out the husband was fooling around with Grace and making all sorts of promises he had no intention of keeping. He owned a two-bit café that survived just because of Grace. Every time she got ready to leave, the guy would pitch a bitch then buy her a few expensive gifts. That muthafucka was a piece of work, you hear me? When I finally put it all together, I found out where she lived and showed up on her front porch one day. We talked through the night. By dawn, I was leaving Sumter with Grace and all the information my client needed to bleed the sonofabitch dry. That was three years ago. She's been working for me ever since."

Grace smoothed the wrinkles out of her blue polyester dress. Mack looked on with his mouth half open.

"Damn! She's definitely good looking."

"You must really like her. You sitting up here with your tongue hanging down to your dick. If you're interested, I'll put in a good word for you."

"I like her a lot. For some strange reason, I get the impression that she's really interested in you. I'd like to get to know her, but I'm not wasting my time if she's hung up on you. Tell me the truth; are you fucking her?"

Wes stared at Mack. Their friendship had withstood whatever life had thrown their way. They knew each other's secrets, most of them, at least. They had always been there for each other, looked out for each other. Most of all, they wanted what was best for each other.

"No, man. I keep telling you, I'm trying to get things right with Marjorie. I don't have time for those games anymore. Marjorie's been there for me through all my shit. The kids are grown, and I want us to enjoy this time. So, if you want me to set you up, I will."

Mack sat quietly. After several minutes, he said, "All right. Set it up."

CHAPTER 40

"PHIXER!" MystikalGremlinz's face lit up like a child meeting his idol when he opened the hotel door and saw Phil. "Please, come in."

By most accounts, Malcolm Graves looked like the typical computer wunderkind, in his brown tweed sports jacket, black t-shirt, and jeans. His brownish-blond hair was in a constant muss and hung over his round, silver, wire-rimmed glasses. He was twenty-two years old but could have easily been mistaken for sixteen. It didn't help that his voice sometimes cracked like a pubescent teen.

The suite's main area was large enough to hold fifty people comfortably. A sofa, two end chairs, and a coffee table were in the center of the room. A small kitchen area was on the left, just as you entered the room. Two partially closed doors on the right led to two private rooms, equipped with a king-sized bed, television, and bathroom.

A laptop and monitor were on the dining table at the back of the suite. Identical images displayed on the monitor and laptop. Malcolm pulled out the chair in front of the laptop and invited Phil to take a seat.

"Welcome to NetVoyager, the first graphical browser for the World Wide Web."

Phil clicked on the links and navigated through the pages. The mixture of bright images mixed with text made the excursion into the virtual world of circuits and switches even more enjoyable. Malcolm referred to the experience as surfing the 'net.

"That's the version we're going to release next week," Malcolm said. "Minus a few bug fixes I'm still working on. I'll be in town until next Friday, so I brought the source code to make the final release build."

Phil clicked on more links, while Malcolm updated him on the meeting with ITI.

"Barring a miracle, it doesn't look like we're going to find what we're looking for before tomorrow," Phil said.

"I guess not."

"There's got to be some way we can buy ourselves more time."

Malcolm leaned against the table. "It looks like I'm going to have to go through with it tomorrow. After the meeting today, I learned that our investors are going to pull out if we don't go through with it. Our competitors are gaining on us. Any further delays would be detrimental, to say the least."

Phil pushed the chair back and stood. "Looks like it's going to be a long night. We need a miracle."

"I hope that miracle comes with food. I'm starving."

Phil patted Malcolm's shoulder. "Look on the bright side. Tomorrow, with the stroke of a pen, you will become the newest member of the Millionaire's Club, and I get to put this case behind me. I won't have to lie to Ann anymore, and my old man can quit worrying about me messing up my good job."

CHAPTER 41

THE WALLS OF THE utility room vibrated as the elevator descended. The door opened slowly, revealing Trace Collinsworth's blue pupil and chiseled tan cheekbone.

He moved swiftly across the hall to the suite, slid the plastic card in the door slot, and waited for the green light. He tried again. The green light turned on and the lock released.

Trace leaned against the door and breathed a sigh of relief. "Finally!" He wiped his brow with the back of his sleeve. "Remember. Enter ... Grab ... Exit."

After his military discharge a year ago, Trace bounced around from job to job and city to city before returning home. He was doing odd jobs when an old Marine buddy who ran a security company approached him about making some easy money. His friend had a client who needed to get their hands on a particular laptop. The client was willing to pay fifty thousand for the job. Half up front. His burglary and espionage experience included swiping a few candy bars from the store when he was a kid and stealing glimpses of the neighbor's wife and daughter taking a bath when he was a teenager. A good paying job had been hard to find, so he jumped at the chance to make a year's salary for a few hours' work.

The blue paper booties on his shoes swooshed and crackled as he walked around the carpeted room. Relying on the skills he learned running recon missions in Desert Storm, he developed an escape route and a concealment location. The escape route was easy but choosing a place to hide, posed a bigger problem. The two bedrooms were the most likely, even though it severely limited his view to the rest of the suite. He walked over to a mirror and pushed it aside. A courtesy umbrella hung from the rod. The space was tight, but it offered the best view of the suite.

Trace unshouldered his backpack and placed it on the dining table. He took a holster from the backpack and clamped it to his belt. Next, he retrieved a twelve-inch black baton with a cushioned handle and leather wrist strap. He pressed the power button and flipped the safety switch on before placing it in the holster. The Annihilator XR-4 packed a 150,000-volt charge that could render a three-hundred-pound man defenseless in seconds.

After he took the job, Trace was told where to find an envelope. Inside the envelope was a key to the room, twenty-five thousand dollars, and instructions on what to take and where to drop it off. The instructions never expressed an element of danger, and it surely didn't say anything about murder. He was relieved. In all his excitement over securing a lucrative contract, he'd forgotten to ask.

He unplugged the cables from the back of the laptop, and then he squatted down to unplug the laptop's power cord from the outlet under the table. He heard someone insert a key into the door. Trace spun around and raced for his concealment location.

Malcolm walked past the closet. He didn't notice the door was partially ajar. Trace looked around for the other guy that had been in the room earlier. He gasped when he saw his backpack on the table.

Malcolm exited the first bedroom then disappeared into the second one. He emerged a minute later and began pulling cushions from the couch.

Trace swallowed hard when he saw Malcolm go over to the table and pick up the backpack. He relaxed when Malcolm tossed the backpack in a chair and continued to look around the table. He finally realized what was going on when he saw Malcolm reach into his coat pocket, pull out a personal digital assistant, and then smile.

"Enter ... Grab ... Exit," Trace repeated to himself when he saw Malcolm heading for the front door.

The thunderous clouds let loose with a loud clack when Malcolm opened the door. He looked back at the window just as the lightning crackled. Malcolm turned to get the umbrella from the closet. The door slammed shut behind him.

Malcolm reached for the mirrored door at the exact moment Trace pushed it aside. Trace and Malcolm stood motionless, staring at each other. Trace closed his eyes and lunged forward. "Who—" Malcolm began.

The sound of lightning and the crackle of electricity emanating from the Annihilator XR-4 made a symphonic boom as Malcolm fell to the floor.

CHAPTER 42

F IVE MINUTES PASSED, and Malcolm still hadn't made it back to the lobby. Phil's pager vibrated. It was Holly. He looked at the glass elevators again. Still no sign of Malcolm.

Wonder what's taking Malcolm so long? Guess I'd better go check on him and call Holly while I'm up there.

Phil was waiting in front of the elevators when the fourth car stopped on the twenty-fifth floor and picked up Trace.

Trace's nerves were still rattled from his encounter in the room. Malcolm had fallen to the floor in a heap after getting clocked and juiced with the Annihilator XR-4. In his haste to get out of the room, he stuffed the laptop in his backpack but forgot to check the guy's vital signs to see if he was alive.

Trace scanned the lobby for the African American who had been in the suite earlier. Three men were at the bar and another was seated at a table, reading the newspaper. He shifted the backpack to his left shoulder and unzipped it. Gripping the handle of the baton firmly, he powered it on and set the safety switch.

When the elevator doors opened at the lobby, Phil was already on his way up to the suite in one of the other elevators.

"Enter … Grab … Exit," Trace muttered to himself as he hurried out a side door.

• • • •

Phil knocked on the door. He thought he heard something that sounded like someone groaning. He knocked harder. "Malcolm, are you all right?"

Malcolm fumbled with the locks and latches until the door slowly crept open. Wobbly and disoriented, Malcolm rubbed his head and leaned against the wall. He had a bulbous black and purple bruise on his collarbone. A welt ran along the bottom of his left cheek.

"What happened?" asked Phil, helping Malcolm to a chair.

Malcolm was still groggy. He grimaced when he tried to turn his head. "I'm not sure. I was getting an umbrella from the closet and out of nowhere, some guy bum-rushed me when I opened the door. I don't remember anything after that. He had a Taser of some sort." He gently touched his collarbone. "He got me pretty good."

Phil picked up the phone to call Holly while Malcolm recuperated on the sofa. Phil was dialing the number when he looked at the dining table. His hands began to tremble as he placed the phone back in its cradle.

"Malcolm, where's your laptop?"

CHAPTER 43

W ES HADN'T TALKED to Robert all week, and according to Grace's latest report, he hadn't been in the diner. An AWOL client always spelled trouble. As the day grew longer, the inclination he'd once resisted to worry had returned and found residence in the pit of his stomach. Short on time and viable leads, he was on the verge of giving up for the day, when he remembered Linda Albright, Robert's co-worker he'd met at Bennigan's. In a few hours, she would be joining her sorority sisters for their weekly girls' night out. With skill and a healthy dose of luck on his side, he decided to drop by and pay her a visit to see if she could shed any light on what was going on with Robert.

Before heading out to meet Linda, Wes called his old friend Vic Bannister. Vic was a partner at a local law firm. He and a group of attorneys at the firm owned a condo. They only used it when someone had to pull an all-nighter and needed a place to crash before court the following morning. They also made the place available to a close-knit circle of friends.

Wes found Linda and her friends seated at the bar. She was an attractive woman in her early fifties, married and divorced twice, with two adult children. Linda was determined to enjoy life on her own terms for once. When Wes suggested they find a quiet place to talk, she happily agreed.

From the second they entered the condo Wes had lined up, the evening proved to be a disaster. After a few general questions, he realized Linda was clueless to everything outside of her department.

"I mind my own business when I'm at work. I just do my job and go home. The less they know about me, the better," Linda replied when Wes asked if she'd heard any juicy gossip about Robert.

As soon as he heard her response, he wanted to abort the mission and take her back to the bar, but Linda had already unzipped his pants and was giving him one of the most bodacious blowjobs he'd received in a long time.

He feigned a back injury when she suggested they extend their play session to the bedroom.

"You poor thing," Linda said, looking up from her kneeled position. She got up and led him to the couch. "Lay on your back right here." She patted the firm leather sofa cushion. "I think I may know just the trick to make you feel better."

Minutes later, Wes watched as Linda bounced, rocked, and grinded her way to an orgasm. She laughed whenever she stopped to catch her breath. It sounded like a cat trying to clear a fur ball from its throat. After her therapeutic ride wound to a close, Linda lay on top of him, breathing heavily into his ear.

Wes stared at the ceiling and suppressed a laugh when he thought about what his friend, Ace, had often claimed: "The letters on their jackets might say Gamma Delta Sigma, but turn the lights off, and you'll find out those letters really mean Greedy Dick Sisters." The Gammas may have earned the title, but they didn't have a lock on the trophy as far as Wes was concerned.

Linda emerged from the bathroom, chewing a stick of Wrigley's Doublemint gum. She smoothed the wrinkles from her Gamma Delta Sigma shirt then put on the matching blue jean jacket that was draped over the arm of the couch. "Your condo is really nice, Wes."

"Thank you. It's a shame I'm not here often enough to enjoy it." Wes grabbed a bottle of water from the refrigerator and drank almost all of it in one long gulp. He agreed wholeheartedly with Linda; it was a nice condo. It had all the amenities that an accomplished bachelor would want. However, he wasn't an accomplished bachelor, and it wasn't his place.

Linda turned her wine glass up and drank the last of the Chardonnay.

"Wine with gum? That's got to taste awful." Wes cleaned the kitchen counter and put the bottle back in the wine cooler

"It's not so bad. I just need to drink something to wet my throat. You sure can take a woman's breath away."

"I'm not sure if I can take credit for that. The way I remember it, all I did was lay there."

Linda walked closer and rubbed her hand on Wes's stomach. She playfully bit his ear and whispered, "Yeah, but you pleased my sweet spot. That's all that matters, right?"

Wes laughed nervously. "I guess you have a point."

• • • •

The neighbor's fishbone tabby scampered across the yard and jumped the wooden fence when Wes pulled his black Eldorado into the covered parking space behind the office. Grace's car was parked in its usual spot, next to the back door.

The office was pitch black, except for a flicker of light coming from Grace's second-story-bedroom window. It was a few minutes after eleven. He knew Grace had been in the bed for at least thirty minutes. She woke up at four o'clock each morning, drank a cup of coffee, read her daily devotional, ironed her dress, and then headed off to the diner.

Wes walked around Grace's red Ford Taurus then tiptoed through the damp grass to get to the back door. He jiggled and sorted through his keys until he found the one for the door's deadbolt lock. He turned on a kitchen light. A note on the counter said his dinner was in the refrigerator.

On the top shelf of the fridge, next to the stacked Tupperware containers, a Saran-wrapped plate of smothered pork chops, mashed potatoes, and green beans greeted his hungry eyes. He was tempted to eat it, but he needed to pay Robert an unwelcomed visit and a heavy meal would knock him out before he even started.

He got the box of Honey Nut Cheerios and a bowl. The encounter with Linda had left him ravenous and reenergized. First, he needed to take a hot, steamy shower. He loosened his tie and unbuttoned the top two shirt buttons. Linda's perfume filled the room.

Grace walked into the kitchen just as Wes placed the carton of milk on the counter. Without so much as a nod to acknowledge his presence, she poured a cup of milk and warmed it in the microwave. The kitchen was quiet, except for the hum of the microwave and the ding of the timer when it shut off.

She sat at the table across from Wes and drank a few sips from the cup. "I see you finally found your way back."

Her ice-like posture and the frigidness of her tone caused Wes's spine to shiver. "I thought you were asleep. I didn't want to disturb you."

Grace twisted her lips into a tight smirk and shook her head. "I cooked smothered pork chops. That's still your favorite, isn't it? I'm not sure of anything these days."

Wes sensed the conversation was headed in the same direction as their last two conversations. "Thank you. I saw it; it looks delicious. Too bad I can't eat it tonight. Something tells me this mess with Robert is coming apart at the seams. I need to get over to his house and see what's going on. I can't leave him hanging in the wind on this, and I sure as hell can't let Phil get swallowed up in it."

"It's always something else with you, Wes. I don't understand it. You'll risk life and limb to save a person, but you never take time to enjoy the pleasure of the lives around you." She set the cup down with a thud.

Wes knew she was right; life had given him much more than he deserved. She deserved better also. He got up from the table. "I'm working on it."

"So, what did you find out from your new lead?" Grace asked over the churn of the dishwasher's rinse cycle. "It must have been a pretty good one because you left Mack and me sitting at the table. He's a nice guy. You could learn a few things from him."

"He's a great guy. As for the lead, it was a disaster."

She stood in front of him. The tips of their noses were inches apart. Grace grabbed the collar of Wes's shirt and pulled it back. "Was she a disaster before or after you fucked her?" She erupted

[182]

into a tirade filled with vulgarity and hurt. Her face flooded with a pain that could only come from a torn heart.

Wes hadn't noticed Linda's lipstick on the inside collar of his shirt. The only defense he could muster was, "Grace, it's not what you think."

Grace ripped his shirt open, sending buttons flying everywhere. She poked her finger hard against his chest. "Lipstick on your chest? It's exactly what I think it is, Wes. This is it. I'm through." She pointed to the door. "I want you out of here, now!"

"This is my damn place. You can't put me out."

"Well, I want you out of here until I can find a place."

The clock in the hallway chimed. It was midnight. "Fine. Stay as long as you need. Just let me shower and get my gear. I've got a missing client to find."

CHAPTER 44

FRIDAY, JANUARY 29, 1993

THE SILENCE in the boardroom was deafening after Malcolm Graves walked out, leaving Jack, Stanley, and Vincent to sort out their next steps.

The daily briefing had been interrupted when Malcolm showed up, bruised, bandaged, and wearing a blue hospital wristband. They were genuinely sympathetic when he told them he had been ambushed. Their sympathy immediately turned to heart-stricken grief when a bruised and bandaged Malcolm told them that his laptop was missing after he had regained consciousness. They plunged from the ledge of grief into the abyss of despair when he explained that all of NetVoyager's source code was on the laptop, and even though WorldNet had a backup, it was an older version from six months earlier.

Vincent ignored the ulcer pulsating on the left side of his abdomen as he sat, seething at the misfortune that had befallen him. His savings and stocks, minus the shares he held on to, had all but vanished into thin air. To make matters worse, he was now on the fast track to becoming the butt of every corporate blunder joke told at every conference and seminar. His story would also become the case study every b-school dissected until the next major fuck up came along.

The classmates and professors who snickered and looked dumbfounded when he parlayed his Stanford GSB valedictorian honor for a job with a failing technology company, would finally get the last laugh. He could have gone with any of the major investment firms or banks in the country, but he'd chosen ITI because it offered the potential for him to do something big. Something on his own. Instead, all his years of planning, maneuvering and out-witting his naysayers had come to a smashing end by some baton-wielding, laptop-stealing thug.

Vincent peered across the table. Any other day, the glum look on Stanley's face would've been grounds for some light-hearted fun, but all he could muster up was a healthy dose of empathy. Stanley was a good guy. His hard work and loyalty were the primary reasons he held the seat to Jack's right, but Vincent knew those qualities weren't enough for Jack to appoint him as his successor; the guy lacked the vision needed to make the company a competitor in the burgeoning technology market.

Although he and Stanley's relationship bordered between professionally cordial on their best days and childish and irreverent on their worst, Vincent wanted to prove to Stanley, once and for all, that he really was a good guy. The projected growth data for the Internet were staggering, even using conservative projection models. Finalizing the deal with WorldNet and delivering the first Internet browser would put ITI at the front of that growth. The final piece in his plan was handing his old sparring partner the keys to the CEO office. It sounded like a damn good gift for a guy who had been a total asshole.

Vincent watched Jack rock back and forth in his chair. The pain on his face caused Vincent to shudder. He understood Jack's desire to get away from it all. After his first meeting with Malcolm, that was all he dreamed about, too.

That dream became even more desirable and tangible when he'd met Roxanne. He felt the sting of the ulcer when he thought of Roxanne. He was barely affording dinner at Frank's. There was no way she was going to stick around after this.

Stanley covered his mouth and smiled when he saw Vincent looking at him. It was the same smile he used to display when he wanted to intimidate his opponent before a match. He felt like Rocky Balboa in *Rocky IV*, after Rocky had taken another one of Drago's bone-crushing punches. Stallone's voice echoed in his mind. *"C'mon. Yuh not so big!"* After the shock from seeing Malcolm's bruises, it felt good to finally find something to smile about. When Russ told him that his guy had run into a slight problem but fixed it quickly, he had no idea that's what he'd meant.

The hardest part of the plan was seeing the pain in Jack's eyes. Stanley was confident that what he was doing was for the benefit of the company primarily, and Jack specifically. Jack had given Vincent more control than he should have. This would prove it.

Jack walked over and stood in front of the portrait of his father. For twenty-five years, he felt the old man staring over his shoulder, mocking him for thinking he could escape the stronghold of his family's legacy. He looked at his father's liquid blue eyes. They were not the eyes of the doting father and husband he had known as a child. Jack Sr.'s eyes were filled with cynicism and regret, the result of being bequeathed his father's chair. He shook his head in resignation. Those were not the eyes he wanted to inherit.

Vincent slammed both hands on the table, breaking the doleful moment. "This is all bullshit. We're being setup. I just know it."

Stanley drummed his fingertips on the table. "Who would want to do something like that?"

Vincent stood up. "I don't know, but I plan to find out."

CHAPTER 45

THE WALKIE-TALKIE on Russ Franklin's desk squawked, and his assistant's voice crackled through the speaker. "Boss, Mr. Martello's here at the front desk. You want me to send him back there to you?"

Russ grabbed the walkie-talkie without shifting his focus from the four monitors mounted on the rack next to his desk. He pressed the orange button. "Affirmative. Send him in. Copy?"

"I copy."

"Ten-four."

Russ knew he was destined for law enforcement the minute he buckled his first toy gun holster around his waist. When he was eight years old, his father had been gunned down in the line of duty by a bunch of thugs robbing a bank. They never caught the bastards, but one day he would, and when he did, they would pay big time.

After a stint with the local police department, he applied and was eventually selected as a candidate in the Secret Service's Criminal Investigative Training Program. He dropped out after six weeks. The drill instructor said his eagerness to catch bad guys made him overlook obvious signs and often led to him overreacting.

"Security means paying attention to details and executing an appropriate response," the drill instructor had told him over and over. When he became ITI's security chief three years ago, he made sure to follow that advice. So far, his attention to detail had only prevented a nosy reporter from getting in without a badge.

Russ also ran a small security company on the side. They did low-budget night security-type work, the kind where the guard sleeps in his car in the parking lot. Business was growing, and he couldn't have been happier. He had picked up two lucrative contracts from Mr. Bricker and Mr. Martello in the same week.

"What in the hell happened last night?" Vincent shouted after he slammed the door. "I paid you to keep eyes on Mr. Graves."

"I did, Mr. Martello. I put my best man on the case. Please have a seat and tell me what's wrong." Russ motioned to the chair in front of his chair. A black canvas duffle bag was in the seat. "Excuse the clutter; it's gotten pretty busy around here lately. I'll take that," he offered.

Vincent handed Russ the black duffle bag Trace had dropped off earlier and then sat down.

"I'll tell you what's wrong. My client, Mr. Graves, was assaulted and robbed while you were supposed to be protecting him."

"We were protecting him, sir. I put my best man on the job, just as you requested. We began our watch at ..." He pulled a notepad from his shirt pocket. "Here it is. We began monitoring activities yesterday at three fifty-five p.m. That was when you, Mr. Bricker, and Mr. Sherman exited Mr. Graves's suite. This morning, at nine oh five, my guy filed a report. He said Mr. Graves went to the emergency room last night at approximately eight thirty. He reported that Mr. Graves had some minor abrasions and contusions, but he didn't think anything of it since he was with a guy from ITI the whole time. He says Mr. Graves arrived at the office with that same guy this morning."

"What are you talking about? What guy? What's his name?"

"He didn't say, sir, but I'll find out. Do you want me to maintain surveillance on Mr. Graves?"

"No. Just find out who this mystery man is. Drop whatever else you're working on, and get me that guy's name ASAP!"

CHAPTER 46

THE BUS'S ENGINE roared as it lumbered through the intersection of Stonewall and Tryon. Phil crossed the street and turned left on Tryon. When he got to the bench in front of St. Peter's Catholic Church, Holly was already there. She was reading the latest edition of *People* magazine. Hillary Clinton was on the cover, smiling and decked out in a tan cardigan sweater.

"Did you follow the route?" Holly asked from behind the magazine.

"I did everything just like you said. What was that all about?"

"Do you know Russ? He's head of security."

"I think so. What about him?"

"That guy creeps me out with the way he stares at people. I believe he has cameras all over the building. I quit using the restrooms after I bumped into him one day. I was coming out of the restroom by the cafeteria."

"We can't be too careful." Phil looked up and down the sidewalk.

"How's Malcolm?"

"Still shaken. He says he thinks he can locate the laptop if they try to connect it to the Internet."

Holly turned to an article promoting the new Kevin Costner and Whitney Houston movie. It was about the attraction between bodyguards and the people they protect. "What do we do now?"

"I've been thinking about that. I still need to check out this event with Jack Sherman. I need you to look into WorldNet's financials for the last year."

"You think Malcolm is behind this?"

"No. Right before the laptop was stolen, Malcolm told me that WorldNet's investors were threatening to pull out if he didn't close on the deal. Let's see if we can get our hands on that list of investors."

CHAPTER 47

THE SOFT GLOW from the light above the kitchen stove and the thirty-six-inch TV gave the living room a movie theater feel. White and red containers of chow mein, Mongolian beef, and steamed rice were scattered across the coffee table. Roxanne sat on the couch with her legs folded by her side, wearing one of Vincent's button-down shirts. The top three buttons were unfastened, allowing her black lace demi bra and round, taut breasts to peep out occasionally.

"Eat up. Your food is getting cold."

Vincent sat slouched down on the couch and stared blankly at the television. "Who can eat while watching this depressing movie?"

"*Trading Places* is not depressing. Besides, you said it was your favorite movie." She laughed as she scooped shrimp fried rice from a container with her chopsticks.

"That was before today. Now, it looks like the story of my life. My fucked-up life."

Roxanne put her container on the table and turned to Vincent. "All right, what gives? And don't try to bullshit me. Trust me. I'll know."

Vincent remained silent.

"I can't help you if you won't say anything."

Vincent traced the outline of Roxanne's face with his thumb. "It won't do any good to talk about it. I'm screwed."

She leaned in and kissed him softly. "It can't be that bad."

"Let's see, the biggest opportunity in my life has been snatched from under my nose. In a few days, I'm going to be the laughingstock of the industry. And, on top of that, I'm bankrupt. Is that bad enough for you?" He finished off his second shot of Maker's Mark.

Roxy remembered Phil saying that ITI was purchasing a company called WorldNet Labs. She wondered if that was the big opportunity Vincent was talking about. She hadn't talked to Phil since their come-to-Jesus dinner with Wes. She was pretty sure he was still mad at her, but it was for his own good, even if their father was lying.

She rubbed the back of his neck. "Yeah, that's pretty bad. What are you going to do?"

"I'm not—" The phone rang. Vincent jumped up quickly. He pushed the containers aside as he searched the coffee table for the ringing handset.

Roxanne found the phone wedged between the sofa cushions. "Here."

"Martello speaking … Hi, Malcolm … No word yet. I've still got my people on it." Vincent listened and replied with a stream of uh-huhs and okays. He hung up and tossed the phone aside.

"More bad news?"

"No. But it wasn't exactly great, either." Vincent rubbed his temple with the heel of his hand.

"Come here." Roxanne beckoned with her finger. She coaxed his head down to her lap and began to rub the nape of his neck and shoulders. "My, you're tense." She pressed her fingertips deeper into his shoulder plexus.

Vincent shut his eyes and moaned as he settled against her warm body. A hint of Red Door perfume tickled his nose.

Roxanne gently massaged his temple. "I know you never imagined this happening when you became a CFO."

Vincent jerked his head from Roxanne's lap. "You mean you know who I am?"

"Yes." She held his gaze as her hand cupped the back of his neck. With a subtle nudge, she lowered his head back to her lap. "Now, from the beginning. Tell me what's going on. Again, don't try to bullshit me. I'll know."

Vincent lay silently. He felt Roxanne's stomach as she took each breath. It was like faint waves coming ashore. He contemplated what to tell her and was fearfully curious of what she already knew. No matter what he said, he was confident she would soon be walking out the door and out of his life for good.

"It was right there. I was on the verge of pulling off the biggest corporate deal since Microsoft's non-exclusive agreement with IBM for MS-DOS. It was going to put Jack and ITI back on the map, and it was going to make me an instant business executive success. I would've had fifteen million the second Jack and Malcolm signed their names on the contract. Then millions more afterward. And just like that …" he snapped his finger, "Poof! It's all gone."

"What's gone?"

"Malcolm's laptop. Someone jumped him in his hotel room and took his laptop with all the software and source code. So there goes my big opportunity … There goes Jack's and ITI's chance to get back on the map … and there goes my future. Fuck!"

Roxanne barely moved her hand as she rubbed the crown of his head. "Vinny, I'm going to need you to start from the beginning. Don't leave anything out. I may be able to help you, but I'm going to need to know everything."

Vincent sat up. He studied her as if he were seeing her for the first time. "Who are you, and what do you know about me? And how do you think you can help me? Don't *you* try to bullshit me … I'll know."

Roxanne paused *Trading Places*. William Valentine had just blown pot smoke into the restroom's vent as Mortimer and Randolph Duke were walking in. She got up from the couch and removed two framed photographs from the top of a bookcase. She turned to face Vincent. In her left hand, she held an eight-by-ten picture of him standing next to a pacific blue 1959 Ferrari 250 GT California Spyder. In the other, he was standing next to a brilliant red 1978 Lamborghini Countach LP400S.

"What are you doing with those?

Roxanne took a deep breath and adjusted her stance. "I was initially sent here to get these. Remington Haas and Associates are reclaiming their assets."

"You're here for my cars? You mean this was all about getting my cars?" He looked like he needed to throw up.

"Yes, that's why I met you initially. But then I got to know you. And then I …" Roxanne hugged the pictures against her chest. She stared at the ceiling. Her right foot tapped the floor.

"Just when I thought it couldn't get any worse. And then what, Roxanne?" Vincent clasped his hands behind his head and fell back against the couch.

"Look, do you want me to help you or not? It won't take me long to find out where the cars are, Vinny. Let me see, now. You say everything you learned about cars you learned at your uncle Tony's garage. I guess I'll begin there. Does that sound like a good place to start?"

Vincent hung his head.

Roxy exhaled loudly. "Listen, I don't want you to lose these beautiful cars. If you don't want to lose them either, then you're going to have to trust me on this. It's going to cost you, though."

"Money is not an issue. If you can bring me that laptop, I promise, I'll reward you handsomely for your services. What about Remington Haas? Won't they be pissed?"

"Leave Remington Haas to me."

• • • •

Roxy's pager lay on the nightstand, buzzing for the fourth time. She looked at it. She could have reached for it if she tried, but she didn't. Vincent's arm was wrapped around her waist. Roxy felt each exhale on the base of her neck as he snored softly in her ear.

The pager's green display lit up, but she could barely make out the numbers. She didn't need to see the number; she knew it was Phil.

He had been paging her for the past five hours. She knew he was calling about the missing laptop. The conversation would have to wait until she saw him at their parent's house in a couple of hours. They were all gathering for dinner to celebrate Phil and Ann's wedding the following Saturday.

Roxy wasn't sure how she was going to tell Phil she had taken Vincent on as a client. Vincent had agreed to pay five million for the return of the laptop. It was a hefty sum, but she wasn't sure if it would be enough of an enticer to get her brother to help, especially since he was dealing with his own set of ITI related problems. And telling him she and Vincent were becoming an item was definitely off the table of available options. She still couldn't believe it herself. *I'm not sure if what I'm feeling right now is love. I just know it feels damn good, and I don't want it to end anytime soon!* She smiled at her own admittance and then nestled against Vincent's bare chest.

CHAPTER 48

SATURDAY, JANUARY 30, 1993

T HE MOUTH-WATERING AROMA of Marjorie's tender golden fried chicken filled the kitchen. She strained the last drops of hot Crisco then dropped the succulent poultry in a pan lined with paper towels. Pots simmered on the stove's burners while an assortment of bowls, measuring cups, and ingredients for the Sock-It-to-Me cake filled the kitchen counter.

Phil waited until his mother was mixing cake batter and talking to Ann—she was seated at the table chopping pecans on a cutting board—before he sneaked past the stove and grabbed a chicken wing. He concealed his piping hot stolen bounty in a napkin and made his way to the den.

"Give me half, or I'm telling Mama," Roderick demanded as soon as he walked into the room.

"Damn, nigga! After all these years, you still begging."

"Give me a piece. Your chubby ass need to cut back anyway. You don't want your tux fitting too tight next week. People laugh when they see fat men in tuxedos. I know I do."

Phil broke off the drumette and handed it to his brother. "Satisfied?"

He joined his other brother, Gregory, on the couch in the den. Greg's wife, Lori, reclined on the chaise lounge on the opposite side of the room. She was engrossed in a corny cable show called *Talk Soup*.

Phil saw Roxy enter the room. He picked up the latest edition of *JET* and flipped through its pages. After paging her a dozen times through the night, she'd finally returned his call at seven that morning.

Roxy casually strolled through the room without saying a word. When she walked past Phil, she nudged him on the shoulder.

Phil finished the article on the swearing in ceremony of the first African American female U.S. Senator, the Honorable Carol Mosely-Braun, then hurried off to meet Roxy.

The basement had once served as Phil's command center. Two long tables were pushed against the wall on the right. A computer, scanner, and printer sat on one table. Spare computer parts and software disks were boxed and scattered on the other. A futon sat against the wall behind the stairs.

Roxy sat on the futon with her legs crossed and her hands clasped around her knee. "Any ideas on who took your friend's laptop? Or where it could be?"

The question caught Phil off guard. He coughed to release the air that was lodged in his windpipe. "How do you know about that?"

"Don't worry about how I know. We just need to get it back."

"We? The last time I asked you for help, you sold me out to Daddy. By the way, I spent all night calling your ass, and you wouldn't even return my call. So where is all this *we* talk coming from?" Phil turned to the computer and tapped the keyboard.

"I really mean *we* this time because *we* have a client." Roxy pressed her glossy lips together into a big smile.

Phil frowned and looked at his sister as if she were an alien creature.

Roxy waved her finger back and forth. "You and me. We have a client."

"How can we have a client when *we* don't have a business?" Phil, nervous about what his sister was getting him into, began to bite his fingernails as he rocked in the chair.

"That's a minor oversight. I'll take care of that. So, are you in?"

"Depends. Who's the client and what does it have to do with Malcolm's laptop?"

Roxy took a deep breath. "It's Vincent Martello."

Phil stopped rocking. "Why would we want to get the laptop back for Vincent Martello? My friend, Malcolm, is the one who got his ass kicked over this. If anything, he's the client I'm helping."

"I'll help you find it for Malcolm if you help me find it for Vincent. Okay?"

Phil looked at the floor and shook his head slowly. "Honestly, it doesn't matter who we help. I doubt if we're ever going to solve this. In the past two weeks, I've learned that I'm not cut out to be a detective. The only things I've accomplished so far are getting Mama and Daddy pissed off and causing one of my best friends to get his ass kicked and lose out on a big opportunity. If we're lucky enough to figure all of this out, that's it for me and being a detective. I'm sticking to programming."

"Well, I don't believe that, and you shouldn't either. You're Philander Wesley Jacobson, the Second, the son of Wes Jacobson, and the heir apparent to the great Jacobson and Associates

Investigative Services. If anyone can do this, it's you. I also know if we don't find this laptop, working with Daddy may soon be your next job. And before you brush me off, let me tell you, it's a possibility that could happen sooner than you think."

"Why do you say that?"

"Because ITI won't last six months if we don't find that laptop."

• • • •

Wes and Marjorie sat at the dining room table, surrounded by their four children and daughters-in-law. Greg, Lori, and Roxy sat on one side, while Phil, Ann, and Roderick were on the other. Platters filled with chicken (fried and baked) were surrounded by pans of cornbread dressing, mac and cheese, and bowls of giblet gravy, collard greens, field peas, Kentucky Wonders, and potato salad. A basket of rolls and pitcher of iced tea filled out the table.

Wes, eager to put the disastrous trip to Charlotte behind, arrived home an hour before dinner. The meeting with Linda Albright had left a memory that was nothing short of unpleasant, his relationship with Grace was every bit of a fiasco, and Robert was the epitome of a calamity.

He looked around the table, admiring the children and thinking about the many holidays and Sunday dinners they had shared around that same table. He couldn't exactly remember all the details; he just knew they were good times.

"This is delicious, baby. It reminds me of all those good Sunday dinners we had when the kids were growing up." He smiled. "Yeah, baby, you really out did yourself today."

Marjorie held Wes's gaze; her fork dangled in midair between her thumb and middle finger. "Phil, did you find those books of MiMi's you were asking me about? Your daddy was at the office Thursday evening. Did you go by there and get the keys like I told you?"

Wes forgot to chew the heaping forkful of mac and cheese he'd stuffed into his mouth and swallowed it whole. The lie he'd told Marjorie about working all night at the office was now exposed. He looked around the table and then down at his plate, anywhere to escape Marjorie's icy glare. *Lord, you know I love my son. But right now, I don't care what you do to him. Choke him. Slap a muzzle over his mouth. Anything. Just make sure he doesn't tell this woman he went by the office the other night.*

"No, I haven't had a chance to look for them. I went by Daddy's office, but Grace said she hadn't seen him."

The vein in Wes's neck palpitated.

Phil turned to Wes. "Daddy, do you know where MiMi's—
"

"Wait a minute, Puddin'! I can explain!" Wes wiped his mouth and tried to stand. Before he could get up, Marjorie had already jumped from her chair and was standing in front of him.

"Sit down!" Marjorie poked Wes in the chest, and he sat down. "I don't want to hear shit you have to say!"

Phil looked at Roxy. She kept eating.

When he turned to Roderick, his brother shrugged.

Lori looked as if she was ready to cry.

Gregory looked at him with an expression that screamed, "That's why I don't want any damn children."

[203]

Phil felt Ann rubbing his leg. He put his hand on top and squeezed.

Marjorie ran to the drawer where she stored her dish towels. She fished under some towels and grabbed a Smith & Wesson .38. She stood next to Wes, patting the blue steel barrel against her right hip. "I want your black, lying ass outta here, now!"

"Marjorie, please. Not in front of the kids. I know what I told you, but I swear to you, it's not what you're thinking." Wes let out a deep sigh and shook his head.

"Do you really want to know what I think?" She held the gun up, pointed it at Wes, and pulled the hammer back. "I think you better walk outta here before they wheel your ass out."

"Mama, no!" Roxy shouted.

Ann stood up. Phil started to get up too, but Ann placed a hand on his shoulder. "Sit."

She walked behind Wes and stood next to Marjorie. In a slow, measured tone, Ann said, "Take a deep breath, Mama. You don't want to do this."

Marjorie, her nostrils flaring and chest heaving like a locomotive, showed no sign of comprehending the gravity of the moment or that Ann was standing next to her. She kept her eyes and the pistol trained on Wes.

"Take a deep breath, Mama. Just relax." Ann gently put her hand around Marjorie's and slowly lowered the gun. "That's it," she cooed.

Marjorie fell into Ann's open arms. Her shoulders shook as a tidal wave of tears, birthed from love, pain, fear, and anger, flooded Ann's shoulder.

The children sat around the table, shocked and dismayed. No one spoke.

Wes got up from the table. He walked from the room quietly and solemnly. Marjorie let out an excruciating wail, and Wes dropped his head further into his chest.

He grabbed his car keys from the keyring holder. Before he left, he looked back once more. Roxy had joined Ann; both were attempting to comfort Marjorie, who was bawling uncontrollably.

Phil rushed from the house as Wes was backing out of the driveway. "Daddy, I'm sorry if I said something that I shouldn't have. I didn't mean to cause any problems with you and Mama."

"Phil, it's not your fault. I did this to myself."

"I just wanted to get into MiMi's library to check out something on Jack Sherman."

"You mean to tell me you're still trying to play detective? What you just witnessed in there is the result of me playing detective. That's why I don't want you doing this. Don't take Ann through the same thing I took your mother through."

"Daddy, I know I'm not cut out to be a detective, and I know I will never be as good as you, so you don't have to worry about that." Phil flailed his arms in despair. "I only wanted to see if MiMi had any information about the Sherman family and their connections to some group called the CLANS."

"Are you saying Jack Sherman is a card-carrying member of the KKK?"

"No, not that Klan. I'm talking about the Confederate Loyalists Association of the New South. C-L-A-N-S. Jack Sherman's great-great-grandfather was a founding member."

"What does that have to do with you and ITI?"

"That's what I'm trying to find out. If it doesn't mean anything, I'll leave it alone. I promise."

Wes knew that line all too well. He shook his head and chuckled. "Go to my office and look in the top left drawer. There's a spare key for the library in a small wooden box that looks like a pirate's chest."

Phil's face lit up. "Thank you, Daddy."

"I sure hope you know what you're getting yourself into." Wes shook his head and backed out of the driveway.

CHAPTER 49

SUNDAY, JANUARY 31, 1993

ANN GENTLY CLOSED the bedroom door. She turned around and bumped into Phil.

"Sorry." Phil gave her a quick smack on the corner of her lip. "How is she?" he asked, looking over her shoulder at the closed door.

"She's all right. She just wants to be alone for a while. I called my parents and told them we were spending the night." She leaned in and kissed Phil passionately. "Let's go somewhere so she can have some peace and quiet."

Phil cupped her butt with his palms and drew her closer. "You're the greatest, baby."

They walked into the den. Roderick was reclining in Wes's chair. Roxy occupied the left side of the couch. Although his brother and sister were labeling their parent's latest spat as "no big deal," Phil noticed they'd both decided to spend the night.

Phil leaned over and whispered to Ann, "So much for a night of peace and quiet with these two in the house."

Everything was going well until Roderick and Roxy got into one of their usual spats. It all started when he accused Roxy of hiding a secret relationship. "Roxy, it's all over your face. Believe me; I know that look when a chick is on a new daily dick regimen."

Roxy burst into laughter. "How would you know? None of the women you date ever stay around long enough to even begin a regimen."

[207]

They went back and forth for several more minutes, then Roxy grabbed her keys in a huff and announced she was going out and would return later.

Roderick looked at Phil. "You can believe her if you want, but she's not coming back." He shook his head. "Nuh uh. Not tonight."

• • • •

It was a few minutes past midnight when Phil arrived at Wes's office. He flipped a row of switches, and the room lit up. Six bookcases were placed around the room.

The redolence of books, old newspapers, and polished wood greeted Phil when he opened the door to MiMi's library. The small room had become a national archive of sorts. Graduate students from universities as far away as London, England, visited the library to glean insight from MiMi's grassroots research.

In many academic and legal circles, MiMi was considered an authoritative source when it came to understanding the machinations and systematic influence of the Klu Klux Klan on legislative bodies and courtrooms throughout the South.

MiMi was working as his grandfather's research assistant when J.D. took his first civil rights case. Through her research, she befriended many Negros who worked for prominent white families. Through the firsthand accounts of housemaids, butlers, and nannies, she uncovered the intricacies of the way communication flowed between the Klan, business leaders, law enforcement, and elected officials.

The library took up half the first floor of what was once the original law office. When the law firm moved downtown, the two-story brick building became the headquarters of Jacobson and Associates Investigative Services.

The Jacobson family had maintained a business on Parrish Street since 1910. Phil's great-grandfather, Samuel Jacobson, was in the group of entrepreneurs that first established businesses along the famed thoroughfare in the area dubbed *Black Wall Street.*

Phil started with the bookcase nearest the door. He traced his finger along the leather and cloth-covered book spines, looking for the set of burgundy and black journals that MiMi titled *The Secret Life.* Some scholars referred to the collection of registries as the umbilical cord of the Klan. He found the books on the top shelf of the last bookcase.

He dropped the books on Wes's desk and began to pore through each of them. The books contained a registry of names and family relationships of known segregationists and KKK members from as far back as the 1880s. The journals were constructed from personal letters, notes, and oral accounts of former slaves. They created the quasi-tracking system to ensure their children knew the "good" white people from the "not-so-good" white people.

Phil flipped through the pages of the first book. *Allen ... Davis ... Gilbert.* Each page outlined the descendants, their spouses, and their children. It also included notations about their occupation and closest associates. He perused the second journal. *Little ... Marshall ... Pringle.* He had often heard accounts of incestuous marriages, especially among white aristocrats. MiMi's books brought the fact to light in a visual display that left Phil astounded.

Phil thumbed through the last volume. *Sawyer ... Sellers.* He fist bumped the air when he found Luke Sherman, Jack's great-great-grandfather. The Sherman family tree filled two pages, front and back. He traced through the family tree until he found Jack Sherman. His name appeared in a small box underneath his parents, Jack Sr. and Sarah. Jack's box was there all by itself. No boxes appeared beside it or below it. Jack was the period on the Sherman family legacy.

There was a notation next to Sarah's name that Phil couldn't decipher. MiMi was traveling and wouldn't be back until next week. Whatever it meant, it would have to wait. He copied the page and placed the book on Wes's desk.

Phil folded the paper and put it in his back pocket. He was going to cross-check the names with the Rowdy Rebel board once he got back to his apartment, to see if he could make heads or tails out of Jack Sherman's CLANS association. He was locking the office when a car passed and blew its horn.

Phil turned around quickly.

"Goodnight, Wes!" The driver waved.

Phil, amused that someone had mistaken him for his father, waved and hollered, "Goodnight!"

CHAPTER 50

"GOOD JOB, EDDIE ... No, you've been a big help. I'm sure we'll be able to narrow it down from here."

Russ held the phone from his ear and stretched until he was able to press the buttons on the control. Four grainy black-and-white images popped up on the monitors.

"Uh huh ... uh huh ... I'll be sure to let him know ... Stay by the phone."

After he hung up, Russ poured a cup of coffee and then leaned back to watch the monitors. Sunday evening to early Monday morning were the hours he liked most. He believed those were the best hours to commit a crime in the workplace because that was the time people dreaded going to work the most. He figured if he was smart enough to know that, surely some conniving bastard was thinking the same thing.

Russ flicked a switch. Four camera angles of the parking garage's first floor appeared. He reached into a greasy white paper bag and pulled out a donut. Glaze splattered everywhere as he stuffed half of it into his mouth. When he saw the black Trans Am pull into the handicap space, Russ raced down the corridor, dusting the crumbs from his shirt.

"Mr. Martello! Mr. Martello!"

"What is it, Russ?" asked Vincent. He looked like he hadn't slept in days.

A bead of sweat ran down the side of his face and fell to the floor. "I was just about to call you. Eddie just called."

"Who's Eddie?"

"Eddie's the guy I had working detail the other night. He says he's positive the guy who was with Malcolm at the hotel works here. He says it's a black guy, but he doesn't know his name."

"I see."

"Eddie felt bad that he didn't know the guy's name. Who can blame him? They all look alike to me, and it's hard remembering those weird names. Anyway, he says he talked to the head security guy at the hotel. The hotel will give us a copy of the tape. It'll take a day or two to pull the tape and make a copy. Eddie says he'll pick it up as soon as it's ready. If that's all right with you, of course."

The elevator arrived, and Vincent got on. "Nice work, Russ. I think I may be able to take it from here. I know just the person who can help us find our mystery man. Have your guy pick up that video from the hotel. We'll need it for evidence."

Russ saluted. "I aim to please, Mr. Martello."

CHAPTER 51
MONDAY, FEBRUARY 1, 1993

ROBERT TURNED THE KEY counter-clockwise and pushed open his office door. He fumbled with the key then finally removed it from the lock. When he turned around and saw Vincent sitting behind his desk, he gasped, clutched his heart, and backed into the door.

Vincent chuckled and sat up straight. "Didn't mean to frighten you. Come in. Close the door."

Robert closed the door. "I guess I was more shocked than frightened." He saw Vincent was still sitting in his chair, so he stood in place in front of the door. A briefcase swung gently from one hand; a set of keys dangled from the other.

"Shocked to see an old friend? We are friends, aren't we?" Vincent's hand glided over a desk-sized calendar. When it came to a stop, the handle of a brass dagger letter opener was resting neatly beneath his palm.

Robert noticed the letter opener in Vincent's hand but didn't give it a second thought. "I thought we were. Unless you're telling me you have a reason to believe otherwise." He'd come to the conclusion that Vincent Martello was a man of contrasting signals, and despite the knife-like object beneath his hand, Vincent's true feelings were evidenced through his photogenic smile.

"Come on, Robert, you know I'm just busting your balls, right? And why are you standing there with that odd look on your

[213]

face?" Vincent grabbed the letter opener and stood up. "Take a load off. Have a seat. This is your office, isn't it?"

"Of course, it is." Robert placed the briefcase on the floor, threw his keys on the desk, and then walked over to the coat stand in the far corner of the office. "It's just that I wasn't expecting to see you when I opened the door. I take it you aren't just dropping by for the hell of it."

"Touché, Robert. Touché. I know you haven't seen much of me lately, but like I told you before, I'm orchestrating some major moves around here. Once again, I'd like to say thank you. You've played an integral part in helping me sort through some of the bullshit."

When Vincent had approached him about getting rid of the resumes, Robert was more than a little scared. In fact, it was fear that had driven him to seek Wes's help. Looking back, his nervous response seemed rather childish. Robert blushed. "It wasn't a problem at all."

Vincent walked behind Robert's desk. A window spanned the width of the office. He looked down at the congested streets and the stream of pedestrians scurrying up and down the sidewalk to get to their offices. "I hope my tokens of appreciation haven't disappointed you. Do you have any idea what most people would offer up for a senior-level promotion, with designated parking and an office with a window overlooking downtown?"

Robert stood next to Vincent. With each passing day, he'd grown to regret involving Wes in something that turned out to be nothing more than a case of overactive paranoia. "I'm sure the sky's the limit. Just so you know, I couldn't be happier. Thank you."

[214]

Vincent wrapped an arm around Robert and gave him a bear hug. "What good is a friend if he can't lend you a hand to lift you up or get you out of a jam, right?"

"Right. So, what do you need from me?"

Dimples deep enough to make a Hollywood heartthrob envious, dotted Vincent's chiseled cheeks. "Ahh! Spoken like a true New Yorker. That's why I like you, Robert. You cut through the bullshit and get right to the point."

Robert shrugged. "Old habits are hard to break. What sort of problem are you dealing with this time?"

"I believe you might want to sit down first." Vincent, still holding the letter opener, pointed to the chair. "After all, this is just as much your problem as it is mine."

Robert sat down slowly, keeping an eye on the opener's blade as it glistened under a beam of sunlight. "My problem?" A noticeable rasp and uncertainty had replaced his once resonant and confident tone.

"Yes, but no need to worry; I'm not blaming you, personally." Vincent stood in front of the desk, zeroing his sights on his confused accomplice. "Not yet, that is." His ever-present engaging smile was nowhere in sight.

"I don't understand."

"I'll help you. A business partner of mine was in town last week. He came here so we could close a lucrative business deal he and I had been working on for over a year. The night before we were supposed to sign the contract, someone assaulted him in his hotel room and stole a very important item that is critical to our agreement."

"I'm really sorry to hear that, but I don't know what any of that has to do with me and why it's my problem."

Vincent walked around the desk and stood inches in front of his visibly nervous friend. He leaned back against the desk, clasping his hands in front, at his waist. "It's your problem because I've been informed that the only person seen with my partner during the time of the assault was a black guy who works here."

Robert raised his arms, palms out. "Well, it wasn't me," he protested.

"I never said or implied that it was you."

"No, you didn't. But you said it was my problem, and I still can't figure out how that's possible."

"It's your problem because when I asked you to hire all these black motherfuckers, I expected you to hire some people I could trust, not some ghetto, gangster sonofabitch, looking to knock people off for a goddamn laptop!" The outer rims of Vincent's ears turned redder than beets as his frustration began to build.

"I *did* hire trustworthy people," Robert objected. "I handpicked many of them myself, and those that I didn't came through reputable contacts."

Vincent leaned closer and poked the tip of the letter opener just below Robert's collarbone. Robert flinched and retreated as far as he could into the chair's leather backrest, but Vincent pressed the dagger harder into his shoulder. "Evidently, someone is playing you for a chump. I suggest you find out who this punk is, and find him in a hurry. If this deal blows up in my face and I go down, my friend, I promise you I'll take you down so far, Hell will seem like a penthouse. Is that clear enough for you?"

Robert felt drops of perspiration trickle from his armpits, down to the waistband of his boxers. His starched white shirt clung to his skin. "Vincent, honestly, I don't know who would've done such a thing, but I promise you I will get to the bottom of this."

Vincent stood up and tossed the letter opener on the desk. He looked at Robert. The photogenic smile was back. "I knew I could count on you, my friend."

CHAPTER 52

MALCOLM PRESSED ENTER, and the screen went black. Then three messages scrolled up:

Dialing...
Connecting...
Searching...

After going over the details, PhantomPhixer was convinced the burglar had come specifically for the laptop. The number of people who knew Malcolm was in town could be counted on one hand. That meant the guy who attacked him and stole the laptop was working for someone close. Their chances of locating the guy were less than encouraging since Malcolm hadn't gotten a very good look. They agreed; they stood a better chance of locating the laptop. To do that, they needed to find it as soon as it dialed into the server at Malcolm's office. It had taken the entire weekend, but Malcolm had finally finished writing a program to monitor the server and then broadcast an alert once the laptop's digital name had been recognized.

He grabbed a slice of cold pizza and was headed to the refrigerator when he heard a knock at the door.

"All I need are clean towels today," Malcolm announced as he opened the door.

"I'll be sure to tell the maid." Stanley smiled. "May I come in?"

"Sure. Come in, Stanley. Sorry about the mix up. What can I do for you?"

The suite looked like a tornado had gone through it. Empty pizza boxes, potato chip bags, and soda cans were scattered everywhere. Malcolm cleared a spot on the couch for them to sit.

Stanley gave Malcolm a soft pat on the knee and grinned. "Malcolm, I was thinking that maybe I could do something for you."

Malcolm shuddered. He wasn't some sort of a germaphobe, more like an introvert. "Something like what?" He scooted to his right to put more distance between them.

"Like finding your laptop."

"I don't know if that will be necessary. You see—"

"With all due respect, Mr. Graves," Stanley interrupted, "I have resources at my disposal who are experts when it comes to matters like this. I am surprised that Vincent hasn't offered you similar assistance. Then again, what can you expect from a guy who offered you a godawful proposition in the first place, right? Take it from me; he's been thinking only of himself through this entire negotiation."

"I'm not sure I know what you mean."

"What I'm saying is this isn't the big break you and your friends think it is. I believe Vincent is pulling a fast one on you. You're going to feel like a fish out of water, working at ITI. Our corporate culture is too constrictive for a guy with your abilities. Trust me, after this is all over, you'll only end up being Vincent's lackey. I know that's not what you want. Am I right?"

Malcolm shook his head. "No, not at all."

"Here's what I want to do for all the parties involved, especially you. Let me put my people on the case. If they find the laptop before Friday, we'll hold onto it for a few days. Vincent won't have any choice but to withdraw the offer. Come next week, we can go over the terms of an offer I'd like to propose. Instead of the hundred million for the software and forcing you and your team to come play in our sandbox, how does sixty million and royalties in perpetuity just for the software sound? That way, ITI will have the product we need, and you'll have more money than you could ever spend. And don't forget, the freedom to work on your next big idea."

Stanley stuck his hand out.

"We have a deal?"

CHAPTER 53

PHIL WAS OBLIVIOUS to the cacophony of sounds generated by the noonday downtown traffic as he sat on the bench, waiting for Holly. He was still trying to make sense out of what was going on with his parents. His father was gone, and his mother was doing her best to act as if it didn't bother her, but her tear-blistered eyes were a dead giveaway.

On top of that, Roxy was acting weird, or at least weirder than normal.

Ann had remained caring and understanding about his family's dysfunctional behavior. Although, he wouldn't have blamed her if she had changed her mind.

"Earth to Phil." Holly waved as she sat beside him.

"Huh?" Phil snapped out of his daze and looked up at Holly. "Oh! Hey, what's up?"

"I wish I had better news for you. It looks like we've hit another brick wall with WorldNet Lab's financials. Their only funding came from an investment firm operating a blind pool. I guess the firm had some investors who were looking to hedge their bets on an unknown startup and didn't want their friends to know about it. Even if they weren't using the blind pool to hide their identities, we would still run into a brick wall because the funds were transferred from a Swiss bank account."

Phil knew Vincent was the blind investor. Now wasn't the time to tell Holly that Roxy had wrangled him into taking Vincent on as a client. "That's okay. Now that I think about it, that's not going to lead us anywhere."

"So, what now?"

"I'm headed over to Malcolm's after work. He finished that tracer hack. We're assuming whoever stole the laptop did it so they could access the Internet. Malcolm created a hack to trace the laptop back to the switch the modem uses to originate the call."

Holly looked at her watch. "I've got to get back. What do you want me to do?"

Phil fished the folded pages from the pocket inside his coat and handed it to Holly.

"What's this?" She slipped the pages into her purse without looking at them.

"Those are the pages from a book collection my grandmother calls *The Secret Life*. It's a copy of the Sherman family connections. At least the ones she knew about."

"What do you want me to do with it?"

"Let's see if Jack Sherman has any personal relationships with those banks."

"You think there's a family connection?"

"I think it runs much deeper than a family connection."

Holly, sensing the seriousness in Phil's tone, looked up and held his gaze. "What do you mean?"

"I'm saying I just stumbled across some interesting info that points to Jack Sherman being a member of a group called the Confederate Loyalists Association of the New South. And, from the looks of it, this group appears to be some sort of secret segregationist group."

Holly's hands flew to cover her dropped jaw. "You can't be serious!"

"Not only am I serious, it seems they're asking Jack Sherman the same question we're asking: Why is he hiring all of these minorities?"

CHAPTER 54

TUESDAY, FEBRUARY 2, 1993

"THAT'S ALL RIGHT, DARLING," Senator Sherman said as he pushed the door open. "No need to waste precious time introducing me. Cousin Jack's office is always open to family. Ain't that right, Jack?"

Jack looked up from his newspaper. "Close the door, Beau. What unfortunate deed did I do to deserve this visit?"

"I just came by to drop off your speech for the keynote next week." He handed Jack a folder.

"No offense, but I prefer to write my own speech." Jack placed the folder on his desk.

"No offense taken, but this isn't a call you can make. The guys in banking are ready. We can't afford anyone going off script on this one. You'll need to get that typed on your personal letterhead."

Jack unsealed the envelope and read the pages.

"These workforce reduction numbers are outrageous. If we go through with this, the African American workforce numbers will cripple those communities. They're barely surviving as it is. This will devastate them. It's not good business, Beau. I won't be a part of this." Jack threw the speech back.

Beau looked at Jack with disgust. "My daddy was right all along about you and Uncle Jack. He always said y'all loved them niggers better than your own family." He picked the papers off the floor and rolled them up.

"And your daddy fell in love with every strung-out call girl he met." Jack sneered. "By the way, send my regards to your mother. Which one was she, now?"

"Let me put this in terms you can understand, Jackie Boy. If you don't go through with it, you'll be out of business by the end of the week, and the vultures will be picking at your carcass by the end of the month." Beau threw the rolled-up pages back at Jack and walked out.

CHAPTER 55

IT WAS SUNNY and pleasantly mild for a February morning. The air smelled of an early spring season, even though the groundhog had seen its shadow. Holly was sipping on her second Coke of the day when the bells at St. Peter's Catholic Church began their melodious announcement of the day's tenth hour.

"Do you think Russ is on to us? Phil asked Holly when they met up at the bus stop.

"I don't think so." Holly looked up and down Tryon Street. "Why do you ask?"

"He gave me a strange look this morning, real suspicious-like."

"That's how he looks at everyone." She reached inside her purse and handed Phil a yellow Post-It note with three names on it. Next to each name was a series of numbers and letters. A dollar amount appeared under each name.

Phil glanced across the table after studying the note for several seconds. "What's this?"

"The first two are Jack Sherman's cousins. His aunt Martha's sons, Howard and Robert. Howard is chairman of the board at Trans-Continental Bank, and Robert is the CEO of American National. The third guy is Ned Bailey. I'm pretty sure his family is listed in your grandmother's journal as well. Ned is chairman of the Securities Exchange Commission. He's a longtime friend of Senator Bill Sherman. Remember, he's the guy we saw last week at Garrison's. Senator Sherman and Jack Sherman are also first cousins.

"All signs point to these three guys as the ones responsible for creating the off-the-book accounts that fund the ITI account. I'm assuming Ned is responsible for funding the account at Chase Mercantile. The CEO is married to his sister, and I'm sure he didn't want to do anything to piss off Ned or the Exchange, if you know what I mean. They're a rather well-connected family, wouldn't you say?"

"How did you figure it out?"

"I hacked into the payroll department's system and traced my payroll check. It was routed to the account at American National, same as your check."

Phil looked at her out of the corner of his eye.

"Sorry for not asking you first."

He shook his head and smiled in admiration. "Damn, you're good. What did you find out?"

"Not much else." Holly turned up the red can and took a huge gulp. "Did you know they're paying you less than the other white guys in your position?"

"I know you think I should be surprised. Unfortunately, I'm not." Phil leaned forward and looked up and down the sparsely occupied sidewalk. "Knowing it doesn't make it feel any better, though."

A bus pulled next to the curb and opened its doors. Holly shook her head. The driver closed the doors and revved on to the next stop.

"Your grandmother's book is fascinating! Did you know Jack Sherman's aunt Martha married General Robert E. Lee's grandson?"

"How ironic. They keep telling us the North won the war," Phil said.

"What are you talking about, the North *did* win the war."

"Not as long as the descendants of southern Confederates run the banks."

Holly checked her watch and stood up. "What do you want me to do?"

"Let's see what else we can find about this group called CLANS." Phil stuffed the Post-It note in his pants pocket.

Holly finished off the last of her soda and threw it in the trash receptacle next to the bench. "When does Jack speak at the conference?"

Phil saw a familiar glint in her eyes. He hadn't known her long, but he'd seen that look enough times already to know she was crafting a plan. "A week from today. Why?"

"I've got a plan. See you tomorrow."

Holly turned to leave. She took a few steps then stopped.

Phil looked around with alarm. "What's wrong?"

"Let's switch routes on the way back and confuse the shit out of Russ," she said with a devious smile.

CHAPTER 56

WEDNESDAY, FEBRUARY 3, 1993

HOLLY WALKED into the executive suite just as Mary Winters was turning on her computer. After twenty years as Jack Sherman's personal secretary, Mary was considered as much an institution as the company itself. She was a pleasant woman, who prided herself on handling all of Mr. Sherman's affairs, public and private.

Handling the schedule for the head of one of the country's most trusted and well-known companies had had its rewards, even if the last three years had bruised her psyche and created a stubborn gray hairline along her temple. She was determined to greet each day with a smile, a positive attitude, and a healthy application of Clairol #5. Her profession was undergoing a technology upgrade that felt more like an alien takeover. All the essential tools she once relied on daily were being dumped into a funny-looking box called a computer. As hard as she tried, the adjustment wasn't going well. A job that had once given her a sense of satisfaction and accomplishment, now made her feel awkward and useless, not to mention afraid. She was too embarrassed to tell anyone about her fear of computers.

Holly discovered Mary's secret when she saw the older woman struggling to remember the steps to print a document. From that day on, Holly had become her guardian angel.

Holly looked around to make sure they were alone then hurried over.

"Mary, has anyone from the Help Desk Support Team been by to service your computer?"

Mary picked up the notebook next to her keyboard and browsed through her latest entries. She shook her head. "No."

Holly leaned closer and whispered, "You mean no one has been up to configure the new hardware drivers?"

"Not a soul." Mary's eyes grew as big as poker chips. The whites of her eyes poked above her half-rim glasses. "I just turned it on. Did I mess something up?"

The computer chirped in response to Mary's inquiry.

Mary dropped the notebook, placed her hand on her chest, and backed away from the computer as if it were about to explode.

Holly waved her hands wildly. "No, no, no! Everything's fine. You didn't mess up anything." Suppressing a laugh, she walked around the desk and took a seat in front of the computer. She pulled a diskette from her purse. "They should have installed them yesterday. I'll install them for you. It shouldn't take long."

"Sure. I'm so glad I can count on you to look out for me, Holly."

Holly inserted the blank disk in the computer. "It's a good thing I got here when I did."

"Thank you, Holly! I've got to print a speech for Mr. Sherman to proof. I sure wouldn't want to lose it, like I did that memo I typed last week." She placed a hand on Holly's shoulder. "Thanks again for helping me find it. I thought I'd lost it for good."

Holly smiled politely and patted her hand. "Grab a cup of coffee while I take care of this. It shouldn't take long."

"Can I get you anything?" Mary asked as she exited.

[230]

"A Coke, please."

Holly felt bad about lying to Mary, but it was the only surefire way to access the files on her computer. Jack trusted no one but Mary to type his speeches. Holly navigated to the directory where she had instructed Mary to store all her files.

She scrolled through the files until she found the one she was looking for. After copying the file to the diskette, Holly dropped the disk back into her purse and then began playing a game of Solitaire on the computer while she waited for Mary to return.

CHAPTER 57

STANLEY UNZIPPED the duffle bag and placed the laptop on the desk. He was in the private office he maintained on the first floor, next to the mailroom. The space had been used for storage, but he had cleared it out and changed the door, so it looked like the other mechanical room doors.

He flipped open the cover and powered on the computer. Stanley chuckled. The look on Vincent's face when Jack asked for a status was priceless and funny as hell. The young punk's expressions and excuses had grown more pitiful each day.

After eighteen months of being squeezed out and embarrassed by Vincent because he had the goose with the golden egg, Stanley finally felt a sense of satisfaction in knowing that he was holding the golden ticket in the end. It felt better than he imagined, especially since Vincent was getting a fair share of comeuppance in the process.

He unplugged the cord from the phone then plugged it into the laptop's modem. Next, he found the icon of the opaque globe transposed on top of a green "N." Stanley clicked on the icon. He heard the modem dial then buzz and squawk. A box popped up on the screen.

CONNECTED!

Stanley clicked on the hyperlinks and navigated through the web pages.

Vincent will be history by Friday. All I need to do is break the good news to Malcolm tomorrow night. Once he hears I've found the laptop, the deal is mine for sure!

• • • •

"So, you're saying you're going to sign a deal with Stanley if he finds it?" Phil shouted from the couch. He was waiting on Malcolm to change so they could grab a pizza and a few beers.

"It's definitely appealing."

Malcolm emerged from the room in a shirt that looked exactly like the one he'd had on previously, except it wasn't as wrinkled. "I'm getting tired of working on this web browser, anyway. I came up with this cool idea this weekend when I was creating the tracer program. I'd like to work on it and let ITI go on with the browser. Even if they screw it up, they still owe me."

"Has he called to give you an update?"

"No. I haven't heard from him since that meeting."

One of the computers on the table began to chirp. Malcolm raced to the table.

Phil jumped up from the couch. "What is it?"

"The laptop just dialed into the server. Someone is using it to access the Internet." Malcolm activated the sniffer program to identify the circuit where the call originated.

The black window scrolled as the sniffer program spit out its data.

"Where is it?" Phil looked over Malcolm's shoulder.

"Hold on. Let me run the circuit ID through the phone company's database. It'll give me the service address."

Malcolm entered another string of commands. The screen went black, and then the address and customer information appeared at the top of the screen.

Malcolm looked over his shoulder. He looked as if he'd just seen a ghost. "What do we do now, Phixer?"

Phil said nothing. He stared at the message on the screen.

Caller: Intellect Technology Incorporation

Address: 444 N Tryon Street

CHAPTER 58

GRACE STOOD in front of the mirror, massaging and stretching the puffy area under her eyes. The swelling had gone down a little. She dabbed a dollop of Oil of Olay on her finger and then rubbed it on a small pimple on her chin. Next, she rubbed cream on the dark splotches on her cheeks.

She let out a long sigh. "Covering up tears, pimples, and blemishes. How depressing," she said to the woman in the mirror. "Not only is it my daily routine, it's the story of my life."

Monroe Thomas, her high school sweetheart, was a pimple in every sense of the word. She'd stayed with his trifling ass for fifteen long years, enduring every excuse for why it was never the right time to get married. When Monroe said he was making a quick run to Atlanta for the weekend, she assumed it was to buy a wedding ring and find a place for them to make a fresh start. He never returned. After months of covering her tears, she eventually heard from him; he'd met someone and had gotten married.

If Monroe was her pimple, Tony Winslow was surely her ugly blemish. She liked Tony, but she was never in love with him. She finally gave in to his sexual advances one night after work. It wasn't because she was overly attracted to him. To be honest, she hadn't ever been attracted to him. It wasn't because of the gifts he showered on her. They were all hand-me-downs, bargain goods, anyway.

After years of being tormented by memories of Monroe, she'd made up her mind that it was time to break free, once and for all. The orgasm she'd had that night on the backseat of Tony's car was more than an emotional release; it was revenge. The thought of Monroe standing outside the car, watching as Tony passionately thrust every single inch of his swollen, vein-popping manhood into her luscious love sanctum made her screams of ecstasy more fulfilling.

Moans of satisfaction soon gave way to sobs of helplessness. Tony's constant jealous tirades, followed by intense sex, had driven her to leave. Promises to do better and gifts, including a house and a car, changed her mind. She'd been covering her tears for eight years, when Wes arrived and rescued her from Monroe, Tony, and Sumter, South Carolina.

Grace applied the finishing touches to her makeup, got dressed, and headed out for dinner alone. She hadn't spoken to Wes since the night she'd put him out, and she hadn't stopped crying since. Wes wasn't a pimple or a blemish, but life without him in it was destined to leave a scar.

Grace heard a knock at the back door when she reached the bottom of the staircase. She looked through the peephole. It was Wes's friend Mack, her boss.

"Sorry, I'm late. I see you're all ready to go!" Mack said when she opened the door. "I told Wes to tell you I'd be here at seven thirty, but traffic was backed up on the Andrew Jackson. By the way, thank you for accepting the dinner invitation. I know I should have asked you myself, but Wes has a better way with words."

Grace knitted her eyebrows together and scrunched up her nose. "I'm not sure I heard you right. Did you just say you were here to take me out?"

"You mean Wes didn't tell you?" Mack looked embarrassingly uncomfortable. "Please forgive me. He told me he had arranged everything with you."

"It's not your fault."

They stared at each other for a few awkward seconds that seemed like an eternity.

"Forgive my rude manners. I don't know where my mind was. Please, come in." She opened the door. "When did you last talk to Wes?"

"Earlier today. In fact, he asked me to give you this."

Mack handed Grace a pastel yellow envelope with her name written across the front.

A smile formed in the right corner of her mouth. Wes had remembered how much she loved pastel yellow envelopes. She opened the envelope and unfolded the sheet of paper.

Dear Grace,

Saying I'm sorry seems trite, but those are the only two words that come close to expressing the remorse I have felt since Thursday. As much as I have tried to forget the look of disappointment that swept across your face, it has been etched indelibly in my memory.

Ever since that night you asked me to take you away from Sumter, I have always wanted to show you that a guy could love and appreciate you without attachments or demands. Our feelings got the best of us, and things went much further than either of us anticipated. For that, I am truly sorry.

I don't blame you for putting me out. I would have done the same. You deserve a man who can treat you better. One who can give you his all. Even if I tried, I could never accomplish such a task.

Grace, if there are any two people who were meant for each other, it's you and Mack. He's not me, and for that, you should be thankful. He's a great guy and a wonderful friend. He's deserving of someone as caring and loving as you.

I didn't tell him about us. I hope that can be a secret we keep between friends.

Love,

Wes

P.S. If Mack doesn't have a problem with it, I sure could use an experienced female assistant.

Grace sniffed then wiped a tear from her right eye with a napkin. She put the note back in the envelope and stuffed it in her purse.

"I accept your invitation, Mr. McIntyre. I can't stay out too late; Doug will have a fit if I'm late in the morning." Grace smiled bashfully.

"Please call me Bobby. As for Doug, I'll take care of him."

CHAPTER 59
THURSDAY, FEBRUARY 4, 1993

H OLLY CUPPED HER HAND over her mouth to keep from spitting out the soda she was drinking. "The laptop is here in the building? Are you frigging serious?"

Phil shrugged. "It was here last night. Malcolm traced the call back to the switchboard, which means it was routed through the PBX system."

Holly's plan to slide another inconspicuous message under Phil's door before he made it into the office had derailed when she saw his door open and the lights on. The office wouldn't begin to show signs of activity for another thirty minutes, so they closed the door and huddled in his office to discuss the latest updates.

"Any idea who it is?"

"Just the usual suspects. No real leads to go on, though." Phil paused to contemplate his next question. "Can you hack into the PBX system? If we can get our hands on the system call log, we can see what extension they were using."

"It's been a while since I've hacked a PBX system. I'll check it out tonight."

"Thanks. We're running out of time, and we need every break we can get."

"Here." Holly handed Phil a brown interoffice delivery envelope.

"What's this?" Phil asked while opening the envelope.

[240]

"A draft of Jack Sherman's speech. Before you read it, I need to warn you; it's terribly offensive and frightening."

"Thanks for the warning. But, trust me, I've seen my fair share of offensive, racist material. It doesn't scare me." Phil pulled the pages from the envelope and began reading. By the time he finished, he could no longer hide his anger and disbelief. He attempted to say something, but the words he was looking for escaped him. Phil closed his eyes, pinching the bridge of his nose.

Holly folded her arms across her chest and leaned back against the door. She looked on helplessly, nodding her head. "I told you."

"This is more serious than I thought. He's calling for a destabilization of the workforce as a way to counter gains made through affirmative action legislation."

"Did you see that outlandish claim he made about businesses having to hire more people to account for the lack of productivity brought on by hiring affirmative action candidates?" Holly walked over to the desk and pointed to a paragraph near the bottom of the second page. "Right here is where he really chaps my butt. 'Many hiring managers state that their payrolls have doubled in the past year. This can primarily be attributed to the loss of productivity caused by hiring individuals whose only tangible skill is that they're minorities.' That's some racist BS, and he knows it."

"That isn't the only shit Sherman's spreading. Why did ITI go through the effort of hiring me and all these other minorities, if all they're going to do is lay us off in the end? Doesn't that sound like a strange thing to do? Especially since we know he was getting money under the table from family and friends to hire us in the first place."

Holly combed a strand of hair behind her ear with her finger. "What are you suggesting we do?"

"We've got to get that laptop back." Phil gathered the pages and secured them in his briefcase. "If we can find it before Stanley or Vincent, then we might have a chance at convincing Jack Sherman not to go forward with this speech."

"You're the PhantomPhixer. If anyone can pull this off, it's you." Holly winked and walked out.

CHAPTER 60

"**O**KAYYY … OKAYYY …" Vincent said in that tone every parent makes after being bombarded with relentless requests to go outside. "I'll be down there shortly … Yes, I still want to see it … No, no. There's nothing wrong ... Really. I'm fine, Russ … See you in a minute." Vincent dropped the phone handset back into the cradle. "As if I didn't have enough problems in my life already."

Two years, seven months, and eleven days. That's how long it had taken to bring his brilliant idea to fruition. Unfortunately, none of that mattered if he couldn't get his hands on Malcolm's laptop within the next twenty-four hours.

He pushed open the double glass doors of the security office suite. The lights were on, but the place looked deserted. The morning crew was out, making their second patrol of the morning. A counter with overhead cabinets was to his left. On the counter was a box with two stale powdered donuts inside. A stainless steel dual pot coffeemaker was at the far end of the counter. A half-full pot of coffee, so thick and black it could lubricate a Hemi engine, was on the top warmer. Someone had attempted to cover up the burnt coffee smell with pine-scented air freshener. It resulted in a smell so nauseating, Vincent had to cover his nose and mouth with a handkerchief to keep from emptying his stomach. He darted through the door to his right, hung a quick left, and raced for the door at the end of the hallway.

Russ opened the door before Vincent had a chance to knock. "Right in here, Mr. Martello. I've got everything all set up for you."

"Good," Vincent replied between deep breaths to fill his lungs with non-lethal air. "I don't have a second to waste." He stuffed the handkerchief inside an inner coat pocket.

A thirty-two-inch television was mounted high on the front wall. A grainy black and white still frame with PAUSE stamped in the top corner displayed on the screen.

Vincent stood in front of the TV with his arms folded. "Show me what you've got."

Russ controlled the remote and narrated from the rear of the office. Vincent ignored Russ's hapless observations, focusing his attention, instead, on the details of each frame.

When they got to the footage of an African American man exiting the elevator with Malcolm, Vincent moved closer to the television screen. The black guy held Malcolm up with one arm while pressing his other hand against Malcolm's midsection. It was difficult to see if he had a gun, the lighting was poor and the picture was grainy. The video transitioned to a camera located at the hotel's entrance, where the lighting and picture were noticeably better. Malcolm and their mystery man came into view. Their heads were lowered as they made a mad dash for the exit. Vincent had all but given up hope on IDing their suspect, when the thief looked up, right into the camera.

"Stop!" Vincent commanded. "That's our guy."

"Do you know him?" Russ stood next to Vincent, eagerly awaiting his next command.

"No, but I've got a damn good idea who will. Get me a printout of that frame ASAP."

Russ moved quickly to open the door. "Will do, Mr. Martello!"

CHAPTER 61

"THERE'S A ONE-WAY TICKET to Leavenworth with your name printed on it, you wannabe gangster." Vincent smiled at the glossy black-and-white photo Russ had dropped off at his office.

He pressed a button on the phone. "Marcia, call Robert Berry. Tell him I need to see him in my office ASAP."

Vincent looked closely at the man in the photograph. The picture was fuzzy but not so distorted that he wouldn't be able to ID him in a police lineup when the time came. The more he studied the photo, the more he noticed something vaguely familiar about the man, especially his eyes. He held the photo up an elbow's length away to get a better view. "Why do I feel like I know you? It's like we've crossed paths. But where?"

"Excuse me, Mr. Martello. Mr. Sherman is here to see you," the secretary announced through the intercom.

Startled by the interruption, Vincent sat up in his chair and hurriedly stuffed the picture into the top desk drawer. "Please, send him in."

The disconcerted look etched on Jack's face when he entered the office didn't come close to expressing the anxiety and distress he was going through. His normally tanned skin appeared pale and jaundiced. His energetic blue eyes were now sunken and dull.

"Come in. Have a seat. You're here an hour earlier than I anticipated, and by that down-in-the-dump look on your face, I definitely understand why." Vincent greeted his mentor with a good-natured grin, hoping it would extinguish his fears.

Jack ignored the small talk and got right to the point of his visit. "Where are we on WorldNet?" His voice sounded gravelly and exhausted, like he hadn't slept in days.

"We've got a good lead on the suspect, sir. I should have a name shortly. After that, I'll contact the authorities so they can make an arrest and retrieve the stolen property," Vincent replied, hoping the welcoming news would shake Jack out of his current stupor.

"Uh huh." Jack's tone was distant, and so were his thoughts. "Vincent, I've been your biggest supporter — "

"Don't think for a minute that I don't appreciate that and everything else you've done for me," Vincent interrupted.

Jack stared at the floor, rubbing his chin. "I know you do," he said in a soft, reserved tone that was more introspective than an acknowledgment.

"C'mon, Jack. Cheer up! Haven't you heard a word I've said? We're about to apprehend the punk who stole Malcolm's laptop. This time tomorrow, we will have put all this behind us. I assure you, we'll be focusing on bigger and better things."

Jack placed both hands on Vincent's desk and leaned forward. "I'm glad you said that because that's the reason I'm here. I stopped by to let you know that tomorrow, deal or no deal, I will be stepping down, effective immediately. For all our sake, especially yours, I hope you're right about tomorrow."

• • • •

Vincent downed a shot of bourbon. It was his second shot since Jack had dropped the breaking news in his lap and walked out without so much as an explanation for the hasty decision.

The urgency in finding their suspect and recovering the laptop and its prized contents had risen to a new stratosphere because of Jack's epiphany. The pressure was enough to make even the most self-confident man wave a white flag and surrender. He'd thought about it a time or two, especially after the attack on Malcolm. But life had taken an unexpected turn since meeting Roxanne.

He glanced at his watch. "Hurry up, Robert!"

The door opened. Robert's long leg burst in, followed by the rest of his body as he squeezed through the tight doorway and past the secretary. A gas bubble exploded, making his stomach rumble like an off-balance washing machine. A smile that was already pitiful drooped lower. The secretary closed the door, pretending not to have noticed.

"Robert, you're just the man I need to see." Vincent grinned and gave Robert a playful pat on the arm.

"I came right up," Robert stuttered, still reeling from Vincent's ruthless behavior during their last meeting. Just to be safe, he looked out the corner of his eye to see if Vincent was holding anything sharp.

"Can I get you something to drink?" Vincent pointed to the assortment of crystal canisters lined across the top of the minibar.

"No, thank you. I can't drink on an empty stomach." Robert checked his watch. "You do realize it's only a quarter to eleven, don't you?"

[247]

Vincent chuckled. "It's after five o' clock somewhere." He returned to his desk and removed the photo from the drawer. "We can drink later. The booze will taste better anyway. I needed you up here because I was able to get ahold of a photo of our suspect. Can you believe he looked right into one of the cameras at the hotel? He's a pretty stupid crook, right? Anyhow, I need you to ID this guy for me." He handed Robert the eight-by-ten glossy.

Robert let out a small gasp when he saw what appeared to be a younger looking Wes staring back at him. He glanced across the desk to see if Vincent had noticed his surprised reaction.

"So, who is he?" Vincent asked when Robert looked up.

"I don't know," Robert lied.

"What do you mean you don't know him?" Vincent shouted, no longer able to conceal his frustration. "You hired this black piece of shit. It's your fucking job to know who he is.

Robert swallowed hard. *"I guess you'll believe me now,"* he heard Wes whisper from the distant ether. His Adam's apple bobbed up and down at the sound of Wes's voice. "Honestly, I've never seen him before. I can't say that I recall anyone fitting his description around here."

"That's not what I'm hearing." Vincent slammed the drawer shut and stood up. "I've got reliable sources telling me they've seen *that* guy in *this* building." He poked the air and stabbed the desk to emphasize his point.

"I'm not saying those people aren't telling you the truth. I'm simply saying, for some people around here, one black man's face is the same as any other. As far as they're concerned, we all look alike." Robert lowered his shoulders and exhaled. "Just a few more hours; that's all I'm asking. Give me a couple of hours to ask around. If he's here, I promise you I'll find him. The last thing you want to do is arrest the wrong guy. You may never find your laptop if that happens." He allowed the silence to penetrate. Convincing Vincent to give him more time was his primary objective. That and calling Wes as soon as he got back to his office.

Vincent considered his options. If Russ and his security flunkies fingered the wrong guy, it would only make matters worse. He couldn't afford to let the laptop slip through his fingers because an overzealous bunch of Barney Fifes miscalculated. "Can you find him?"

"I'll do my best." Robert allowed a small grin to escape as he turned to leave.

"For all our sake, I hope your best is good enough," Vincent shouted before Robert opened the door.

CHAPTER 62

DURHAM, NC

WES SAT IN HIS OFFICE, legs propped on top of the desk. He'd been in the same reclined position for the past several hours, looking out the window, watching the sun ascend over the horizon. The last bit of fog had dissipated an hour ago. Now, the sun's beam was inching its way to the heel of his shoe.

The front door was locked tight, and the waiting room was darker than midnight in Gotham City. A faint, bitter aroma of day-old coffee lingered in the air. The receptionist hadn't been in all week. He'd met her at the front door when she arrived for work at the beginning of the week, handed her a check, and gave her the rest of the week off.

A window provided the only light in what was an otherwise dark, empty, silent office. He wanted it that way. Silence was nature's way of comforting a soul in chaos.

He looked up and over his shoulder at the clock on the wall behind his desk. He let out a slow, laborious exhale. "Damn, not even ten o'clock. Looks like it's going to be another one of those slow, drag-through-hell days," he mused aloud, returning his attention to the heavenly view outside his window.

With a casual laziness, Wes drummed his fingers across the faded yellow pages of a thick leather-bound journal that lay open on his desk.

"As if I wasn't going through enough shit already. Puddin's gone stone outta her goddamn mind. I can't believe she kicked me out after all these years." He shook his head in disbelief. "And in front of the kids, too."

A vision of Linda Albright smiling, with his head buried between her titties appeared in his mind's eye. "She must've found out about Linda. That's the only thing it could be. But how? That was a spur of the moment meeting. I didn't see any familiar faces in the bar. And I paid the bar tab with cash just to avoid getting a receipt. We didn't stop anywhere after we left. We spent the rest of the night at—"

Wes slammed his fist down on the open journal.

"That lowdown muthafuka, Vic! I should've known better than to ask his snitching ass for a favor."

Wes felt his pager vibrating on his hip. He popped the pager from its clip, held it at a distance, and then moved it back and forth like a trombone slide to get a good look at the numbers. Keeping his eyes on the digital readout, he fumbled around the desk with his other hand, looking for his glasses. Then he remembered they were on top of his head and pulled them down.

The blurry numbers sharpened as they came into focus.

"Now, he pages me!" Wes exclaimed as soon as he recognized the number.

Robert was turning out to be the worrisome client Wes had always suspected. Nevertheless, he was relieved to see Robert was finally resurfacing after being AWOL for over a week.

Wes reached for the phone. A pain shot through his lower back. He dropped the handset as his body stiffened against the penetrating spasms above his tailbone.

He sat motionless, his face flush against the desktop, sucking in small gasps of air through clenched teeth.

Wes considered his current situation and began to pray. "Lord, I know I deserve a whole lot more than this pain. And when you take into account all the trifling, low down things I've done, I oughta be the last one asking for mercy. But seeing as though I was only doing this to keep my son from following in my footsteps and engaging in the debauchery that comes with it, can you please not withhold your grace? Ease this afflicted child's pain one more time, if You would be so kind. Lord, and while you're at it, can you please soften Puddin's heart, so I can go back home before Mama comes home because you and I both know, I'll never hear the end of it if she finds out I've been staying at her house. Lord, I guess what I'm saying is I don't care how you do it, just get me home and back to my bed."

The pain finally eased after a few minutes. With one hand pressed firmly against his side, he gingerly lifted himself upright.

The phone handset was on the desk, in the same place he'd dropped it. Carefully, he reached for the handset and brought it to his ear. He pressed the hook switch a few times with his thumb to get a dial tone.

Robert answered after the second ring, his voice frantic and high pitched. "Wes, you've got to come quick. They're on to us! They're going to kill me!"

"Robert, slow down! Who's going to kill you?" Wes felt a sharp prick in his back. He grimaced and rubbed his back gently.

"I don't want to call any names. They might be listening."

"Mmm hmm..." Wes said with a calmness that bordered on indifference.

Years of experience had taught him maintaining one's composure was the best position to take whenever a troublesome client dropped off the scene unexpectedly and then called unexpectedly, claiming his life was in jeopardy. It was an occurrence that had happened more times than he cared to recall.

"Wes, I swear to you, everything was going good."

"You don't say."

"Next thing I know, they're telling me some black guy stole a computer, and they're holding me responsible for finding him because I was responsible for vetting all the black employees."

Wes frowned with skepticism. "How are you supposed to find out who did it? I'm sure they gave you a picture or description of the suspect, right?"

"No. They didn't give me anything." Robert closed his eyes and prayed Wes would believe the lie he'd just told. *God, if you get me through this phone call, I swear I'll tell Wes as soon as I see him.*

"What do they expect you to do, pick someone out of thin air? Are you telling me everything?"

"I swear I didn't do anything wrong." Robert's voice trembled.

Wes took a couple of deep breaths and massaged his temples with his thumb and middle finger. "Robert, do me a favor; stop telling me you haven't done anything wrong. If you haven't done anything wrong, you wouldn't be calling me."

Robert sniffed. "I know you don't believe me, but I'm telling you the truth. It wasn't my fault. You're all I've got, Wes. They're going to kill me. They told me so."

[253]

Wes got his notepad and looked around for a pen. "Who is this 'they'? And how far to the top are you talking?"

"All the way to the top." Panic caused Robert's normally deep voice to squeak. "Starting with Jack Sherman himself."

"Why would Jack Sherman and those guys want to kill you? As far as they know, you did exactly what you were asked to do. If anything, we have proof that they never attempted to hire students from black schools. That's got to be worth something, right?"

He reached for a pen that was lying in the journal's gutter. Wes examined the page for the first time. Near the top, among the notes, dates, and carefully drawn lines, a name stood out like a donkey running in the Kentucky Derby: JACK SHERMAN JR.

A box was drawn around the name. Solid and dotted lines connected the box with other boxes on the page. He traced a line from Jack's box up to the two boxes above it. Based on the names and dates of birth, Wes concluded these were Jack's parents.

Eager to find sanctuary and a listening ear, Robert offered up every tidbit of information he could remember that didn't include Wes's son. "They're saying some black ITI employee stole a laptop, and I put the guy up to it. They're going to kill me if I don't return it."

Wes held the phone away from his ear. His brow wrinkled from the curious frown pasted on his face. Surely, Robert wasn't talking about Phil.

He looked at the book and remembered Phil saying something about Jack Sherman and a secret group.

"Don't move, Robert. I'm on my way!"

CHAPTER 63

"LOOK OUT, KAREN! A ghost is creeping up behind you," Dana announced when she saw Phil enter the break room.

Karen looked over her shoulder, "Oh, my God, you're right! And it looks just like Phil."

The two ladies erupted in high-pitched laughter.

"Haha. I see you two are full of jokes today," Phil retorted, taking a seat at the head of the table.

"Just saying you have been pretty invisible around here lately." She winked at Karen, who replied to the coded message with a sneaky grin of her own.

"Okay! Okay! I know I've been out of pocket for a few days. I'm just trying to tie up some loose strings before the wedding this weekend."

He considered Dana and Karen as friends. Not only were they friends at the office, he and Ann had gone out with both and their dates a few times. He'd even thought about sharing his suspicions with them but decided it would be best to wait. Dana was an undercover conspiracy theorist, with a tendency to overreact because of some self-initiated fear.

"I don't know what loose strings you're tying up, but it definitely looks like you're untying a certain admin assistant's loose bras and panties."

Karen raised her hand, palm out, and Dana gave her a high-five slap.

"Holly's just a friend," Phil objected. "She's helping me with something."

"Mmm Hmm!" Dana replied. The tone of her voice and the expression on her face were dead giveaways. She was not convinced.

Phil ignored the not-so-subtle insinuation. "Pass the popcorn, please."

Dana filled a white Styrofoam cup with popcorn and passed it to Phil. "Here you go, Mr. In Demand."

"What is that supposed to mean?" He poured out a handful of puffy white corn kernels and poured a few in his mouth.

Dana opened a packet of sugar and sprinkled it over her popcorn. "Just saying a bunch of people have been looking for you today," she said between chomps.

"People like who?"

"Darnell and Jerome, for starters. I ran into them at lunch, and they both asked if I had seen you. They said Robert Berry was looking for you."

"Yeah," said Karen, jumping into the conversation. "And Leslie asked me the same thing when I went down to HR a little while ago."

"Well," Dana said, ready to up the ante, "Robert stopped by my office right before I came here. And he asked me if I had seen you today."

Phil's throat was dry, and his stomach was turning flips. "What does he want?" he asked with hesitancy.

"He didn't say, but it must be serious. As long as I've known Robert, he's always been a rather laidback dude, but he seemed pretty discombobulated."

Phil knew he needed to get out of the office before Robert cornered him. Dana and Karen weren't prying, but it was obvious they wanted to know more. He didn't have time to feed their curiosity. He had to get busy feeding his own.

Phil stood up and tossed the cup in the trash.

"Where are you running off to now?" asked Dana.

"If Robert's looking for me, I guess I better see what he wants," Phil replied on his way out the door.

CHAPTER 64

THE CAMARO'S ENGINE had barely come to a stop by the time Phil was out of the car and through the front door of his father's office.

"Grace? Daddy? Anybody here?" he shouted on his way to the kitchen and some of Grace's 7-Up pound cake.

He sliced a chunk of cake and placed it on a napkin while he went to get milk from the refrigerator. A bowl of flaky, tender fried chicken greeted him when he opened the fridge. Phil grabbed a drumstick and placed it between his teeth while he got the carton of milk. On his way to get a cup, he noticed a family-sized bag of potato chips lying on the counter, folded and clipped closed with a plastic clamp. He got a cup and was halfway across the room when he turned around and picked up the bag.

"Phil, slow down, baby!" Grace kidded when she entered the kitchen. "You're going to make yourself sick, stuffing all that food down at once. You must be nervous about the wedding. You only eat like this when you're nervous." Grace wrapped an arm around his shoulders and hugged tightly.

"Have you seen Daddy?" Phil stuffed the last piece of cake into his mouth and wiped his hands.

"I haven't seen him, but I have talked to him. He's at the main office. Been there all week."

"Damn! I was hoping he'd be here." His body went limp as the last grasp of hope fizzled out.

"I'm sure he'll be here tomorrow," Grace said enthusiastically, hoping to cheer him up. "Your wedding is the day after tomorrow, and he's not missing it for anything. It's all he seems to talk about."

Phil leaned back against the pantry door. "The way shit's spiraling out of control, I doubt if there's going to be a wedding," he mumbled, staring at the floor and shaking his head.

"What do you mean there's not going to be a wedding? Of course, there is. Why wouldn't there be?"

Phil looked up, right into Grace's waiting stare. He stumbled to find an answer, but all he kept hearing was, *"Don't do anything to mess up this great opportunity."* His father's warning had been on a constant loop since he sped out of the office garage.

Grace frowned. "Phil, sweetheart, you don't look so well. What's the matter?"

Feeling deflated and defeated, Phil slumped his shoulders. "I just messed up big time. Daddy told me not to do something, but I did it anyway. Now the thing he told me not to let happen is about to happen. Daddy's going to go crazy. He'll probably kill me for sure this time. Then, Mama's going to look at me all pitiful-like and declare I can't help it that I'm acting just like Daddy. Once Ann sees this mess, there's no way she's going through with a wedding. No one in their right mind would. I'm screwed."

Grace dismissed the woeful response with a wave of her hand. "First off, your mama's right, you and your daddy are opposite sides of the same coin. How neither one of you notices it is beyond me. As for Ann, there's no way she's going to pass up a chance to marry a good-looking, intelligent, and kind man like you.

"Now, as for your daddy and how he's going to get mad if something happens: If you want my opinion, I think that as long as it hasn't happened yet, then you're smart enough to make sure it doesn't happen. I know your daddy thinks you're smart enough. He brags about you all the time. So, if he told you not to let it happen, then doggonit, don't let it happen."

The last two weeks had been one continuous chase, and the only thing Phil figured he had to show for his efforts was becoming the hunted. He knew if he was going to have any chance at turning things around, he was going to have to face his fears head on. "You're right, Grace! It's time I handle my own problems, instead of asking Daddy to fix it every time. That's exactly what I'm going to do, but I'm going to need your help with one little thing, though."

"Sure. What do you need?"

"I need Robert Berry's address."

Grace stopped stirring her tea. "Who is Robert Berry? And why would I have his address?" she asked with a noticeable hesitancy.

Phil walked around to the opposite side of the island counter, where Grace was standing. He smiled to suppress laughing at the shocked expression she couldn't hide. "Come on, Grace. I know you know Robert Berry. I know you've been babysitting him every time he goes into the diner."

Grace's hands flew over her wide-open mouth. Her saucer-sized eyes stared at him as if he were some sort of alien.

He leaned on the counter on one forearm. "I also know Daddy and Robert know each other well enough to have drinks together, which means Daddy knows where Robert lives. You and

I both know Daddy wouldn't take a meeting without first knowing where the person lived and worked."

Grace stood mesmerized by Phil's revelation. Then she remembered what Wes had said, *"I know my son. He's not going to quit until he gets to the bottom of this shit. When that day comes, I just want to be sure that he doesn't find my ass in the middle of it."*

Grace laughed and shook her head in disbelief. "Lord, have mercy! Your father was right all along."

"Right about what?" Phil frowned, trying to decipher her coded message.

"Nothing. Let me go get that address for you." Grace walked off, still shaking her head and laughing.

CHAPTER 65

THE DUSKY SKY — a gradient mixture of orange, purple, blue, and black—created a soothing backdrop for the airport lights and the full moon that hung over the skyline. Phil zipped past cars and eighteen wheelers as he headed northwest on Interstate 485.

He glanced over at his sister. "C'mon, Roxy, what's up?"

"Nothing. Just drive, okay?" Roxy replied, staring straight ahead.

Phil drove on, peeking over at her every few minutes, but saying nothing.

His sister was getting harder to understand by the day. When he called to tell her his plan and ask her to ride along so he could update her on the laptop, he knew she'd jump at the chance. As expected, she was gung-ho about the whole idea.

She was far from excited when he'd picked her up. He attempted to make small talk and even went so far as to tell her about the laptop being in the building and what he'd learned about Jack Sherman and his upcoming speech, but she just sat there, never interrupting, staring into the distance.

They slowed down in front of a house. The red brick ranch-style house sat on a spacious, neatly manicured two-acre lot. Spruce trees outlined a cemented path to the front door. Evenly trimmed hedges created a four-foot border along the front of the house.

They passed a matching brick mailbox. "Eleven thirty-four. This is it. This is Robert's house."

"So, what's your plan now, Lil' Wes?" Roxy asked, surveying their surroundings.

Phil ignored her sarcasm. "I can't just walk up to the door and ring the doorbell and say, 'Hi Robert. I hear you've been looking for me.'"

"Why not?"

"Because you never go into a place blindly. Daddy never does it, and I'm not going to do it, either." He looked up and down the street. We can't stay here. I saw a park on that road we came in on. There's got to be some nature trails that run through those trees. I believe I see an opening over there." He pointed to his right. "We should be able to find a spot that will give us a good view of the house and provide plenty cover."

"Boy, I didn't come out here to entertain you by playing some undercover Rambo game. I am not walking through them damn woods. I don't walk through the woods in the daytime; so, you know I ain't going in there at night." She frowned and twisted her lips.

Phil turned around and drove to the park. He pulled into the parking lot and parked in front of three picnic benches covered by canopies.

He killed the engine and then turned to his sister. "For the record, I know you're only interested in getting the laptop back for Vincent. To be honest with you, it doesn't even matter, I just want Malcolm to get his code back so he can sell his software, and I can move on. If we get the money, I'd take it and start my own business so I wouldn't have to put up with this bullshit again." He popped the trunk and climbed out.

Phil went through a final check of his knapsack. All the essential stakeout tools—a flashlight (with new batteries), mosquito repellant, and a pair of binoculars—were on hand. Next, he lifted the trunk's floorboard and pulled out a plastic case that was about the size of a cigar box. He retrieved the revolver from the case, loaded it, and threw it in his duffel. When he closed the trunk, Roxy was leaning against the rear fender with her arms crossed.

"I can't believe I'm letting you talk me into this crazy idea."

When they reached the entrance to the trail, Phil turned on the flashlight and looked through the trees to see if he could see Robert's house.

"Follow me. This is the trail that leads to Robert's house."

Roxy clutched Phil's hand and followed the flashlight's beam. Pine cones crunched and twigs snapped as they walked carefully down the manmade trail. Phil stopped ten feet from the trail's exit and set up their stakeout location. Robert's house was across the street, about half a football field distance away.

Roxy started slapping her forearms. "Dammit! I don't know why I listened to you. Got me out here in these damn woods, with all the damn mosquitoes!"

Phil opened the knapsack and tossed her a can. "Here's some mosquito repellant. Don't spray too much. The wind will carry the scent."

Roxy sprayed her arms and her circumference.

"I told you don't spray too much," Phil whispered in a gruff tone.

Roxy gave the spray top two quick pumps and handed the can back to Phil. "So what do we do now, Lil' Wes?"

"I'm going to wait, while you annoy the hell out of me for the rest of the night."

CHAPTER 66

VINCENT PACED the width of his office, rotating a pair of Baoding balls in his right hand. It was after five, and he still hadn't heard from Robert. "I trusted him. He was running errands and doing grunt work when I got here. I got him a corporate credit, and this is how he pays me back?" He switched the steel balls to his other hand and continued pacing.

After the meeting with Robert, he'd been behind locked doors all afternoon.

Pacing … Drinking.

Contemplating ... Drinking.

Plotting ... More drinking.

By six o' clock, it was apparent Robert wasn't coming and was more than likely hiding out somewhere. His plans for a future with Roxanne were slipping away with each passing minute. It was supposed to be their last night at Frank's for a long while. Instead of planning a celebration, he now wondered if there was such a thing as a future without Roxanne at his side to share in it.

Vincent leaned back in his chair and downed the rest of his bourbon. He'd drank enough so that his drunkenness was like the message in the side view mirror: closer than it appeared.

His anger boiled as he looked across his desk at the spot where Robert stood earlier. "Robert, how could you do this to me? I trusted you, and what did I get in return? You lied to me. You looked me right in the fucking eyes and lied. I knew it as soon as you said it. I saw how you ..."

He frowned as he tried to bring the memory into focus. Frame by frame, he replayed the whole scene. Then he remembered handing Robert the photo. "The sonofabitch flinched when he saw it! He knows!"

Thirty minutes later, he'd finalized the plans for his next move. He called Roxanne before heading out. His body and soul melted at the sound of her voice. They made plans to meet later at Frank's. Then Roxanne brought up the missing laptop.

"I believe I'm really close to finding the laptop. I'll know a lot more by the time I see you at Frank's. Just sit tight, Vinny. I got this."

"Roxanne, you don't understand. I've got everything riding on this, most of all, you. I love you. How can I just sit here?"

Roxanne's heart leaped to her throat then plunged to her clitoris. She pressed the phone against her pelvis and moaned before placing it back to her ear. "Vinny, I don't date clients; so, if you want me as bad as you claim, I'm going to need you to sit still so I can close your case."

"But, Roxanne, you don't understand," Vincent pleaded.

"No! Listen to me," Roxanne interrupted. "You've been drinking. I can tell by the way you're talking. I don't want you going anywhere but home. Promise me you're going straight home."

Neither said anything for twenty stiflingly silent seconds.

Finally, Vincent said, "I promise."

He hung up the phone then poured another drink. With one long gulp, he downed it all. Then he set the tumbler down hard against the desk. "I promise ... I'll do everything in my power to give us the future we deserve."

The liquor ignited a healthy dose of boldness to go with the fear and desperation that was also raging. He grabbed the Smith & Wesson Model 64 from his bottom desk drawer and stood up. "Robert, you better hope that laptop turns up before I find you."

• • • •

Vincent turned off his headlights and drove slowly past Robert's house. He noticed the house was dark, except for two rooms on the left wing. He rounded the cul-de-sac, parked in front of the house, and got out.

He looked down both ends of the street. There were two houses further up the street, on the right, near the entrance. Robert's house sat between two huge vacant lots. On the other side of the street, branches from a big oak tree covered the nearest street light.

On a hunch that it might be worth his while to take a look inside before ringing the doorbell, Vincent staggered across the yard. He was halfway across when a security light blinded him in his tracks. Vincent stood wide-eyed like a deer on a dark interstate with an eighteen-wheeler bearing down on it. He remained motionless for all of five seconds then stumbled awkwardly for cover.

He found refuge in a darkened corner against the hedges. His heart was beating faster than a locomotive rolling through the cornfields of Nebraska. Billows of bourbon-laced steam—from the double shot of Maker's Mark he'd drank on the way over—rose from his lips and nostrils and then drifted into nothingness.

Vincent breathed a big sigh of relief when he realized he was all alone. He leaned forward, rested both hands on his knees, and took a couple of big breaths.

It was a chilly Carolina night. The half-moon hovering above a water tower in the distance provided just enough light to make a flashlight unnecessary. The first room with a light was twenty feet ahead. As much as he wanted to take a look inside, the security light kept him barricaded in the corner. With nothing else to do, he crouched down and waited for the light to go off.

His thoughts quickly turned to Roxanne, or more specifically, the thought of losing her. The last few weeks had been nothing short of fantastic. The smell of her perfume mixed with cocoa butter still lingered in his memory. He longed to taste the saltiness of her sweat and the tanginess of her love juices. The sex was great, but it was all the other things he'd learned about her that interested him most. Never had he encountered a woman so ruthlessly cunning, ambitious, and passionate. She was truly his equal. As much as he wanted to believe Roxanne's feelings about him were mutual, there was no way she was going to stick around once he was penniless, unemployed, and a laughingstock. He squeezed his eyes shut and shook his head in an attempt to drive the depressive thought from his head.

"Robert, you gotta come through for me. If you help me get the laptop back, I'll let bygones be bygones. I swear to you. Just help me get it back. Please!" he prayed softly.

The security light shut off. Vincent stood up and shook the stiffness from his legs like a sprinter standing at the starter's block. Taking every precaution not to trip the sensor again, he pressed his back against the manicured shrubbery and inched his way to the first window. He searched the curtain-covered window for an opening that would let him see inside. As hard as he tried, he couldn't see a thing. The curtains were drawn tight.

He squatted down on his hands and knees and bear crawled to the next window. There was an opening about two inches high between the bottom of the blinds and the window sill. Vincent lifted his head above the window sill. He gasped and then ducked down quickly; Robert was sitting at the kitchen table. He thought about what he'd just seen and slowly lifted himself again. There was Robert, still sitting in the same face-down-on-the-table position. Judging from the empty liquor bottle, he wasn't going to be lifting his head any time soon.

Using the blade of a pocketknife, Vincent popped the screen out of its groove and placed it aside. He nudged the window up a few inches. Robert let out a snore that sounded more like a boar grunting than anything else. He removed the revolver from the inside pocket of his jacket and used the nose of the gun to lift the blinds. The house was still and quiet, except for an occasional glass-rattling snore from Robert.

"Robert, we need to get an early start in the—" a male voice said.

Vincent snatched the gun out of the window, causing the blinds to flop down and bang against the window.

He stepped back a half-step.

Out of nowhere, a roach flew into his face and landed on his lips. Vincent sputtered, spit, and flung his arms excitedly as he continued to back away from the window. The roach fluttered and crawled its way onto his nose, then his eye.

He stopped suddenly when he realized he'd tripped the security light once again.

In the midst of all the commotion going on in the house, Vincent heard his name.

Robert and his accomplices were on to him. Had Robert been setting a trap for him by pretending he was sleeping? How many people were inside?

Fear gripped him. It felt as if his legs were about to collapse under the pressure. It would be only a matter of seconds before they were outside.

Vincent looked up at the glaring light and shielded his eyes.

He heard a loud *POOF!*

Everything went black. Scared out of his mind, Vincent closed his eyes and fired at the house before spinning on his heels and running for the car.

CHAPTER 67

W HEN WES ARRIVED at Robert's house, Robert was nursing a bottle of Jack Daniels. By the time he was walking out to go meet Vic Bannister, Robert was sitting on the couch, well on his way to a drunken stupor.

"Wes... *HICCUP*... tell me; is all this my fault? I know it ain't ... *HICCUP* ... 'cause you'd tell me if it was, right? *Youuu* damn right, you would!"

Wes looked at the empty bottle on the coffee table and shook his head. "That goddamn Jack will make a fool outta you every time."

He grabbed the empty bottle and left Robert sitting on the couch. "Sit tight. I'll be right back," he shouted before closing the door.

Thirty minutes later, Robert started paging him. By the time Wes returned, Robert had paged him twenty times.

When Wes walked in, Robert was sitting at the kitchen table, muttering to himself. A bottle of Crown Royal sat before him.

"You're not going to have to worry about anyone else killing you, you're about to kill your damn self," he said, nudging Robert on the shoulder.

"Either way, I'm dead," Robert slobbered. Ashy white streaks ran down his cheeks.

Wes looked at him sternly and said, "And as long as you keep wasting time trying to convince me that it isn't your fault, instead of telling me what is your fault, you might want to add me to the list of possible killers."

"You wouldn't kill me, would you, Wes? Remember, you said we weren't just doing a good thing; we were doing the right thing. You wouldn't kill a person for doing right, would you?"

Wes ignored the question. "Why were you paging me so much?"

Robert turned solemn. "I was afraid," he said. Then his chin fell against his chest and stayed there.

"I told you I would spend the night. I hope you don't make me regret making that decision." He took Robert's glass. "Something tells me this is going to be a long night," he said on his way to the guestroom, while Robert slept it off.

Wes was happy to find a comfortable bed after sleeping on that old, lumpy mattress at his mother's house. He sat on the edge of the bed, with his arms folded across his legs, staring at the floor. He began to pray. "God, I know I was wrong for sticking my nose in Your business, but please don't hold it against me for trying to steer Phil away from following in my steps. I know what a toll this work has taken on me. I don't want the same for him. If I'm wrong, I'm sorry. I was only doing what I believed a good father would."

A tear rolled down his eyelash and fell softly against the carpet.

He reached for his handkerchief on the nightstand. That's when he saw the envelope inside the black notepad.

In his rush to get back to Robert, he'd forgotten all about the envelope he'd gotten from Juanita, an old friend who worked in the county's records department. She'd been there for years and pretty much ran the place. So far, she'd trained her last five managers.

He unsealed the envelope and pulled out two sheets of paper. Each was a photocopy of a birth certificate.

"I'll. Be. Damned. Right under their noses," he mumbled as he looked back and forth between the two pages.

Wes walked down the narrow hallway to the kitchen.

"Robert, we need to get an early start in the—"

He stopped when he saw Robert lying face down on the table, snoring. The blinds banged against the windowsill. Wes looked up. The blinds were swinging. He heard someone outside the window.

"Robert, get up! Somebody's outside!"

He pulled Robert up by the shoulder, causing the chair to tumble over on its side. Robert's arm flew wildly, knocking the bottle of Crown Royal off the table. Stumbling backward, they bumped hard against the wall, then fell into a heap on the floor.

Wes rolled from under Robert, then scrambled to take cover behind the chair.

"Wes, you gon' *prah'tek* me?"

Wes looked over his shoulder. Robert had managed to stagger to his feet and was leaning back against the wall. He heard glass breaking and something that sounded like a man screaming.

"Robert, get down!"

Wes scrambled on his hands and knees to get to Robert. He fell flat on his belly and covered his head when he heard the earthshaking boom of a pistol, followed by the loud clatter of glass hitting the floor and splintering.

He looked up just in time to see Robert's legs buckle underneath him, and he began a slow slide down the wall, falling to the floor.

A hole about the size of a poker chip was in the wall. Just below it was a splotch of blood. Crimson trails streamed down the wall.

Wes crawled to the wall then raised up on one knee and turned off all the kitchen lights.

Using the chair as a shield, Wes pushed it toward the window. He snatched the nickel-plated snub nose .38 from the holster strapped to his right calf. He looked out the window, but all was quiet and dark. A car's engine roared in the distance.

Robert moaned with agony as the pain from the wound and his drunken stupor collided in his throat.

Wes raced back to Robert and turned on the lights. Robert lay writhing in pain, with a bullet wound to the shoulder. Wes found a pillow cushion and propped it under Robert's head. "Robert, you better not die on me. If you do, I swear to God I'll yank you from the heavenly gates and kick your ass for all the shit you've put me through."

CHAPTER 68

EXCEPT FOR ROXY'S annoying gripes—the mosquitoes, the chilly temperature, and, finally, Phil's lack of preparation in planning a stakeout (she was hungry, and he hadn't packed any snacks)—the evening was actually quiet and uneventful.

Roxy lobbed her next complaint when she leaned against a tree and took a shoe off. "My feet hurt!" she announced, wiggling her toes.

Phil slammed his fist to the ground. He'd reached his limit. As much as he didn't want to believe it, his father had been right all along. Conducting an investigation with a woman, especially his sister, was a disaster. "What the fuck do you want me to do about it?"

Roxy, sensing her brother was no longer in the mood for constant badgering, relaxed and let out a big sigh. "I don't want you to do anything. I apologize if I'm getting on your nerves."

Phil looked over at his sister. "It's okay. Sorry for hollering at you."

Roxy had always been the take charge type, the one who always had a plan laid out, and the one who always had an answer ready. The past few hours, she'd been nothing close to her normal self. Of course, with Roxy, one was never sure if she was using the moment to hone her acting skills.

After a brief silence, Roxy let out a small, exasperated sigh. "I still don't know how you call yourself planning a stakeout and you don't bring chairs and something to eat."

Phil dug into the pocket of his hoodie and pulled out a candy bar. He broke it in half and handed her a piece. "Okay. Will that hold you?"

Roxy grabbed it. "I knew your greedy ass was hiding some food. You can't fool me."

Phil was chewing on a big wad of chocolate, peanuts, caramel, and nougat when Wes's Eldorado came barreling down the street and swung into Robert's driveway.

Phil swallowed the oversized chunk of candy. "Roxy! That's Daddy!"

"Tell me something I don't know. I told you Daddy was lying. Do you seriously think he's unlocking Robert's back door to go in and talk about worker's comp cases? You're going to listen to me one of these days, little brother."

"So, what do we do now?"

"Once again, this is *your* stakeout. Far be it from me to tell you what to do. Last time I said something, I damn near got my head chewed off."

"Shut up, Roxy. Just shut up. We're going to wait a little while longer. Okay?"

Roxy checked the time on her pager. Her thoughts went back to Vincent, the pressure of not finding the laptop and having his big deal falling apart were causing him to fall apart at the seams. She wanted nothing more than to come through for him, if for no other reason than to get past her "no dating the client" policy, and the five million he had agreed to pay.

Neither were going to happen if they continued to sit in the dark. Finally fed up, she said, "Phil, it's nine thirty. Don't you think it would be better if we focus our attention on finding the laptop? If we find the laptop, are you seriously going to care what Robert Berry has to say? And, for what it's worth, will it matter what Daddy has to say?"

Phil shined a pen-sized flashlight on his watch. "I guess you're right."

A car turned onto the street as he packed his things. The headlights looked like panther's eyes as the car prowled toward them.

Roxy gasped and covered her face.

"What?" Phil tried to stand up but stumbled over himself and fell backward.

"That's Vincent's car."

Phil scrambled to his feet. The black Trans Am turned its lights out, making it nearly impossible to see. It rolled around the cul-de-sac then parked in front of Robert's house.

Vincent exited the car, clad in official henchmen attire: black jeans, black turtleneck, and a black leather jacket.

Roxy couldn't see his face. There wasn't much light, and they were standing at an awkward angle. It didn't matter; she knew it was him.

Vincent started for the front door then crossed the front yard.

With each step he took, Roxy's heart plummeted. Emotions she'd been avoiding for the past few days erupted, and the incapacitating numbness every lover feels at the first sign of betrayal flowed through her veins like hot ice.

A high beam security light snapped on as he walked across the lawn.

Vinny, I love you! Please don't do this! Roxy shouted to herself when she caught a glimpse of Vincent's profile as he ran for cover. She gasped.

Phil rushed to her side. "Did you get a good look? Is it Vincent?" he asked excitedly, barely able to keep his voice above a whisper.

Roxy looked on helplessly, shaking her head ever so slightly.

"What do we do now?" Phil looked around wildly.

"What do we do now?" Roxy frowned. "You've been the one masterminding this whole operation from the beginning, remember? You tell me."

Phil searched through the duffel bag until he found the pellet gun. He stuffed the gun into the pocket of his hoodie and started to walk away.

"Boy, where do you think you're going with that toy gun?"

"What does it look like I'm doing? Since I can't get any help from you, I'm going to stop that deranged sonofabitch myself."

"Not with that pellet gun."

Phil stopped and then looked back over his shoulder. "You have a better suggestion?"

[279]

She dug through her purse and pulled out a leather-covered cylinder. "Here, take this."

Phil grabbed it and held it up to get a good look. "What's this?"

"Pepper spray. That's the real deal, not the kind they advertise in the back of the *National Enquirer*. If you hit him in the face with this, he's going down."

Phil handed Roxy the gun and took off down the street toward the cul-de-sac. When he was parallel to the right side of Robert's house, he darted across the street and hid behind the spruce trees.

Disappointed and hurt, Roxy watched with disinterest as Phil crossed the front yard. She couldn't believe how chaotic things had gotten in the past few weeks. Who would've imagined that the biggest case of her life was going to lead her to the man of her dreams and within a week, she would fall in love and lose it all. *Damn, Vinny! You would have to go and mess up a good thing.*

She'd learned as a small child to be gracious in losing, and she always was, but Roxy hated it, nevertheless. *"If you spend all your time nursing your hurts and disappointments, you'll never have time to nurture your desires and opportunities,"* her acting coach had reminded her when studio executives nixed her role in *LA Law* after she'd been selected. Roxy looked across the street. Phil had already rounded the corner of the house and was stealthily creeping along the darkened perimeter of the house, closing in on Vincent.

From her earliest childhood memories, MiMi claimed that she was the latest proxy of her great-grandfather's spirit. According to legend, Solomon Poindexter was a shrewd businessman, who thrived on catering to the needs of misfortunate souls. Seeing opportunity in any situation was an ability Roxy honed at an early age. This moment wasn't going to be any different.

Just because she'd lost out on love didn't mean she necessarily had to lose out on the five million.

Sure, she was mad at Vincent for lying and attempting to take matters into his own hands. That was a score she would have to settle later. Right now, she needed to make sure they got their hands on that laptop.

She looked on helplessly as Phil, now on his hands and knees, moved in on Vincent like a panther preparing to ambush its unsuspecting prey.

"Phil, you're going to hate me for this, but once you get your cut, I'm sure you're going to forget all about this."

She sprinted across the street to Vincent's car and took a knee behind the front fender. Steadying her elbow on the hood, Roxy gripped the stock with both hands, leveled the pistol, and began a slow, steady countdown in her head.

Four... Three... Two...

When she got to one, she exhaled and pulled the trigger. It seemed as if the pellet were traveling in slow motion.

"Lord, please help a sister out. I promise I won't cheat Phil out of his share," she whispered to herself.

The sound of shattered glass rang out. Everything went dark. Roxy turned and ran for the trail entrance. Her knees buckled when she heard the cannon-like blast of Vincent's .38 echo throughout the street. Fearing the worst, she covered her eyes before turning around. She spread her fingers and peeked through.

[281]

Tires screeched, rocks flew, and a big dust cloud filled the street as the Trans Am sped off. Seconds later, Phil rushed up, gasping for air.

"Wha … Wha … What the hell just happened?"

"I don't know. I stayed over here like you told me," Roxy replied with remarkable innocence. She looked nervously at Phil. "Was he shooting at you?"

"No. I'm not sure he even knew I was there. I don't know what happened, but he started freaking out, swinging his arms all crazy and shit. Then all hell broke loose after that light exploded. I don't know what was going on inside the house. I heard Daddy shouting for Robert to get down, then I heard a bunch of noise, like chairs and glasses falling on the floor. Next thing I know, Vincent fired off a round and then hauled ass."

Roxy blew a small sigh of relief and relaxed.

Phil grabbed his gear, and they made their way back through the trail.

"Now what?" he asked after they got in the car.

"Call Malcolm. Tell him I need to talk to him tonight."

"What are you about to get us into, Roxy? That crazy muthafuka could've killed Daddy or Robert. We need to call the police."

The back door of the house swung open, and Wes rushed out with his flashlight to survey the premises. Phil and Roxy watched as he shined the light on the ground around the window's shattered glass.

"Be quiet. And I'm not getting us into anything. You're the one who dragged me into this. Now, I'm going to get our asses out of it. Call Malcolm when we get back to my place. Tell him I'm on my way. He and I are about to pay Mr. Martello a visit."

Phil smiled. The old Roxy was back.

CHAPTER 69

ROXY AND MALCOLM parked in front of Vincent's townhouse. She opened the vanity mirror and applied a fresh layer of lipstick and gloss then puckered her lips and flipped the visor up.

"You sure you wanna do this?" Roxy asked before opening the door.

Malcolm nodded. "Yeah, I'm sure."

Roxy strutted to the front door, the heels of her shoes clacking against the pavement.

She rang the doorbell then looked at Malcolm with the confidence of a general leading his troops to a sure victory. "Don't say a word."

Malcolm, looking nervous, stood behind Roxy's right shoulder. "Are you sure this is going to work?"

"Trust me; it'll work out fine. Just follow my lead," Roxy said before Vincent opened the door.

Vincent wore a pair of gray warmup pants and a white t-shirt. An oversized towel covered his head and face as he dried his hair.

"Hi. Sorry, it took me so long. I just got out of the shower." Vincent draped a towel around his neck. He reached to hug Roxy but stopped suddenly.

"Malcolm?" Vincent asked quizzically, dumbfounded by his presence.

He stepped back clumsily and shifted his eyes back and forth between his two guests.

Roxy stared at Vincent, her face devoid of any expression. She remained silent as she walked in and closed the door.

"What's the matter, baby? You look like you've seen a ghost. It's just Malcolm and me."

Roxy and Vincent stood in the middle of the living room. Malcolm stood not far behind, his mussed hair covering his glasses.

"Well, I wasn't—"

"Vincent!" Roxy raised her hand as if she were a traffic cop, her palm an inch from the tip of his nose. "Don't say a word, okay?"

Vincent nodded meekly.

"I know you weren't expecting us to show up at your door, at least not together. But, you see, I ran into Malcolm tonight while I was looking for your computer, and he told me the good news. Aren't you excited that he found it?"

Vincent's eyes lit up. He looked at Malcolm. "No fooling? You found it?"

Malcolm flashed Roxy a look.

"Yes," Roxy replied, "and you would have known that if you had stayed in your office like I pleaded with you to do. But *nooo*, you were out pretending to be some kind of hitman."

Vincent's eyes bulged. The vein in his neck began to pulsate.

[285]

"Yes, Vincent, I saw it all. I saw you at Robert's house. I also saw you fire a round into his house and run. I'm sure it won't take the police long to put two and two together."

Vincent looked flushed. "Robert's dead? Please, don't tell me I killed Robert." He bowed his head. "I'm sorry, Roxanne. I don't know what came over me."

"You're sorry? You kill an innocent man and all you can say is you're sorry? I'll tell you who's sorry. Me!" Tears began to stream down both her cheeks.

Vincent wrapped his arms around her and held her tightly. Roxy's shoulders shook as she wailed and cried profusely.

Malcolm ran his fingers through his fuzzy brown locks. Things were not turning out the way he had imagined. He thought about going back to the car and waiting for Roxy, but he kept hearing her say, *"Trust me. I'm a really good actress. No matter what I do, you just follow my lead."*

Roxy broke free from Vincent's grasp with dramatic, yet realistic flair. She wiped away her tears with the back of her hand.

"I wanted to be here for you, but I can't handle a prison romance, Vincent." She sniffed and held back tears. "I'm not cut out for weekend jail visits, talking on two-way phones, and putting money on your books so you can write me letters on bartered stationery."

"Roxy, I never meant to hurt you this way. Something took control of me. I can't honestly explain it. I couldn't stand the thought of losing all that I had worked so hard to accomplish. More than anything, I couldn't stand the thought of losing you. If I had a chance to do it all again, I would give all of it up just to have you.

Roxanne, please forgive me. I love you, and I don't want to lose you."

Roxy looked over at Malcolm, grinned, and took a bow. Then she fished a compact mirror out of her purse and wiped her face with a pink makeup sponge.

Vincent and Malcolm watched on in silence.

When she finished, she cleared her throat and said, "Vinny, I told you I don't date clients, and I will never date a client who won't listen. I brought Malcolm along because I might be able to help you, and I really want to give you one more chance; so, please listen to me." She turned to Malcolm. "Malcolm is willing to negotiate a new deal, and I believe you should take it, considering your current dilemma."

"I'll take it." Vincent held out his arms with his palms up.

"Not so fast, Vinny. Once you're done with Malcolm, there's still some unfinished business between you and me."

"Fine. I'll do whatever you want. What are the new terms you're proposing, Malcolm?"

Roxy waved her hands. "Before we get to that, there's something we're going to need you to help us with."

"Anything. Name it."

"We need you to help us get the computer."

"I thought you said you found it."

"Not exactly. But we know where it is."

"Where is it?"

Roxy looked at Malcolm and winked. "He's all yours. Take it from here."

CHAPTER 70
FRIDAY, FEBRUARY 5, 1993

PHIL STOOD on his tiptoes and craned his neck to see if Roxy and Malcolm were in the crowded lobby.

"Do you see them?" Holly asked as she slid her finger down the list of signatures on the visitor's sign-in sheet.

"They'll be here soon."

Phil and Holly maneuvered past the horde of ITI employees, jockeying for position when the next elevator arrived. They found a bench near the garage door entrance and sat down.

"Holly, I can't thank you enough. Locating that extension was the break we needed last night."

Holly's cheeks turned a dark pink. "I was shocked when I discovered the password on the PBX server hadn't been updated. Once I found the extension, the only thing left was to locate the assigned office. After I found out it was located next to the mailroom, I knew right away Stanley was the one behind it. Anyone who has been here for any length of time has heard Stanley Bricker's mailroom-to-penthouse story."

"I couldn't have done it without you."

"How were you able to extract the laptop from the office without tipping Russ off?" Holly swept her shoulder-length brunette hair behind her ear.

"Vincent helped us with that. By the way, Malcolm says your old buddy Russ was quite helpful. He unlocked the door for them."

Holly cupped her hands over her mouth "You're kidding me!"

"No fooling. They found the laptop in a duffel bag and switched it out with another one that doesn't have the source code. By the time Stanley realizes it's the wrong laptop, it'll be too late."

Holly looked at Phil. "Now that we've recovered the laptop and have a new agreement, what about Jack Sherman's speech?"

"I tossed and turned all night, thinking about it, and I'm still not sure what to do about that."

"You better think of something soon." Holly looked at her watch. "Time is running out."

Marvin strutted through the entrance, talking nonstop to an attractive African American woman, who towered above his diminutive stature.

"I'll get with you later, Jackie. I need to holler at my boy, PJ, for a minute," Marvin announced when he saw Phil.

"I'm in meetings all day. I'll give you a call," Jackie replied as she walked away with a relieved look on her face.

"PJ, I've got everything set for your big bachelor party tonight. Are you ready?"

"Marvin, things have been so crazy these last few weeks that I haven't had time to think about a bachelor party. Besides, I told you it wasn't necessary."

"I've got everything set up. All you need to do is show up. PJ, I promise you, it will be a party you won't forget," Marvin said as he walked off proudly.

Holly placed her hands on the side of her lightly freckled face. Her brownish green eyes danced under the fluorescent light. "Oh, my goodness! Tomorrow's the big day, isn't it?"

"Yeah, it's finally here. I didn't think I was going to make it for a while."

"Ann's a lucky woman." Holly leaned over and kissed him on the cheek.

Phil blushed. "By the way, I really want to apologize for leading you on that night at your house. I shouldn't have taken advantage of you like that."

Holly held Phil's hand between hers. "What makes you so sure I wasn't taking advantage of you?"

CHAPTER 71

ALL THE LIGHTS in the boardroom were off, with the exception of a set of recessed lights, illuminating the east end of the massive table. Jack Sherman sat at the head of the table, his head propped up against his thumb and two fingers. The gloom, despair, and agony that consumed his countenance were even more noticeable against the majestic sunny backdrop above his right shoulder.

He stared across the boardroom at a full-length mirror hanging on the west wall. He ignored the mirror most of the time. Only paranoid narcissists like his cousin, Beau, looked in every mirror they passed.

This morning, however, he couldn't drag his eyes away from it. The more he looked into the mirror, the more he understood why. The reflection in the mirror was his, but the pathetic expression on his face was, without a doubt, his father's. Then his father appeared in the mirror, wearing one of those smirky smiles that had "I told you so" written all over it.

Jack grunted and shook himself free of the trance. "It's five after nine. Where's Graves? He's the one who called this meeting."

"He'll be here. Right, Vincent?" Stanley replied in a tone steeped with smugness.

Vincent raised his head. "Huh?"

Stanley, seeing Vincent's listless and confused demeanor, coughed to suppress a laugh.

"Jack, Vincent and I both know Malcolm's doing everything in his power to find the laptop. I've got people looking into it, and I'm sure Vincent is doing the same, probably more. It hasn't turned up, but I'm sure it will."

Stanley had checked on the laptop one last time before arriving at the meeting. Although no agreements were in place, he would make sure one was drawn up the minute Malcolm walked through the door empty-handed.

He looked across at Vincent. *Enjoy your last minutes, you slick know-it-all punk.* He resisted the urge to lean over the table and say it to his cocky colleague's face. It was tempting, but there would be time for that later.

Jack was the person Stanley was most concerned about. The whole ordeal had taken a toll on his venerable mentor and friend. He looked up to Jack because Jack had done the one thing he, himself, hadn't done when he was dealt the same cards.

After old man Sherman died, Jack stepped in without hesitation and led the company. He regretted not doing the same. When his father died, so did the tavern that he owned and their old neighborhood.

• • • •

Malcolm stepped off the elevator, flanked by Phil and Roxy. A black computer bag hung from his shoulder.

Wes, looking cheerful and relaxed, sauntered off the elevator with a bandaged and heavily medicated Robert in tow. After Wes had discovered that Robert's injury wasn't life-threatening, he called in a favor to a doctor friend who specialized in undocumented office visits.

"Roxy! Roxy!" Phil barked in a loud whisper. "I know you hear me. Don't go in here and embarrass me. In case you forgot, I still work here."

"Boy, ain't nobody gon' mess up your damn job. Besides, how am I gon' mess up a job you don't even know how you got in the first place?" Roxy flipped her hand up like a traffic cop stopping traffic and shot him her infamous "I dare you" look.

"Let's do this," Malcolm said as he opened the door to the boardroom.

CHAPTER 72

MALCOLM OPENED the boardroom door, and a vacuumed gust of wind escaped into the hallway.

Stanley looked up as Malcolm entered, followed by Phil and Roxy.

Vincent rocked and watched with deliberate anticipation as Stanley's expression went from slightly curious to totally dumbfounded.

"Good morning. Sorry, I'm late. I had to apply some last-minute updates to the final release build," Malcolm announced as he sat next to Vincent.

"No way!" Stanley scoffed. "You don't expect us to believe you've written six months' worth of code in a week?"

Malcolm laughed as he unzipped the black nylon computer bag.

"No, of course not. I found my laptop. These nice people found it for me." He pointed to Phil and Roxy, who were standing a few feet away.

"Who are these people?" Stanley began to turn pink around the collar.

"They are the investigators that found my laptop."

"I don't believe it." Stanley jumped up. "What sort of game are you playing, Mr. Graves?"

"Sit down, Stanley," Vincent interjected. "This isn't a game."

Malcolm removed the laptop from the bag and placed it on the table. Stanley looked as if he'd seen a ghost. He backed away from the table.

"Oh, by the way, we found your little hiding spot. I guess once a mail clerk, always a mail clerk, right?" Vincent winked at Stanley.

"Kiss my ass, you lying sonofabitch!" Stanley growled.

"Is this the computer that was stolen or not?" Jack demanded.

"Yes, it is," Vincent replied. "Malcolm's team tracked it down." He looked Stanley squarely in the eye. "I was present when it was recovered this morning."

Stanley squinted his eyes and tightened his jaws as red rage began to engulf his face. "You sneaky sonofabitch. I'm going to kick your ass!"

Stanley stormed to the other side of the table.

Vincent jumped up from his seat and balled his fists. Before Stanley made it to the other side, Jack got up from his chair and stood between his young mentees.

"Stanley! What has gotten into you?" Jack shouted as he put his forearm in Stanley's chest to block his forward progress. Stanley lunged and flung his arms in an attempt to grab Vincent.

"I'm going to kick this greasy-haired wannabe capo's ass! Just let me get my hands on him. I'll pulverize you, Martello!" Stanley took quick, deep breaths that sounded like a bull getting ready to charge. His eyes bugged out like a deranged man and spit gathered in the corners of his mouth.

Jack patted Stanley's shoulder and talked him back to his seat. Vincent kept a sizeable distance between him and Stanley's vice-like hands.

"As I was saying," Vincent continued. "After we recovered the laptop, Malcolm and I renegotiated the terms of the purchase. Instead of acquiring WorldNet, they're going to sell us the software for fifty million, plus royalties in perpetuity."

Stanley, stunned and speechless, sat, staring at the table.

Vincent cleared his throat. "Also, once the sale is finalized, I'll be announcing my resignation, which should make Stanley's transition into CEO much smoother.

Stanley jerked his head upright. Vincent shrugged. "You're the CEO the company needs right now. By the way, the new cost structure is going to leave the company with a substantial cash reserve and provide Jack that nice golden parachute he deserves, not to mention provide me with a handsome buyout for my contract."

Malcolm stood up and carried the laptop to Jack. "Mr. Sherman, I assure you this is the final release build. Like Vincent said, he and I came to an agreement this morning. Your signature is the only thing that's needed."

Jack rubbed the top of the laptop. A wide grin spread across his face; perhaps he could still go through with his plan. He didn't have much time, and he needed to begin right away.

"Get the papers. I'll sign right now."

"Before you sign the papers," Malcolm began. He walked to the door. "There's another issue I want to bring to your attention."

Wes and Robert walked in. Wes was dressed in a blue three-piece suit. The gold pocket watch J.D. always wore during his closing arguments was tucked in his vest pocket. He held on to Robert's elbow with a firm grip. Robert's eyes roamed around the room. The heavy sedatives had left him lucid but not coherent.

"Jack, I believe you know Mr. Berry," Malcolm continued. "It's been brought to my attention that Mr. Berry aided in the return of the computer and sustained injuries as a result of his efforts. He is here today, with his advisor Mr. P. Wesley Jacobson."

Jack shook Robert's weak hand. "Thank you, Robert."

Wes cleared his throat. "Mr. Sherman, on Robert's behalf, I would like to thank Mr. Martello for the generous reward he personally donated for Robert's valiant efforts."

Roxy started clapping. Soon, everyone in the room joined in.

That is, everyone but Phil. He leaned over and whispered, "Just so you know, I think you and Daddy are letting him off too easy. He damn near killed Robert, remember?"

"If I were you, I'd shut up and clap. Especially since your broke ass is about to be sitting on two-point-five million for a mess you needed me to clean up for you."

"Wha—" Phil started to respond, but Roxy shushed him before he could get a word in. His eyes fell on Jack Sherman, and he remembered the speech and Sherman's CLANS connection.

Phil approached Wes and Jack at the front of the table. Wes had a brown envelope in his hand. "Pardon me. Daddy, may I speak to you for a minute?"

"Excuse me, Mr. Sherman." Wes handed Jack a folder. "Please take a moment to look through this. It's some information I've gathered. I'm sure you will find it equally as interesting as I have."

Phil and Wes moved a few feet back from the table.

"What's wrong, son?"

"It's Jack Sherman and that CLANS organization …"

"I know, Phil."

"You know about the CLANS and what they're trying to do?"

"No. I still don't know anything about that CLANS group, but I know plenty about the Sherman family."

"Daddy, that's what I'm trying to tell you, Mr. Sherman and the CLANS—"

"Phil, you're getting worked up for nothing," Wes interrupted. "I've got this. By the time I'm finished with Jack Sherman, he'll be ready to atone for all his family's sins."

"Good. He needs to go to jail for what they're trying to do."

"Wait a minute. I have no intentions of sending him to jail. Not if I can help it."

"Then you need to read this." He held out the folded speech. "You'll change your mind."

"I'll read it, but it's not going to change my mind. Do you think I'm going to allow the same system that enriched Jack

Sherman to pronounce his judgment? That man has made millions, most of it through government connections and at the expense of black folk that look like you. Son, this isn't about justice. This is about payback."

"Mr. Jacobson," Jack grunted and waved the folder, "May I please speak with you privately in my office."

CHAPTER 73

"WHO ARE YOU, and where'd you get this?" Jack threw the folder with the birth certificates on his desk.

Wes, amused by the line of questioning, remained unflappable as he sat in front of the enormous mahogany desk. "I take it you agree with my discovery." A small grin poked out of the left corner of his mouth.

Jack noticed his guest's stoic demeanor. Wes didn't look threatening, but Jack could sense a shrewdness about him. *This guy looks dangerously calm*, he thought.

"Is this some sort of attempt to blackmail me?" Jack asked in a tone that sounded more hopeful than accusatory.

Wes belly laughed.

"Now, why would I want to blackmail a brotha? You are a brotha, right? Or would you rather I see you as a white man? In which case, I guess this would be blackmail."

"Call it whatever you want," Jack said, a note of dejection in his voice. "It can't be any worse than the hell I've already been through. Yes, my mother was a fair-skinned black woman, who passed for white. She and my father kept it a secret from everyone, including me. I was a sophomore in college when my mother finally told me. My father, on the other hand, was madder than a Carolina wildcat."

Wes pursed his lips and nodded. "So, what happened?"

"I met this gorgeous girl named Allison Mayweather and fell in love. She was African American like my mother, only darker. We were going to get married, that is until my father found out and went ballistic. I don't know what he told Allison, but she told me she never wanted to see me again and walked out. I haven't seen her since.

"I couldn't believe what my father had done, considering the fact that he was married to a black woman. After Allison left, it dawned on me that my father, while loving and caring, was ashamed of my mother and me. All the years he'd spent secluding us from his hate-filled brethren in the Family was really him saving his own hypocrisy. I was beyond angry at him. I accused him of not loving me and my mother for who we were. Then I told him I hoped I never became the man that he was.

"I roamed around, mad and confused, for ten years. Then one day, I got a call saying my old man's dead and I've got to come home because he left instructions for me to run the company. When I heard what he'd done, I felt really bad. I thought I'd judged him too harshly. I took the job in hopes of showing him how much I forgave him and to prove to him I was worthy of stepping up to the task.

"What I didn't know at the time was that his generosity came with a huge price tag attached. I looked at my father's picture today, and you know what I realized?"

Wes held his arms out, palms up, and shrugged.

"I realized that I haven't been any better. For the past twenty-five years, my father, in his own unorthodox style, has been teaching me the lesson he failed to grasp. He's been showing me that it is much easier to give voice to a belief than it is to actually live it out. He's taught me that being noble isn't about upholding traditions; rather, it's breaking free of them for the better good."

Wes sat up straight and moved to the edge of the chair.

"Jack, we all have dirty family secrets that get exposed through unconventional methods and often at a time when it's least expected. In my line of work, I uncover secrets that people would rather keep hidden. I find secrets. I don't expose them. I guess you could say it's because I've got a few of my own that I'm hoping never see the light of day. The good thing about finding secrets is that they have a value that you can use for good or bad. I have my faults, but I am an honest man and intend to get an honest value for that information.

"I don't consider what I'm about to ask for as blackmail since it's not for me. I counted student applications from ten different historically black universities that were being dumped without a glance. If you really want to atone for your misdeeds, as well as those of your family, I believe a substantial gift to those schools would be a nice start. I will set up a trust and make arrangements for you to fund each school a million a year for the next twenty years.

"I also want you to use some of your connections for my son's sake. He's really smart, and he wants to go places. So, whenever he's in a place where you can help, I want you to make whatever calls you need to help him.

"If you think any of that is unfair, remember I don't expose, but I can make sure Senator Sherman and the rest of your relatives find out about your daddy's secret. Then you'll see firsthand how they feel about niggers."

Wes stood up. "Do we have a deal?"

Jack grabbed Wes's hand and shook vigorously. "It's a deal, Mr. Jacobson," he said with a wide grin. "Before you go, I have a proposition for you. I promise I will definitely make it worth your while."

Wes considered the request then sat down. "What do you have in mind?"

CHAPTER 74

WHEN YOU'VE LIVED with someone for forty or more years, you have a good sense of their mood and what they're thinking, even when they aren't in your physical presence. Marjorie's and Wes's relationship was the personification of such an axiom.

This time was no different.

Nearly a week had gone by since Marjorie's big blow up. In all their years, they'd always found a way to talk things out.

This time was different.

"Thirty-second floor," the elevator's automated attendant announced.

Wes took a deep breath and blew it out slowly. He stepped off the elevator and strolled into the Mercury Room, an upscale restaurant located on the top floor of the Charlotte Towers.

The maître d', a tall, slender middle-aged guy, was on the phone when Wes entered. He held the handset in place between his ear and left shoulder as he jotted. He looked up with a smile and placed his hand over the mouthpiece.

"I'll be with you shortly, sir," he said in a hushed tone.

"I'm supposed to meet someone here. Do you mind if I take a look around?"

"She's here. To your left, by the window." The maître d' showed him through with a nod of his head and then continued with his conversation. "Yes, ma'am. I've got it. Dr. Cecil Callahan, party of six, arriving at seven."

Wes raised an eyebrow and shot a curious glance at the head waiter. *How does he know who I'm here to see?*

The answer became obvious when he entered the main dining area. Marjorie sat at a table for two to his far left by the window, just as the maître d' had declared. She was also the only diner in the place. It was a quarter past three; the lunch crowd was long gone, and the TGIF worshippers wouldn't be arriving for another two hours, at least.

A panoramic view of the city's skyline served as the spacious room's backdrop. The tint on the window held back just enough of the sun's powerful rays to create a warm custard glow.

Basking in the warm light, he could see how the years had softened her once angular cheeks. Her rich burnt brown tone radiated still.

His knees weakened, and the knot in his stomach that he'd been ignoring got tighter when he saw her. Despite the strong shell and the determined look, he could see she'd been crying. He didn't need a detective or Ann Landers to know he was the reason behind each teardrop.

"Hi, Puddin'. Good to see you, baby." His voice crackled.

"I wouldn't count on that." Marjorie stirred the snifter of Remy Martin and looked straight ahead.

Wes felt his heart fall into a hollow pit, past his stomach, down through his testicles, below his ankles, and shatter beneath his feet.

"Puddin', baby, it's not what you think. I know that sounds like the same old excuse, but I'm telling you, baby, it's not what you think."

Marjorie sat still. Resiliency washed across her countenance.

"Come on, Puddin'. Look at me, baby."

"What do I need to look at your old ass for?" She huffed in exasperation and began to wave her hand busily. "Go on, sit down before you have these nosy-ass white folk all in our business."

"Baby, it's not what you think," Wes said as he slid into the chair across the table. "I promise."

Marjorie stared ahead. "Let's just cut to the chase. I know you're wondering what three questions I have for you. Well, here they are. I'll give them to you slowly. And just so you know, I ain't got time for your bullshit." She gave a single nod and stared him down. "*Why'd* you ask to borrow the condo? *Who* were you meeting that you needed to meet *there*, of all places? And, *what* does this have to do with Philander?"

He wanted to come clean about the whole mess. It was an option he'd considered many times. He was tired of safeguarding his secrets. All the years in the business had taught him one thing: No matter how hard you try to hide your secrets, some sonofabitch was going to find you out. Over the years, he'd told his share of lies. Marjorie had even caught him in a few. They paled in comparison to the multitude he'd told.

But this time, it wasn't about him. Convincing his wife of that was damn near impossible. She'd find a way to blame him. She always found a way to blame him. It was a skill she'd subconsciously perfected.

"Puddin', I don't want to lose you, but if I'm going to lose you, I want you to know I'm going to lose by attempting to be the best man I desire to be to you. So here goes. The answer to your first question: I needed to use the condo to interview a potential lead.

"To answer your second question, which is the one you *really* want to know: The name doesn't matter, but, yes, I did spend the evening alone with a woman."

Marjorie feigned surprise then rolled her eyes with a look that shouted, "Negro, please don't waste my time!"

Wes chuckled and leaned closer to the table. "Listen, baby; I only took her there because I needed to get her on record. I needed to get her to a quiet place because the only place I knew to meet her was that loud-ass Bennigan's place. Do you know they call that place the meat market? They ain't lying, either."

Wes placed his elbow on the table and clasped his hands beneath his chin. He let out a deep exhale and placed his chin on his closed fist.

"Anyway, you know I do background on all my clients. Well, this client started acting strange, and I needed to find out why. So, I brought her there to ask her some questions. That's all it was, nothing else."

Marjorie narrowed her eyes. Wes smiled broadly. He knew she was trying to see the vein in his neck.

"Finally, to answer your last question, because that's the one that will ultimately decide my fate: I had no intention of involving Phil. It just so happened that my client worked at the same company. I did everything I could not to get him involved. I even told him not to worry about it. But did he listen to me? I wonder where he gets that from." Wes looked Marjorie squarely in the eye.

She turned away.

"Puddin', you keep wanting to ignore it, but I know you've got your suspicions about Phil and Ann repeating the cycle. I see it, and I know you see it too."

Marjorie chuckled. "I see MiMi's been talking to you, too. You don't believe all of those old tales, do you?"

"Name one thing she's been wrong about."

Marjorie thought for a minute. "That's my point, Wes. Why shouldn't those children's lives be as equally glorious and challenging as ours?"

"That's not how I meant it. If it makes you feel better. I brought everything to order and was able to gain a few favors in the process. Phil ended up helping me. He was trying to tell me about something he found on that computer of his. Puddin', I'm telling you those computers are something else. Soon, people's whole lives are going to be on display with them damn things."

Marjorie began to laugh.

"I'm serious! And, as for that daughter of ours, I know she talked him into it. I try not to let it bother me because she's only doing it to spite me. I keep telling you this business is no place for women, least of all my daughter."

"Wes, drop it! That's your problem. You're always trying to make sure everyone's life is comfortable until you're missing the joy of the life around you."

Wes folded his arms and frowned.

"Dewar's Scotch Sour, sir?" The waiter placed a glass on a table in front of Wes.

Wes's mouth dropped open. Confused amazement filled his eyes.

"How? How did you know?" he sputtered.

Marjorie saw the look on her husband's face and started laughing uncontrollably.

Wes huffed and shook his head in disgust.

"Vic's double-crossing ass!"

"Now, why are you blaming Vic? He's your friend as well as mine. If you didn't think so, then why'd you ask him to invite me here?"

Wes shrugged. "It was the only way I knew you'd come," he resigned. Then he frowned. "Besides, Vic owed me! I wouldn't be in this mess in the first place if he hadn't told you I asked to use his condo."

"What makes you think Vic told me anything?"

"Puddin', are you serious? Vic's gossiping ass tells you everything. If I were up to anything, do you actually believe I would let Vic know about it? Hell, everybody knows he's still jealous that you married me. That's why he tells you everything. He's hoping if he tells you the right thing, you'll finally give him some."

"How do you know I haven't given him some already?" Marjorie gave him an icy glare.

Wes pulled his chair and sat perpendicular to Marjorie. He tried to grab her hand, but she jerked it away.

"Then I forgive you. There's nothing I can do about it now, anyway. Puddin', you're the one I've always wanted, and you'll forever be the one I love all the way. Baby, you're the one I strive hardest for. If you quit setting expectations for me now, I'll be lost. I haven't done everything right, but you know I've always tried to do my best when it came to you and the kids. If you don't believe any of what I just said then just believe me when I say Puddin', I want to come home … home to you … home to us!"

CHAPTER 75

SATURDAY, FEBRUARY 6, 1993

THE WEDDING RECEPTION was in full swing. The dance floor was packed as the deejay played Frankie Beverly & Maze's "Love Is the Key."

Marjorie swirled a cup of brandy as she and Ann sat at the head table, checking out the view. Phil and his buddies were huddled in a corner, laughing and carrying on like teenagers. Wes was showing Roxy he still knew a few moves on the dance floor, which had her crying with laughter. Gregory and his wife were dancing nearby. Neither looked to be enjoying it. Roderick's latest fling kissed and covered him like a glove, although it didn't stop him from making constant eye contact with one of Ann's cousins. A crowd had gathered around as MiMi held center stage with a young groomsman, showing off one of her patented swing steps.

Ann laughed. "MiMi is a character!"

"She's quite a woman. You and I can only hope we get to enjoy life like she does." Marjorie pondered her thoughts. She leaned closer to Ann. "Philander truly loves you. I know because that look he has, I've seen it before."

"You have?" Ann asked, not hiding her surprise. "When?"

"The night Wes proposed to me in his office. That office was so tiny he barely had enough room to get down on one knee." Marjorie giggled.

"How sweet! That had to be one happy day."

"Happy?" Marjorie shrieked. "Humph! More like mad as hell." She laughed.

"Why?" Ann asked, now thoroughly engrossed in the story.

"The day Wes proposed, I'd just found out I was pregnant. I stopped by the law school to tell him, and that's when I found out he had dropped out six months prior. Talk about mad! He had a job waiting for him at the NAACP's Legal Defense Fund."

"Are you serious?"

Marjorie nodded her head. "Yes. Thurgood Marshall and J.D. were old friends. During one of his trips through Durham, Thurgood stayed at their home. He was so impressed with Wes that, over dinner, he asked him to join his team as soon as he graduated. And that wasn't his only offer. A law firm in Harlem was also calling."

"And he quit law school anyway?

Marjorie popped her lips and smiled. "Child, you know I had to be in love to stick around after he pulled a stunt like that. But I was in love, and Wes's slick, romantic behind didn't make it any easier to walk away after sliding that two-carat diamond ring on my finger and showing me that box filled with cash, all from his first case."

"So, Daddy made the right choice, then."

Marjorie sipped her brandy. "Between you and me, 'bout the only thing he got right that night was asking me to marry him," she said with a wink.

The DJ segued into "Flashlight" by Parliament-Funkadelic. On cue, the dancefloor filled with body-bumping dancers.

Marjorie cleared her throat. "By the way, I've been wanting to thank you."

"For what?"

Marjorie took a deep breath. "The other night at dinner."

Ann shrugged. "Everyone was just sitting there doing nothing. I had to do something." She studied Marjorie for a second. "You really weren't going to shoot him, were you?"

"I sure was," Marjorie said with assurance. "That's why I took all the bullets out the gun before I pointed it at him."

Ann's mouth fell open as she stared at Marjorie, who was holding her chin up in defiance. Marjorie winked and shot Ann a sly grin. They burst into laughter.

After they regained their composure, Marjorie took Ann by the hand. "I'm going to tell you like MiMi told me after Wes and I got married. How exceptional the Jacobson men truly are will be debated for centuries to come. But, rest assured, the record will show one thing that was a constant among all of them. They excelled at marrying super extraordinary women."

With that, she patted Ann's hand and stood. "Now, let's get out there on the dancefloor and dance our asses off like the super extraordinary Jacobson women that we are."

EPILOGUE
SUNDAY, FEBRUARY 7, 1993

R OXY SAT CROSS-LEGGED on the couch, watching *In the Heat of the Night*. She hugged her deco pillow, and a hint of Vincent's cologne brushed the tip of her nose. Her thoughts immediately drifted to the night she'd followed Vincent to his townhouse. That passion-filled weekend turned out to be a whole lot more than she wanted to concede. She closed her eyes and was instantly transported to Vincent's dimly lit bedroom and the king-sized sleigh bed covered with silk sheets.

"That's it, baby. Let me stroke you where you love it most," Vincent had pleaded seductively as her legs draped over his shoulders. A flutter of waves bombarded the top of her pelvis. A jolt of electricity cascaded along the walls of her vulva. She stretched out her trembling legs and panted.

A half hour later, she pulled herself up from the couch and prepared a snack while the tea kettle boiled. A filmstrip with four black-and-white photos, taken during her and Vincent's last visit to Frank's Grille, was clipped to the refrigerator door.

She didn't want to look at it. Looking at it only reminded her of how long it had been since they last talked. Vincent was confident that all would go smoothly, but nearly two days had passed, and she hadn't spoken to him.

Just as she was about to sit down to eat, she remembered the Sunday paper and headed for the front door. Roxy opened the door and froze instantly in her tracks.

[315]

Vincent stood on the threshold. "I wanted to give you this personally." He handed Roxy an envelope. "That's the five million I owe you."

Roxy looked on both sides of the envelope. "Thank you."

"I know you said you didn't want a guy to bring you flowers. So here goes nothing." Vincent took two envelopes from his shirt pocket and held them out like a bouquet. "Come fly away with me."

"What?" Roxy knew it wasn't the proper response, but it was the only one-syllable word she could sound out at the moment. Her tangled emotions freed themselves. She felt the excitement and joy that comes when your heart leads the way.

"You don't need a thing. In fact, we're making the Grand Caymans our first stop, so you can put your check in a secure tax-free account. We might as well take care of that first since it's on the way. I know a great banker, he can set up whatever accounts you need. From there, we're going to Costa Rica. We'll stay as long as you like; then you decide where we go from there."

• • • •

MONDAY, FEBRUARY 8, 1993

Wes leaned against his car and watched the black stretch limo pass through the gate and amble down the mile-and-a-half-long entrance. The car's headlights pierced through the pale glow of the cloud-covered evening sun as it entered the cavernous hangar at Concord Regional Airport.

The limo stopped in front of Wes's car. The driver jumped out and hurried to open the rear passenger door. Jack exited, wearing a pair of faded blue jeans and a blue and green plaid shirt. He pulled down the brim of his khaki-colored fly fishing hat to cover his brown horn-rimmed glasses.

"Are we ready?" Jack grinned like a kid going on his first overnight camping trip.

Wes handed him a white letter-sized folder. "Your new passport and tickets. There's also a matching driver's license and social security card, as well as all of my contact numbers."

"You're quite efficient, Wes. Thank you."

"Things tend to happen quicker when money's no object."

"My lawyer has everything drawn up for the annual disbursements. The only thing that's needed is your signature on the accounts." Jack shook Wes's hand. "I couldn't have done this without you."

"Let's not start patting ourselves on the back just yet. We've got to get you out of here and up to D.C. Your flight leaves in ten hours. Your pilot, Tony, is an experienced pilot, who's used to flying covert missions. He knows everything there is to making a crash landing. By the time you reach Amsterdam, plans for the Jack Sherman memorial service should be well underway."

Wes escorted Jack to the cabin door of the Cessna 425 Conquest. He reached inside his coat and pulled out an index card with an address and phone number written on the front.

"What's this?" Jack asked as he studied the card.

"That is the address and phone number for Allison Williams, or should I say Allison Mayweather-Williams. I called in a few favors and was able to locate her in San Francisco. She and her husband, Johnny, were married for fifteen years until his untimely death five years ago. Cancer. She doesn't have any children. Sounds like she could use some companionship."

"What should I do?" Jack looked at the three-by-five card with astonishment.

"Call her and beg like hell for another chance."

• • • •

MONDAY, SEPTEMBER 6, 1993

Phil exited the Usenet group then closed the NetVoyager browser window.

With Stanley at the helm, ITI's newest product was fast becoming Wall Street's hottest commodity. Despite its rocky beginning and Jack Sherman's untimely death in a plane crash, days after closing the deal with Malcolm and WorldNet, the company was also showing signs of a promising recovery.

The plane crash and Jack's death made national headlines. Hundreds of investigators pored over the mangled plane. Two charred bodies, presumably Jack and the pilot, were found among the wreckage. Both were burned beyond recognition.

Jack was reported to have been on his way to speak with a select group of business and banking leaders at a private event when the plane crashed. There was no mention of the Confederate Loyalists Association of the New South or a State of the Confederacy conference.

Two weeks after Jack's death, Phil walked out of ITI for the last time. His post-ITI career was taking a step forward and upward. He'd reunited with two longtime hacker friends from his first summer computer camp and started a small software development company. With some unexpected help from Uncle Mack, they landed a sub-contracting assignment on a project at NASA Langley.

Phil placed a CD in the carousel tray and hit play. A photograph of him and Malcolm standing under the logo for Malcolm's next Internet venture hung on the wall above the stereo cabinet.

He'd flown to Boston and hung out with Malcolm for a few days. During the visit, Malcolm pitched his idea, an Internet search engine called Youreka! "If the Internet continues to grow at its current rate, locating information will be vital. Who knows, search engines might rule the Internet one day," Malcolm predicted with a grin.

"You've got mail!" announced the computer.

Phil clicked on the envelope. A message from Holly sat on top of a long queue of unread messages. After several attempts at trying to split his portion of the payment with her, she finally accepted a smaller, but generous offer and started her own consulting firm, specializing in network security.

"Companies used to offer rewards for my capture. Now, they're paying me to keep people like me out. Isn't that just amazing?" she quipped one afternoon when they met for lunch.

As for NoMoBoesky, she forged ahead with her mission of exposing corporate corruption.

His briefcase lay on the far end of the desk. He stared it down like a matador facing the bull before driving the sword between its shoulder blade. He took a quick glance at the clock. The red LED lights showed 1:12.

Ann was sound asleep, but he was wide awake. He let out a heavy sigh then reached for the briefcase. He opened it, pulled out a legal-size manila folder, and scattered its contents across the desk: a small stack of case notes (handwritten and computer-generated), two court filings, some newspaper articles clamped together with a paperclip, and finally, two Polaroid photographs.

Roxy had given him the envelope when she stopped by to check out their new place. Although he'd been successful at avoiding the envelope for weeks, he hadn't been as successful in ignoring their conversation that day ...

"Just look over it before you say no," Roxy insisted. Recovering the laptop and securing Vincent's business dealings had stirred the investigative fire in her belly, from a flicker to a blazing flame that had her on a mad search for her next case.

"Roxy, I keep telling you I ain't Daddy. My name isn't Wes Jacobson. I am a programmer, not a private investigator. Besides, you know Daddy would go ballistic if he found out we were in the business. Everybody from Jesus to the Devil knows how he feels about you being in the business. And I'm more than sure he's not cool with the idea of me taking up the business either."

"And I keep telling you that you are an investigator; you just don't know it yet," she replied.

"I won't have time; Ann's about to have the baby, and I just picked up a big contract."

"I'm not asking you to start on it today. Just look at it. I'll be in Barbados for a while. I need to take care of some business and a whole lot of pleasure."

"Roxy, you can't be serious," he pleaded in dismay. "You can't just drop a case in my lap and leave. I'm telling you, I don't think I'm cut out for this."

Never one to give up easily, she relented, finally, by saying, "Tell you what, I'll be back on Labor Day. When I get home, I'll call you. If you answer the phone, then I'll know you're in. If you don't, I won't bother you about this again. Deal?"

She held out her hand.

After a brief hesitation, he shook it.

"Deal."

"And for the record, if you decide that you don't want to help, I won't stoop so low as to tell Ann that you lied about how you came into your little cash windfall," Roxy teased before leaving him alone with the envelope.

Phil looked over the items. Unsure of where to begin, he decided to start by reading the court filings. The state had filed criminal charges against Helen Shipley for fraudulently claiming an injury in order to receive tens of thousands in disability benefits each month. A civil suit, seeking $1.5 million in damages was pending in another court.

According to the newspaper articles, the State looked to have an airtight case. Their certain victory hinged on a video of Helen Shipley walking out of the mall with her husband, standing upright and without the use of her walker. Helen Shipley's attorney countered that no one could be certain it was his client because you couldn't see her face. However, the district attorney pointed out that Dennis Shipley, Helen's husband, was easily recognizable, and based on that, it had to be her.

With the trial set to begin in six weeks, Helen Shipley's attorney had hired Roxy to find anything to help prove his client's innocence.

Proving Helen's innocence was not going to be an easy task. Based on her own admittance, she had exaggerated the extent of her injuries but held steadfastly to the claim that she still experienced pain daily and could not stand up straight nor walk a long distance without her walker.

Although the money had come in handy, she stated profit had never been her motive. She was addicted to pain medicine, and prescriptions were like her limitless supply of golden tickets to visit Willy Wonka. She also admitted to being at the mall that day with her husband and wearing an outfit like the one shown in the video.

Six hours later, Phil was still at his desk, going over everything for the umpteenth time. This time, he started with the photographs. A white wide-brim sun hat shielded the woman's face all the way down to her chin. Then a statement Helen had made flashed in his mind.

He flipped through the notes until he found it. Helen claimed she and Dennis had exited the mall from the west entrance around ten thirty that morning. He studied the picture closer. It was too grainy to make out the fine detail, but he was certain he could prove the picture he was looking at wasn't taken from the west side of the mall at ten thirty in the morning.

The phone rang, interrupting his thoughts. Absentmindedly, he reached to pick it up.

Before Phil had a chance to say anything, Roxy cooed, "Hello, Wes Jacobson."

PERRY BUSBY is a data analyst consultant, and founder of Intellect Technology. Having worked in both the private and public sector, his portfolio resembles a Who's Who list of technology pioneers and innovators, with such notable organizations as IBM, NASA, and the Federal Reserve Bank included on the list. An accomplished analyst, he has led data migration and data analysis projects for several local and state government agencies throughout the United States. In 1996, his passion for politics led him to establish a data analysis services for political campaigns.

Perry is an advocate for STEM, STEAM, and other innovative programs that introduce youth to science and technology, dedicating his time and service to many worthwhile programs. He served as Program Director for the 5th Ward/HP i-community, a 3-year, $3M philanthropic program sponsored by Hewlett-Packard. He served as a board member on the Houston IT Empowerment Consortium (HITEC), a think-thank of non-profit organizations focused on addressing technology issues within urban communities. In 2000, he established the Association of Minority IT Professionals (AMITP), a social networking organization aimed at bridging relationships between minority IT professionals, small businesses, and corporate decision-makers. In 2004, the Congressional Black Caucus (CBC) recognized Perry for his efforts and inducted him into their Community Technology Champions inaugural class.

After thirty-five years of writing computer code, he now turns his keyboard and attention to writing stories about a career that has been just as adventuresome as it's been nerdy.

A native of Beaumont, Texas, Perry and his wife, Nancy, currently reside in Fort Lauderdale, Florida.

CPSIA information can be obtained
at www.ICGtesting.com
Printed in the USA
FFOW02n2158300318
46051357-46957FF